What People Are Saying About
Carnival of Lies

The background detail of *A Carnival of Lies*, much of it from hitherto untapped sources, of the complex development in Nazi Germany between 1939 and 1945, is so insightful that no one interested in the subject can fail to profit. Totalitarianism has never seemed more subtle, insidious and in the end more terrifying. This is **an outstanding book, beautifully written and absorbing.**
    J.K. TAPLIN

A most unusual and compelling book: the author, by the device of the fictional autobiography of an undercover agent in Nationalist Socialist Germany in the years from 1933, portrays with unembellished clarity the horrors of the Nazi machine operating at the national and individual level, with the contrast of those whose faith in humankind— even when they perish—outlasts those terrible years. **Highly recommended.**
    ALAN SCOTT, CVO, CBE, lately Governor of the Cayman Islands

Vernon Anley's nightmarish narrative about a nation led into infamy gallops on at a pace and style guaranteed to hold the reader's attention from the start. A romance set against the backdrop of the Holocaust grips the imagination with horror and compassion. From the moment the first page is turned we are witness to a chronicle of man's inhumanity to man, based throughout on carefully researched historic facts. **A powerful story of human survival against all odds and a triumph of hope over despair.**
    RAYMOND ZALA

A CARNIVAL OF LIES

A
CARNIVAL
OF
LIES

VERNON L. ANLEY

Wipf and Stock Publishers
199 W 8th Ave, Suite 3
Eugene, OR 97401

OTHER TITLES
by
DR. VERNON ANLEY

An Unholy Love

A Divided Universe

It Happened in Hanoi

The Orange Tree and Other Stories

The Last Song

for more information visit:
www.vernonanley.co.uk

Know, my son, with how little wisdom
the world is governed.
COUNT AXEL OXENSTIERNA

⌘ ⌘ ⌘

Occasionally words must serve to veil the facts.
But this must happen in such a way
that no one becomes aware of it;
or, if it should be noticed, excuses must be at hand
to be produced immediately.
MACHIAVELLI

⌘ ⌘ ⌘

If a way to the better there be,
it lies in taking a look at the worst.
THOMAS HARDY

⌘ ⌘ ⌘

A Carnival of Lies is based on
one of the most tumultuous and horrific times
in human history—the Holocaust—
and is, as a result, **graphic in content**
in its portrayal of stories of man's inhumanity to man.

Foreword

When writing an autobiography the "times" are for the most part a subordinate clarification of the "life," but in times of great upheaval the perspective is reversed and one is called to write not a "life" but a "life and times." Although the book carries much historical detail, I have not included a bibliography or listed the archives and documents that provided the background for the complex developments in Germany between 1939 and 1945. My intention from the beginning was not to write another history but to uncover what hitherto had been experienced but not properly known.

The book carries a graphic and detailed reconstruction of life in Dachau and Auschwitz. One of the more pervasive myths of our era is the absolute authority given to first-person testimony of survivors of concentration camps. Primo Levi was haunted by the sense that his own account of Auschwitz was that of an "anomalous minority." Since one of the Nazi mechanisms for controlling prisoners depended on isolating each of them as much and for as long as possible to keep them ignorant of the full scale of their predicament, the testimony of any single survivor is both partial and unrepresentative and in need of supplementation from other sources and narratives.

Although Russian, Polish, and German archives have revealed many little-known facts about Hitler's Germany and his network of camps, this book does not claim to be an original piece of historical research. In literary terms the book is concerned with the drama of life, with what results through the characters, their decisions, their actions, and not only because of them but also because of their defects, their oversights and failures to act.

1

The *Geheime Staatspolizeiamt* (Secret State Police or Gestapo) arrested my father in the Adlon Hotel in Berlin in the summer of 1933. When he asked why, he was told, "We do not give reasons." Even then Hitler was sufficiently powerful for the Gestapo to act with impunity.

My father was taken to Gestapo Headquarters in *Prinz-Albrecht-Strasse*, where he was interrogated. Hanging on the wall in front of him was a map of *Russia and the Neighboring States.* It showed the still independent countries in central and Eastern Europe incorporated into the Third Reich. That map, so brazen in its presumption, confirmed my father's belief that Hitler intended to wage a war of conquest.

A Section Chief in the Security Service told my father that he had been overheard speaking disparagingly of Hitler. He was guilty of *unerhörte Verleumdungen* (unheard-of-calumnies) that he would be listed as *Deutschfeindlich* (an enemy of Germany) and that he was to leave the country immediately. The interrogating officer was unaware that Otto Wagener, Head of the Nazi Party's Economic Section, had invited my father to Germany and that he was a guest of the Reich Corporation of German Industries. My father, who had listened to these accusations in silence, finally rose from his chair. He was a big man, used to authority, and in faultless German suggested that before more was said that the *Sturmbannführer* (Major) telephone Herr Wagener, who immediately ordered my father's release.

The man who spoke against my father was Herr Nagel's chauffeur. Herr Nagel was a close personal friend and the director of a heavy machinery company. The chauffeur had overheard the two men talking and reported that my father had criticized Hitler for letting a "punishment expedition" of SA run riot in Okrilla, a large engineering plant in Dresden. The episode is noteworthy only in so far as my father's release and the chauffeur's dismissal would have been unthinkable a few years later when Himmler became Chief of the German Police.

⌘ ⌘ ⌘

I first went to Germany in 1937 when I was eighteen. I stayed with the Nagels, who had a large property west of Münich near Utting on the Starnberger See. Alex, the Nagel's younger son, and I were the same age and quickly became good friends. At that time Nazi coercion was undertaken by simple injunctions or by subtle means of social reinforcement. Commands were given not to listen to Radio Moscow, to give the Hitler salute, and to be a good citizen by attending NSDAP meetings. No one foresaw the consequences of voting for Hitler or for the introduction of the Third Reich—until it was too late, by which time a great many Germans had learned to temper their love of militarism on the cold steppes of Russia.

By 1937 people had a good idea of Hitler's intentions. He had torn up the Treaty of Versailles and began to rearm as he had prophesized in *Mein Kampf:* "W*ir wollen wieder Waffen!*"—We will have arms again! Despite the supra-patriotism in the pre-Nazi years, people were apprehensive about the scale of Hitler's rearmament program. German industry was turning into a war machine. Hitler's appeal to the mystical community of the *Volk* was his argument for anything he wanted to undertake (a claim he expressed in the messianic formula: "As I am yours, so you are mine."). The endlessly reiterated slogan, *"Ein Volk, ein Reich, ein Führer,"* became a call to arms.

The *Volk* was scattered beyond Germany's existing boundaries— wherever, in fact, German-speaking settlers had established themselves. Hitler's self-proclaimed mission was to gather all these far-flung *Volksgenossen* into the one Reich and to provide the *Lebensraum* which this vastly increased population would need. He did not mince words explaining how this additional territory would be secured.

"The military exploitation of our resources cannot be undertaken soon enough or on too large a scale. If we do not succeed, in the

2

shortest possible time in turning the German army into the world's finest army, Germany will be lost. All other considerations therefore will have to be subordinated to this mission."

When Rudolph Hess, Hitler's inseparable secretary, asked the rhetorical question, "Why don't you (the Nazis) reduce your population instead of demanding more room? Why, on the contrary, is the new Reich taking steps to increase its birth rate?" Hitler answered, "Because we do not understand why one of the most valuable peoples in the world should go under; a people to whom man owes his greatest cultural benefits and progress, the most glorious contributions to his literature, to music, to the graphic arts!"

Hitler's warmongering was background noise for Alex and myself. We heard the stomping of Nazi boots, the metallic rumbling of heavy vehicles, and saw cavalry riding well-fed horses, but neither of us grasped what was happening. In fact, very few people saw the consequences of voting in the Third Reich. There was no real comprehension of what Hitler actually stood for and no real understanding of what Nazism was.

⌘⌘⌘

I returned to Australia in time for my first term at university. One of the set tasks for students of German was to read German newspapers and periodicals. They made depressing reading. In the eighteen months between my first and second visit to Germany Hitler invaded Austria, undermined the Czech Republic, and secured Mussolini's signature on the Anti-Comintern Pact, which bound both parties not to sign a treaty with Russia. On the domestic front the Jews were being forcibly emigrated and harassed. *"Wenn's Judenblut vom Messer spritzt,"* sang the Stormtroopers, *"dann geht's noch mal so gut"* (when Jewish blood spurts from the knife, things will go better still).

The poet Heinrich Heine predicted a hundred years earlier that revolutionary forces in Germany were biding their time to break out and fill the world with terror: "When ye hear the trampling of feet and the clashing of arms, ye neighbors' children, be on your guard...

German thunder is of true German character: it is not very nimble and rumbles along somewhat slowly. But come it will, and when ye hear a crashing such as never before has been heard in the world's history, then know that at last the German thunderbolt as fallen." All the signs were that Hitler had lifted the thunderbolt and was about to hurl it.

⌘ ⌘ ⌘

In July the following year I returned to Germany and was immediately struck by the number of people in uniform. The uniforms were an ugly shade of brown, a color personally chosen by Hitler. In Münich, as in all other cities of Germany, every billboard and shop window carried posters of Hitler, with captions such as, *Volk will zoo Volk, und Blut zu Blut, dem Führer dein Ja* (People to people, and blood to blood, Yes for the Führer) and *Weltmacht oder Niedergang* (World power or ruin). Buses, trams and taxis carried placards saying that the driver was for Adolph Hitler. At the station loudspeakers carried slogans about "honor" and "freedom." Nazi propaganda was everywhere. Even tubes of toothpaste and children's toys were decorated with swastikas and eagles. Invisibly, like the static electricity growing in the air that presages as summer storm, the atmosphere of oppression and violence was growing.

Alongside images of Hitler were inflammatory pictures of Jews. Anti-Jewish signs with messages such as "Jews Not Wanted Here" and "Entry Forbidden to Jews" and "*Juda Verrecke*" (Jewry Perish, literally, "Croak") were commonplace in restaurants and hotels. SA men bared the way in to Jewish shops. Placards on the highways leading to towns all over Germany declared: "Jews Enter This Place at Their Own Risk" and "Jews Strictly Forbidden in This Town." Dangerous bends carried the warning notice: "Drive carefully. Sharp curve—Jews 75 mph!" It was the start of that ineluctable process that ended five years later in the gas chambers of Auschwitz.

The Nagels' estate ran down to the Isar River. The house was built by Crown Prince Fredric of Prussia in the eighteenth century as a hunting lodge. It had been much enlarged, and little of the original building remained. The Nagels were proud to be German, proud of their culture, and regarded Hitler a dangerous upstart who would lead Germany to ruin if given half the chance. In spite of their deep-rooted dislike for the Nazis the family was careful not to criticize the government. A neighbor had involuntarily said "Shame!" while looking at a Nazi slogan chalked on the walls of a building and had been arrested for "spreading false and agitational political rumors." Herr Nagel continued to greet people in a courtly manner by tipping his hat, thus circumventing the "German greeting" (i.e., "Heil Hitler" and the submissive one-armed salute), although this worried his wife. The Gestapo was everywhere. To express oneself against the system was to invite persecution. Each time someone cautioned his neighbor or friend he was strengthening the general atmosphere of fear.

An example of how efficient the Gestapo became by reason of rumor and fear was a doggerel whispered by quite ordinary people:

Lieber Gott mach mich stumm
Dass ich nicht nach. kumm
(Dear God make me dumb,
So I don't have to go to Dachau.)

Dachau is a beautiful old town set in the rolling hills north of Münich. Alex and I often walked up the cobblestone streets past cross-beamed houses to the onion-dome tower of St. Jacob's and the remains of the Renaissance Palace. The southwest wing overlooks Dachau and the north face of the Bavarian Alps a hundred kilometers to the south. Neither of us wanted to go the neighboring village of Prittlbach to see the concentration camp. Little did I know that several years later I would see Dachau from the inside when I would be taken into "protective custody" in Dachau before being transferred to Auschwitz.

As long as we stayed on the estate we could ignore the mass meetings and slogans, the Gestapo, and their terror tactics. Theatres showed only newsreels of militarized masses at Party Rallies and children in the *Jungvolk* throwing hand-grenades and firing machine guns. The Hitler *Jugend* gave Hitler an inexhaustible reservoir of ardent young fighters. Every German boy belonged to a branch of Hitler

Youth from the time he was five until he was eighteen and every girl until she was twenty-one. Hitler said he wanted "a violently active, dominating brutal youth" whose education and training "must be directed towards giving them a conviction that they are superior to others." The schools obliged. They gave Hitler his "new species of man."

But that summer was memorable not just for the anti-Semitism and general breakdown of trust and social communication. I met Alex's cousin, Marian Adel, the most beautiful girl I had ever seen. I had seen pictures of her at home. Our mothers had been childhood friends in Bavaria and wrote to each other from time to time. Marian's dark eyes and long hair had not changed, but she was now eighteen, a young woman. We were inseparable. By the time I left Germany we had fallen in love.

Marian left Berlin to live with the Nagels after the universities introduced the so-called "Aryan paragraph," excluding anyone with Jewish blood from lectures and student organizations. Her father, a doctor, had been struck off the medical registers earlier that year and imprisoned on the trumped-up charge of boycotting German pharmaceutical preparations. Because Marian's mother was Aryan, they were allowed to keep their home, although she was hounded by the police and endured repeated house searches.

During my last week with the Nagels, Alex's older brother, Karl, had a young SS officer to stay. Claus Buchheim was tall, blond, and blue- eyed. He was a graduate of the Hitler *Jugend* and had commanded one of the Hitler Youth Patrols. Now, aged twenty-three, Claus was a dedicated SS man. From the moment he saw Marian he could not stop looking at her.

Physically Claus and I were much alike. At a distance we might have been mistaken for brothers. I had had my nose broken in a boxing match, which gave a slight cast to my face, but otherwise we had much the same coloring, features, and build. Boxing was the only sport I was any good at, but I often wondered, sitting with gloves on, waiting for the fight before mine to end, why on earth I did it. But once in the ring I enjoyed facing up to an opponent. I was never conscious of pain, even with a torn ear, a broken nose, and split lips.

Claus, on the other hand, was not someone who would take kindly to being put down, physically or verbally, and would avenge himself when you dropped your guard. He never stopped talking about the superiority of blood over brain, the glory of war, and the mystical connection between *Volk* and the *Führer*. No one found these topics the least bit interesting, but being a friend of Karl's we listened politely. Later on I met a lot of SS like Claus. Almost without exception they were conceited and arrogant, without imagination, and with a blind trust in Hitler.

Because the SS was at Hitler's sole disposal he did not have to account to anyone for the use to which the SS was put. One of its first tasks was the persecution of the Jews. Claus's own anti-Semitism did not surface until one evening when he joined Marian and I in the garden. It was a lovely evening, the twilight air shimmering in the afterglow of the sun. The adage of three being a crowd was apt, but we accepted his presence without comment. Claus immediately began talking about Hitler. "The *Führer* is building a new Germany and a new World. He has rebuilt the army in order to make the Fatherland strong. Today it is the warriors who rule. We Germans have a special mission for all other nations. One day those who oppose us will recognize the enemy within. They will join us to bring down the Jews. The Jews are the lice of civilized humanity. All of us, and not just the Führer, are Jew-haters."

I looked at Claus. He was one of those people whose lips become moist when they talk, with the humidity collecting in the corners and bursting there in tiny bubbles. Catchwords that carried the Nazis to power had assumed for Claus the status of unquestionable truths. Like millions of others, he had been seduced into identifying with Hitler's purpose: world domination, beginning with the elimination of those whose bloodline was a threat to the purity of the master race. Committed to the illusion that only ideas backed up by force can be successful, Claus was ready to open the gates to violence and terrorism, torture and concentration camps.

"And what," I asked, "will this supra-world state of yours be like?"

"Ah," he said, "nothing less than a single world empire. We are experimenting, but experimenting on a scale never dreamt of before. For the first time we are attacking the biological structure of the human race. We have started to breed a new species of *homo sapiens*. We are eliminating the undesirable strains. We have begun the task of exterminating the gypsies; the Jews will be next. Parallel to the work of elimination we are building up a new racial aristocracy. Our Elite Guards (by which Claus meant the SS) will only be allowed to marry subject to strict eugenic criteria; the bloodline of both partners will be analyzed and submitted to a special board for approval. The next step will be the compiling of a card index for the whole nation..."

Claus must have seen me smile.

"You may smile. But not until every family is registered and its heredity known can we weed out the Jews."

Marian stopped. We all stopped. She looked at Claus and, for a moment, I thought she was going to slap his face. Then she said quietly, "I am a Jew."

Claus looked stunned. His mouth opened and then closed again. For a moment I thought he was going to apologize. But then he stiffened, gave a curt bow, and walked off. He did not speak to either of us again.

The next time I saw Claus was at Friedrichshafen, when Marian and I were escorted off the train at the German Swiss border.

2

On 1 October 1938 Hitler invaded Czechoslovakia. Marian had told me a few weeks earlier that Karl's regiment, the SS-Deutschland, had moved to the Czech border, so I knew something was afoot. Hitler justified the invasion by saying it was necessary to protect the Sudeten Germans, a German minority of less than 3 million occupying the outer rim of the Czech Republic. He had used the same argument a year earlier to arouse public support for the Anschluss. Although Hitler told the Reichstag that "Germany neither intends nor wishes to interfere in the internal affairs of Austria," he demanded that the Austrian Government lift the ban on the Austrian Nazi party and for good measure sent several armoured divisions to the Austrian border on the pretext of coming to the defense of the nationally-minded Germans in Austria.

To shore up his government von Schuschnigg called for a plebiscite to decide whether the country was in favor of an Anschluss (as Hitler declared) or a free and independent Austria. Hitler called for Schuschnigg's resignation and demanded the plebiscite be called off or he would send in the army.

Schuschnigg, in his farewell speech over radio Vienna, made a desperate attempt to set the record straight. In a voice breaking with emotion he said that German stories of disorder in Austria were lies "from A to Z" and that he had been forced to nominate Seyss-Inquart as chancellor. He ended his address with these words: "President Miklas of Austria has asked me to tell you that he has yielded to force. Because we are unwilling even in this terrible situation to permit at any price the shedding of streams of blood, we have ordered Austria's armed forces to withdraw without resistance in the event of an invasion.... And so I take leave of Austria with words of farewell which I offer from the depth of my heart—God protect Austria."

But as he spoke, motorized columns of German infantry were crossing the border.

Whatever the Germans thought about Hitler's methods, they were jubilant in the hope of seeing the old dream of a united Germany and Austria fulfilled without bloodshed. In the euphoria accompanying the annexation there was an orgy of sadism and killing. Crowds gathered to enjoy what was known as "scrubbing parties," in which Austrian Jews, forced to put on their best clothes, were made to scrub the streets with small brushes and water mixed with sulphuric acid. In Währing, one of Vienna's wealthier districts, women were made to scrub the pavements in their fur coats while Nazis stood over them and urinated on their heads.

Carl Zuckmayer, the German playwright, who was in Vienna at the time, noted in his diary that "the underworld has opened its gates and let loose its lowest, most revolting, most impure spirits. The city was transformed into a nightmare painting by Hieronymous Bosch, the air filled with the incessant, savage, hysterical screeching from male and female throats…in wild, hate-filled triumph."

Jews who could not prove their Aryan descent for eight generations were rounded up, sent to Dachau, or shot. Wives whose husbands were arrested received one of two printed slips. The first read: *The relative of…is informed herewith that he died today at Dachau Concentration Camp.* The second slip attached to a small parcel read: *To pay 150 marks for the cremation of your husband—ashes enclosed from Dachau.*

Hitler took Austria without losing a soldier. Germany not only acquired an additional 6,500,000 people and Austria's iron and timber resources, it now sat at the gateway to the Balkans, controlling the transportation and communications hub of south-eastern Europe. As an added bonus, Germany hemmed in its next victim, Czechoslovakia, on three sides.

The annexation of Austria was a warning that councils of prudence reinforce the designs of dictators unless backed up by force. It was a warning, even as Hitler aimed his guns at Prague, that was ignored. All that summer we listened to Hitler haranguing the Czechs for their supposed mistreatment of the Sudetens. He brought the crisis to a head by calling for the cession of Sudetenland. "My patience is now at an end. Peace or war. Either Herr Benes will give the Germans their freedom, or we will go and fetch this freedom for ourselves.... We are determined! Now let Herr Benes make his choice."

Chamberlain was so alarmed by the prospect of war that he flew to Germany the next day to see Hitler. Thinking he had struck a deal, he returned to London and after talking to the French, agreed that those areas where the German population was more than 50 percent should be ceded to Germany, a decision the Czechs were forced to accept by an Anglo-French ultimatum.

On hearing that the Czechs had accepted Chamberlain's proposal, Hitler wasted no time in demanding German occupation of the entire Sudetenland. The British cabinet decided that it couldn't accept Hitler's terms and informed France that if she went to war with Germany as a result of fulfilling her treaty obligations, Britain would stand beside her. But lulled by a speech made by Hitler in which he said that after solving the Sudeten question, Germany had no more territorial demands in Europe, Chamberlain and Daladier (without any Czech representative being present) agreed that Germany should take over the Sudeten German areas. Two days later the Münich Agreement was signed without Russian agreement. As a result Russia was irretrievably alienated, giving Hitler everything he wanted.

The pact of Münich is signed, wrote General Jodel in his diary. *Czechoslovakia as a power is out...The genius of the Führer and his determination not to shun even a world war have again won victory.*

In just three days, without firing a shot, Hitler had acquired 11,000 square miles of territory and a network of fortifications, eight million subjects, the Skoda works (whose production of munitions surpassed the total output of British arms factories) and the gold and currency reserves of the Czech National Bank.

On their return from Münich Chamberlain and Daladier were greeted with rapture. It was left to Churchill to utter a warning. "You were given the choice between war and dishonor. You chose dishonor and you will have war." An unhappy truth confirmed by Field Marshal Keitel at Nuremberg. When asked if Hitler would have attacked Czechoslovakia if the Western Powers had stood by Prague, Keitel replied, "Certainly not. We were not strong enough militarily. The purpose of Münich was to gain time and to complete the German armaments."

Australian newspapers reported these events, but Europe was far away and the memory of Word War 1 was still very alive. It seemed impossible that just 20 years later we would go to war again. But anyone with ears to listen could hear the drums of war beating in the background.

3

When Hitler became Chancellor in 1933 his appointment created a surge of optimism for the future. The seemingly endless squabbles of national politics in Germany were over; at last something was happening. But there was more. Democracy was finished; from now on dictatorship would rule. To emphasize the point the Nazis organized a huge rally in Nuremburg. Half a million party members and 60,000 boys selected from the Hitler *Jugend* attended to hear Hitler speak. Each boy had a knapsack and a blanket roll on his shoulder and carried a knife in a sheath with the inscription *Blut und Ehre* (Blood and Honor). War prefers its victims young, and it would not be disappointed. As the flags swept by, the staffs wreathed with the green oak leaves of victory, everyone shouted wildly *"Seig Heil! Seig Heil!"* Young Germany was on the march, and young Germany looked very strong.

These were the halcyon days of the Third Reich, when it seemed as though Hitler might actually be making good his promise to create a new German utopia. The six million unemployed had found jobs in the armaments industry; the humiliating Versailles treaty had been torn up; and the German army, once a mere shadow of its former self, was again the most dangerous war machine in Europe.

With virtual control over the administration the Nazis undertook their first and most important task: Aryanizing and removing from the Jews their means for survival by taking over their businesses and appropriating their bank accounts. In Australia we were scarcely aware of German anti-Semitism until the SS unleashed *Kristal Nacht* (the Night of Broken Glass). In cities and towns all over Germany people were awakened by the noise of shattering glass and the cries of men and women being beaten to death. Organized to look like a spontaneous outburst of rage in response to the assassination of a German diplomat in Paris by a German-Jew angered over the deportation of his parents, mobs of SS looted and destroyed Jewish homes, businesses, and synagogues. Thirty thousand Jews were deported to concentration camps and several hundred murdered. Marian's brother was among those killed. He had tried to help a woman being dragged from her house by a gang of 15-year-olds dressed in the uniform of the Hitler Youth and was beaten to death.

Marian wanted to return to Berlin to live with her mother, who had now lost a husband and a son. But the Nagels would not hear of her leaving in spite of the danger to themselves. It was not just the Gestapo they had to be careful of, but Germans who chose to side with the police. Denunciations from the general public were more useful to the Gestapo than the regime's own spies. Ordinary Germans, boys and girls among them, had participated in *Kristal Nacht*, while thousands of others had watched without lifting a finger. A clipping from *Der Stürmer* showed spectators lining the streets watching the deportation of Jews to Dachau and Sachsenhausen. It was taken in front of the SS quarters in Nuremberg. Below the German eagle was a banner: *By resisting the Jews, I fight for the Lord.* Jew baiting had entered the public domain.

In Germany the only criticism of *Kristal Nacht* was limited to the destruction of property and the Gestapo's bad taste in using the well-furnished, public city buses to transport the Jews to Grünewald station. There was not a word of condemnation by the Church. Just the opposite, in fact. The Protestant churches declared that the Jews were *geborene Welt-und Recisfeinde* (born enemies of the world and of Germany) and incapable of being saved by baptism owing to their racial constitution. Archbishop Konrad published a letter blaming the Jews for Jesus' death, implying that the Nazis were right to mistreat them. The Lutheran bishop, Bishop Otto Dibelius went further, saying that the Jews played a "corrosive role" in society and that their "dying out" would be a good thing. If Germany's moral beacons shared Hitler's anti-Semitism, could less have been expected from their parishioners?

Psychologists and historians have tried to understand Hitler's hatred of the Jews, but as with most obsessions, it was the product of fears and desires. Those who say he was taken over by an evil spirit are as close to the mark as anyone. His countless references to Jews make it plain that "the Jew" was not a real-life figure but a demonic concept hovering, so to speak, over his unconscious. This "mystical" anti-Semitism seems to have identified itself in Hitler's psyche with Wagnerian mythology. Parsifal carried the SS vision of a new aristocracy of blood and soil. *Untergan* (metaphorical destruction) became a blueprint for the *Endlosung*, Hitler's "final solution." It was fitting that Hitler himself played the role of one of Wagner's heroes at the very end. Just as Siegfried and his lover Brunnhilde were consumed in a funeral pyre, so too Hitler and Eva Braun were to be immolated together in the *Götterdämmerung* that was Berlin.

4

In spite of the hue and cry by the outside world after *Kristal Nacht,* or perhaps because of it, Göring, on Hitler's instructions, issued a statement saying, "Should the German Reich come into conflict at any time in the foreseeable future with a foreign power, the first thing we Germans would obviously think of would be our final reckoning with the Jews." The *Schwartz Korps,* the official paper of the SS, filled in the details. "The Jews are to be driven from our residential districts and exterminated in the same way as we are accustomed to exterminating any other criminal—by fire and by sword. This will result in the actual and final end of Jewry in Germany, its absolute annihilation. *Sterben Juden!"* (Death to the Jews!).

Marian wrote to me saying that she had given up hoping that the persecutions would stop.

> Hitler is firmly in the saddle and never loses an opportunity to turn all his enemies into Jews. Today the *Stürmer* carries the headline: "Synagogues Are Dens of Thieves." In the course of the last few days anti-Semitism has been officially instituted in Italy as well. Anyone who commits the slightest indiscretion can expect, at the very least, a raid and search of their houses, or deportation to a concentration camp. Where will it all end?

The literature of anti-Semitism is vast, its details endless, but one thing is clear: German anti-Semitism was animated by a rationale quite different from the banal category of ethnic slurs. The Nazis were certain that the Jews were not just an inferior race like the Slavs and blacks, but were more dangerous, because they were a universal destructive parasite who cleverly adapts to become almost indistinguishable from the host society in order to destroy the healthy texture of that society from within. Their extermination was spoken of in terms of hygienic medicine: Jews were labelled "a dangerous bacteria." *Entlausung* (delousing) was the terrible realization of an ideological metaphor that saw its fulfillment in the gas chamber. It was a mechanism that functioned to justify the rational of euthanasia, deportation, Germanization, and extirpation of anyone considered to be worthless.

On my first visit to Germany I was aware of the anti-Jewish mind-set. It was widespread in all sectors of German society, young and old. A child's letter that appeared in *Der Stürmer* before I left read as follows:

Gauleiter Streicher has told us so much about the Jews that we absolutely hate them. At school we wrote an essay called "The Jews are Our Misfortune." I should like you to print my essay. Unfortunately many people today still say that God created the Jews too, and that is why they must be respected. But we say that since vermin are animals they are also destroyed. The Jew is a half-caste.... He has a wicked book of laws called the Talmud.... In Gelsenkirchen the Jew Gruenberg sold us rotten meat. His book of laws allows him to do that. The Jews have plotted revolts and incited war. They have led Russia into misery. In Germany they gave the communist Party money and paid their thugs. We were at death's door. Then Adolph Hitler came.... Heil Hitler."

This pathetic garbled letter shows just how far anti-Semitism had affected a child's stream of consciousness; and since the stream involves succession and direction, how difficult it would be for the adult to regard the Jews any differently.

One can't be sure of the exact moment when Hitler made up his mind that the Jews must be physically destroyed, but it could not have been later than 1941, when he gave his killing squads, the *Einsatzgruppen*, orders to shoot the Jews. But the ground was prepared for what Hitler called "the solution of the Jewish question in Europe" long before this.

In one of Marian's letters, just before the outbreak of war, she said that the Foreign Office had set up a new section called the German Department. Its purpose was to oversee the "elimination of the destructive influences of those alien sections of the nation which represent a danger to the Reich." The Jewish "problem" was no longer a question of "whether" but of "how."

The answer to Marian's question, "Where will it all end?" had to wait until SS Captain Rudolf Höss visited the small Polish district town of Oswiecim, 50 kilometers southwest of Krakow.

5

I was in my study when I heard that Britain had declared war on Germany. Chamberlain's announcement to the House of Commons was replayed over and over again:

That was the final note (referring to a communiqué to the German Government asking them to suspend all aggressive action against Poland). No such undertaking was received by the time stipulated and consequently this country is at war with Germany.

With these words our lives became subject to events over which we had no control. Marian and the Nagels were now the enemy. Alex, who hated guns and uniforms, was going to carry a rifle—just as I would have to. People talked about patriotism and dying for one's country: no one spoke about killing for one's country.

I tried calling Marian, but it was impossible to get a connection. I was not able to talk to her until I got to Germany seven months later. One of the unseen consequences of war is the splintering of relationships—within families, between friends and those who love one another.

Germany invaded Poland on September 1, 1939. If any country had good reason to fear Germany, it was Poland. The Poles had received territory at Germany's expense at Versailles, the loss of which was more resented in Germany than any other part of the Treaty. Immediately after the invasion of Czechoslovakia, von Ribbentrop told the Polish Ambassador in Berlin that Germany wanted the return of Danzig and for East Prussia to be connected to Germany. Hitler pressed these demands, adopting the tactics used to precipitate the Sudeten crisis, accusing the Polish government of terrorizing the German population of Danzig. In a speech to the Reichstag he gave warning of his intentions by denouncing the Ten-Year Non-Aggression Pact with Poland, regardless of the fact that it did not permit abrogation without notice.

To protect his back Hitler negotiated a nonaggression pact with Stalin. Stalin's signature (10 inches long, an inch high and a tail 18 inches long) convinced Ribbentrop that Stalin would stick by Germany come what may. Both countries pledged not to attack each other for 10 years. In a secret protocol Russia agreed to respect Germany's "interests' in Poland for a free hand in Finland, the Baltic States, and 77,000 square miles of Poland. In plain language the Pact meant that Germany and Russia agreed to a virtual partition of Eastern Europe between them. The most short-lived and cynical treaty of the century was also one of the most dramatic diplomatic coups in history. At a stroke it ensured that Russia was solidly "neutral" in favor of the Nazis and removed the danger of a second front—the only obstacle that Hitler took seriously.

Six days after Stalin guaranteed Hitler a free hand in Poland Hitler issued his "Directive Number 1" for the conduct of the war. Hitler told his generals, verbally and in memoranda, that "it is important that the responsibility for the opening of hostilities should rest unequivocally with England and France," and that in the first instance, "purely local actions should be taken against insignificant frontier violations."

The most notorious of these "local actions," which allowed Hitler to lay the blame for the outbreak of war on Polish "atrocities," took place at Hochlinden on the Polish border. A company of Polish speaking SS seized the German customs post in a staged skirmish with border officials. Six prisoners from Sachsenhausen concentration camp were dressed in Polish uniforms, given lethal injections of cyanide, shot, and laid on the ground to suggest they had been killed while attacking the post. The German press and some foreign correspondents were taken to the scene and reported the staged "outrage" as evidence of Polish provocation.

Hitler, in a characteristic note of truculent self-defense, blamed the invasion on the Poles for launching an offensive attack. "This night, for the first time, Polish regulars fired on our territory. Since 5.45 a.m. we have been returning the fire, and from now on bombs will be met with bombs." It was not true.

But at dawn on the morning of September 1, German land forces supported by hundreds of bombers and fighter aircraft swept into Poland. It was the largest army of invasion which had at any time in history been hurled on the first day of war against another country. The Polish troops on the frontiers were overwhelmed. In Oswiecim, as a Polish Mounted Artillery Division retreated in the direction of Krakow, they were astonished and dismayed when the inhabitants began firing at them from the windows. They were Polish citizens of German descent, who in this fashion announced their allegiance—a fact not lost on Himmler when he decided to open new concentration camps in Upper Silesia.

Within a week the German armies had bitten deep into Poland. The Polish army was rapidly pushed back eastward to a natural line of defense along Poland's rivers, but had little hope of holding out without outside help from Britain and France.

On September 27 Warsaw radio ceased to play the Polish national anthem and Hitler entered the devastated capital. Meanwhile Soviet troops entered Poland from the east. Intent on "Sovietizing" their newly acquired lands, Khrushchev, sporting military uniform and a pistol, unleashed depredations every bit as cruel as those of the Nazis, eliminating anyone that might oppose Soviet power and deporting nearly one million Polish children, women, and men to the most inaccessible parts of Asiatic Russia.

"The final solution of the Jewish people," that sinister and terrible phrase used to disguise plans for the extermination of the Polish elite and all men, women, and children of Jewish blood was entrusted to Himmler and his vassal, Reinhard Heydrich. They unleashed motorized formations of *Einsatzgruppen* (Action Squads) who carried out mass shootings and deported millions of Poles from their farms and homes. Since even the *Einsatzgruppen's* dedication to murder could not clear Poland of all its Jews, Heydrich had the Jews in rural areas rounded up and concentrated in a few of the larger towns. This was a first "interim measure," pending the realization of the top secret "final measure" which, he said, would take rather longer to achieve. In the meantime the "racially valuable elements" were to be "extracted from the hodgepodge and Germanized."

Just how many Polish, Ukrainian, and Russian children were torn from their parents and taken to Germany after being examined by "experts in racial science" is not known. The search-and-find register at Arolsen set up by the Allies after the war lists a quarter of a million names of children sought by parents from Poland and the Ukraine. The true figure is probably double.

The newspapers gave daily accounts of the German and Russian advance through Poland, but we heard nothing about the Einsatzgruppen, although anti-Jewish outrages (atrocities and the burning down of synagogues) were reported from time to time. Uppermost in my mind was the fear of Marian being arrested. After the attack on Poland, the situation of the Jews became more and more threatening, because they became subject to new polices that aimed to "ethnically segregate," i.e., to deport and resettle. Marian, with millions of others, faced arrest and deportation to Jewish "reservations."

6

I enlisted after graduating in December 1939. My preference was the Navy, not because I loved the sea, but because if I had to fight, I did not want to fight on land. I could not imagine myself pointing a rifle at Alex, his brother, or anyone else.

I received a letter from the Army early in the New Year asking me to report to an office in North Melbourne. On arrival I was taken to see Major Barret, and quite unexpectedly, my German tutor from university. Barret introduced himself and then Professor Duldig, "Who I think you know?"

Professor Duldig and I spoke in German. He said that he had been asked to assess the German language skills of four or five candidates but had not been told why. Duldig, who knew my mother was from Bavaria, told Barrett I had grown up speaking German and that testing was unnecessary. After a few minutes Barret took me next door, where I had a conversation in French with a teacher from the Alliance Francaise. At the time I thought I was being tested for a job as a translator. A few weeks later I received another letter asking me to report to the army barracks in St. Kilda, from where I would be taken to an unspecified camp for training. What kind of "training" was not mentioned.

⌘ ⌘ ⌘

On arrival in St. Kilda I boarded a bus with 14 other recruits for a camp near Seymour 100 kilometers north of Melbourne.

The following morning our commanding officer, Colonel Richman, a large man with prominent eyes, told us that we were to be trained as spies and saboteurs. We were, he said, a very secret group. "Not only do you not exist, you never will have existed. You will remain for always unknown and unacknowledged. There will be no awards, no glory, and no medals."

We were divided into two groups: No. I Special Wireless Section, and our group, known simply as Section X. The Wireless Section was trained to intercept enemy wireless transmission. After their initial training, they served in Egypt and Greece, where they monitored German and Italian messages. When Australia declared war on Japan after the attack on Pearl Harbor, they returned to Australia to become part of MacArthur's top secret Intelligence Unit. One of their more decisive intercepts resulted in the death of Admiral Yamamoto, Commander in Chief of the Combined Japanese Fleet and the architect of the attack on Pearl Harbor. An intercept revealed Yamamoto's flight plan, which allowed his plane to be shot down over the Solomon Islands. His death was a major psychological blow for the Japanese, who had been told of victory after victory even after Midway and Guadacanal.

Our group, Section X, was recruited to work for British Intelligence. For 12 weeks we learned about espionage and sabotage, evasion, escape, and capture. We had lessons on weapons and explosives, tap codes and shortwave radios, booby traps, how to pick locks, and extract letters from envelopes using a sliver of bamboo. We were taught how to get through a hostile interrogation and the codes of the Geneva Convention, how to communicate using microdots (photographs are reduced down to microscopic size, concealed under stamps, on top of punctuation marks, or under the lips of envelopes), and dead-letter drops. It was drilled into us that spies must lead a double life. As a spy, one had to live the life the Germans thought you were living; and this second life had to become as real as your actual life.

⌘ ⌘ ⌘

I flew to Switzerland in March 1940, a few days before my twenty-second birthday. Brian Connolly, head of the Economic section in the

Australian Legation, met me at the airport in Bern and took me to an office in Marktgasse, where he had set up a dummy company called Lloytron Chemicals.

At first meeting Brian was not a person one would remember easily. Middle-aged with an air of abstraction, wearing glasses, and eyes some miles away in thought, Brian appeared to be a rather weary academic. But he didn't miss a trick. Although he had no previous connection with the secret services, he performed with extraordinary skill the multiple roles of field collector of intelligence, covert diplomat, analyst, and disseminator. The Australians had no separate operating area in Europe but worked with the British. Although Brian was guided by SOE (Special Operations Executive), and the intelligence material gathered was sent to London for processing and appraisal, he had his own communication network and ran his own agents.

Brian had rented an apartment for me in Köniz, near Kirchenfeld, the diplomatic quarter of Bern. Bern had the atmosphere of a suburb rather than a capital and I quickly found my way around.

1940 was a critical time for Switzerland, sharing as it did its borders with Germany. Hitler said that the German part of Switzerland should be incorporated into the Reich, which encouraged the *Frontisten* (Swiss Nazi parties) to call for unification with the new, powerful Germany. On the whole the Swiss were very well informed about the Nazis (there were German émigrés everywhere) and with the exception of the *Frontisten* wanted to maintain their neutrality.

I spent my first few weeks growing another skin, that of Albert Oeri, a Swiss national and representative for Lloytron. The most tedious part of the disguise was memorizing the chemical formulas, composition, and properties of Lloytron's fictitious products and their uses. But when I left Bern in early April, I was confident in my new role and eager to enter Germany—and see Marian again.

7

If Germany was at war, nobody had told the Berliners. People sat outside in the spring sunshine drinking coffee and reading newspapers. The flower ladies in the *Potsdamerplatz* made nosegays behind buckets of violets and roses, and the cafés and shops were crowded. The only indication that things were not quite normal was the large number of soldiers from the barracks in Pankow. There were more riding boots on the streets than in the Pampas, but no horsemen. But no one took much notice of the men in uniform, and apart from looking well-turned-out, they did not seem to have much purpose about them.

I called Marian as soon as I arrived in Berlin. I said I was a friend of Alex's and kept talking until I heard her give a little gasp and knew that the penny had dropped. Our conversation was quite ordinary, relying on intonation rather than words to close the distance between us. Hearing her speak again was magic. The child in Marian, her openness and trust, was still in her voice. I desperately wanted to tell her that I loved her and that I had set my mind on getting her out of Germany. But it was common knowledge that phones were tapped by the Gestapo. One never knew who might be listening.

I found a small apartment in *Rosen Strasse*, not far from the old Imperial Palace. The apartment was on the second floor, sparsely furnished, with high ceilings. It had a view of the stock exchange and behind it the spires of the cathedral. For a long time Rosen Strasse was called *Hurengasse* (prostitute alley), but the girls had long since disappeared. The apartment was to be my home until the building was destroyed by a British bomb four years later.

Rosen Strasse was not a popular address for most Berliners because it was where the office for the Jewish Social Services was located. I must have passed the five-storied building a hundred times without giving it a second glance.

But in 1943 Rosen Strasse became the center of an around-the-clock street protest that forced the Nazi leadership to change its plans. In the autumn of 1942 the decision was taken to include "temporarily exempted" intermarried Jews and their children in the Final Solution. Most of Germany's remaining Jews were in Berlin. They had been temporarily exempted from deportation because they were from Jewish-German families, or because they worked in the armaments' industry.

Hours before daylight, a battalion of SS men, led by the elite *Leibstandarte* SS Hitler, fanned out across Berlin in a fleet of 300 trucks to capture the city's last unsuspecting Jews. The Gestapo's code name for this massive arrest was the "Final Roundup of the Jews," and for thousands, this was the beginning of the end. Warned that running meant getting shot, the Jews were crammed into the omnipresent trucks face-forward into the backs of those in front of them and taken to various collection centers, but mostly to the Jewish Community Center in Rosen Strasse.

At the first rumors of arrest ran through Berlin, Germans married to Jews flocked to Rosen Strasse. Day and night for a week hundreds of German women married to Jews staged their protest, calling out, "We want our husbands back!" Time and again they were scattered by threats of gunfire, and time and again they advanced, calling for their husbands to be released. Göebbels was forced to climb down—an amazing *vote face*, considering that by 1942 the machinery of the Final Solution was operating at full capacity, with more than 2,700,000 Jews killed in that year alone. The Jews that survived the Roundup owed their lives to the defeat of the German Sixth Army at Stalingrad. Both Hitler and Göebbels knew that continuing support for the war was just as necessary as the calibre of armaments: there was no way that Göebbels could whip up enthusiasm for an even harsher war in the face of the 200,000 soldiers lost while antagonizing non-Jewish Germans by deporting intermarried Jews.

It is difficult to imagine an act more dangerous for German civilians than an open confrontation with the Gestapo. Although only partially successful (half of the 8,000 Jews arrested were deported and immediately gassed, and the hard labor alternative for those who lived was intended only as a short step preceding death), the rescue of the Jews by their German partners was the only German protest against the Nazi Party. It suggests that Nazi anti-Semitism might never have developed into genocide had the German people not acquiesced to the social isolation of the Jews, the prerequisite for deportation and mass murder.

8

My assignment was straightforward. Allied intelligence had learned that German factories were planning to move beyond the range of air attacks from Britain. I was to find out the relocation plans of chemical and engineering works in Hamburg, Bremen, Hanover, Braunschweigm and Magdeburg (all on the flight path from London to Berlin). I was skeptical that industry was planning so far ahead, particularly in the light of Hitler's victories. But I was wrong. Factories making parts for JU-88 dive-bombers were relocating to Brünn, Graz, and Vienna. In fact, all but the smallest factories had contingency plans. AEG, Krupp, and Messerschmitt had already sent people to Czechoslovakia and Poland looking for sites.

I gave myself a week to get settled. Berlin was not the Berlin of my father's day. Nearly all the writers, musicians, artists, and intellectuals who made Berlin the city it was were either exiled or forced to flee. Brecht escaped to Prague, Kurt Weill and Kandinsky to Paris. Einstein, after being told his Jewish throat would be cut, to California. Schönberg, expelled from the Academy of Arts went to New York, as did Otto Klemperer and Bruno Walter. Thomas Mann, Stefan Zweig, Freud, Zola, and Gide had their books burnt in the *Bebelplatz*, an episode that has come to be known as the *Bücherverbrennung*. The empty spaces in the library were filled with copies of *Mein Kampf* and anti-Semitic literature chosen by Göebbels. The book burning was a first tentative rehearsal for Auschwitz. As the poet Heine observed, "Where you burn books, you burn people."

Before leaving Berlin for Hamburg I got in touch with my only contact in Germany, an SS officer recruited by British Intelligence. Although it is universally respected in espionage work that every agent should keep clear of other agents, I wanted to know who I was dealing with in case I should ever need his help. Max Neuemann was a catch for the British. He had access to files dealing with the occupied territories as well as internal security. Max had been to school in London, where his father was an attaché in the German Embassy. He returned to Berlin in 1930 to study law but became disillusioned when forced to adopt a political ideology cast in terms of "race" and "blood." After graduating he was recruited by the Ministry of the Interior. A good-looking man, short and powerfully built, Max was fluent in Russian, French, and English and very anti-Nazi.

We arranged to meet in a small bar in the shadow of the S-Bahn railway viaduct near Wertheim's department store. Behind the bar was a large picture of the Führer as well as a printed sign that said, *Always give the Hitler Salute.* Max said that the proprietor was no friend of Hitler's but that after March 1933 everyone had to toe the Nazi line. It seemed that everyone in Germany was somebody different before Hitler became chancellor.

Max confirmed what I had heard, that the borders were closed to Jews. There was only one way out of Germany, by cattle truck or goods train, and only one place to go, German-occupied Poland—and die of hunger and deprivation in one of the ghettos. Deportees rarely got more than 15 minutes to get ready (depending on the locality) and were forbidden to take anything with them. Nazis took "strength through Joy" groups through the ghettos to show them that Jews— *Volksschädling* (pests harmful to people) were not fit to live. Dressed in rags, emaciated, and starving, the inhabitants scarcely bore any resemblance to human beings. The secret of how ordinary people become murderers or condone murder lies in just such a transformation. A displacement is brought about in a person's mind by divesting all human attributes from the future victim so that other characteristics can be imposed upon him.

⌘ ⌘ ⌘

Almost all agents are given a field of work broader than they can cover, and I was no exception. Brian gave me few guidelines about the operational side of my work.

I left for Hamburg towards the end of April with no clear plan in mind. It was not difficult to locate weapons factories or learn their relocation plans. Information gathering is mostly humdrum. Quite often one source will pass you onto the next. In those early days of the war few people thought to conceal what they were doing or where they were working. I made no sales but didn't expect to. Lloytron's prices were deliberately uncompetitive.

While I was in Hamburg von Ribbentrop announced that German forces had invaded Holland, Belgium, and Luxembourg. The German Blitzkrieg took everyone by surprise. Ribbentrop said that Germany had "unimpeachable proof" that the Allies were planning an imminent attack through the Lowlands into the German Ruhr—a complete fabrication.

In little more than a month German troops were in Paris. Göebbels noted the event enthusiastically in his diary:

The world can speak of nothing else but our capture of Paris. The German flag flies over Versailles. Triumph. It makes one's heart beat stronger. The Führer calls to tell me about the capitulation of the French; he is deeply moved.

Stalin was too, but with some anxiety. "Couldn't they (the Allies) put up any resistance at all?" he asked Khrushchev. "Now Hitler's going to beat our brains in."

When the Germans entered Paris, cinemas all over Germany showed pictures of Nazi legions marching under the Arc de Triomphe. First came the dusty tanks, clanking savagely, followed by the motorized divisions and behind them gray-clad goose-stepping infantry.

By nightfall the Germans held all bridges and key points and set up their headquarters in the Hotel Crillon next to the American Embassy. German propagandists took over the radio stations. They told the population that the Germans wished them no harm and that they had been poorly led by Jews who had betrayed France.

The French Armistice delegation was escorted to an unknown destination to meet with Hitler. To make German revenge complete, the "unknown" destination was a railway car at Rethondes, northeast of the forest of Compiègne, where in 1918 Marshal Foch dictated surrender terms to the Germans. It was now Hitler's turn. Before entering Foch's private car, Hitler, in uniform, walked slowly over to a great granite block and read the inscription engraved in high letters: "HERE ON THE ELEVETH OF NOVEMBER 1918 SUCCUMBED THE CRIMINAL PRIDE OF THE GERMAN EMPIRE ... VANQUISHED BY THE FREE PEOPLES WHICH IT TRIED TO ENSLAVE."

In a gesture of defiance Hitler placed his hands on his hips and planted his feet wide apart. Then, turning his back on the inscription, strode contemptuously towards the car followed by his aids. There was no negotiation. Hitler dictated the terms personally. The French fleet was to report to such ports as the Germans might designate. The use of aircraft was forbidden and all transport facilities were to be placed at the disposition of the Germans. Alsace and Lorraine were to return to Germany, and France itself would be divided into an occupied and an unoccupied zone.

Hitler had brought the Third Republic to an end in a matter of days. Although it had sadly faded away during an evening of defeat, it had, for the great part of its existence, ranked among the great Powers of Europe. France would have to wait another five years before it could regain its place in the world.

9

I returned to Berlin in time to see Hitler's huge victory parade on the 6 July. Hoping the Gestapo would not be so diligent during the celebrations I had arranged to meet Marian at Ochel, a small village a few miles from the Nagels' estate.

Hitler's route from the Anhalter railway station to the Wilhelmsplatz was converted into a carpet of flowers by the *Bund Deutscher Mädel* (League of German Girls). The streets were lined with people waving Nazi flags, shouting *"Heil Hitler"* and singing the "Horst Wessel" song. Facilities were provided throughout Berlin to ensure that those unlucky enough not to catch sight of their Führer could listen to the accompanying commentaries. In addition to the radios required by law in restaurants and cafés, loudspeakers were mounted on lamp-posts and billboards. Anyone inclined not to listen could expect a hefty fine from one of Göebbels' radio wardens.

Göebbels' deep, booming voice, always magniloquent, reached ludicrous heights, declaring that Hitler stood "before the throne of the Almighty."

Julius Streicher outdid even Göebbels. He told the German Academy of Education that, "It is only on one or two exceptional points that Christ and Hitler stand comparison, for Hitler is far too big a man to be compared with one so petty."

Hans Frank, the Bavarian Minister of Justice, capped even this sycophancy. He claimed that Hitler had been sent to Germany by God. "Hitler has received his authority from God. Therefore he is the champion, sent by God, of German Right in the world."

People outside Germany may have found this adulation ridiculous. But it was a mistake to think of these panegyrics as mere words or names. They were far more than that. They were images connected with a living individual by the bridge of emotion. It gave Hitler enormous authority. He had Germany in his hands, and it was his to do with as he pleased.

The train ride to Münich was uneventful. I took a bus to Ochel and walked to the bridge outside the village where we had arranged to meet. There were times when I thought I might not see Marian again. I saw Herr Nagel's car and waved. As soon as Marian stepped out of the car, we ran into each other's arms. It was one of the sweetest moments in my life.

Shy, slight of build, with brown eyes set in an oval face surrounded by long dark hair, she was even lovelier than I remembered. There was so much to say, and so much that could not be said, that to speak at all was to miss saying anything that really mattered. I said I would bring her a Swiss passport when I returned to Germany in a couple of weeks.

Herr Nagel, who had accompanied her, said he would drive her to Berlin to avoid the Bahnschutzpolizei.

I asked about Alex and Karl. Karl's SS unit was attached to the 28th Army and Alex was with general Kluge's Fourth Army. Both brothers had taken part in the assault on France, but the family had heard nothing since. I asked him if Hitler's success would curb his persecution of the Jews. Herr Nagel said, "No." He had met Hitler in 1934 at the Industry Club in Düsseldorf where Hitler told a selected audience that if there was another war it would mean the end of the Jews. "If I can send the flower of the German nation into the hell of war, without the smallest pity for the spilling of precious German blood, then surely I have the right to remove millions of an inferior race."

⌘⌘⌘

Returning to Berlin, I took the night train to Zurich. I thought about my plans to get Marian out of Germany. There was little time to lose. The Nazis saw intermarried Jews and their *Mischling* (mongrel) children as especially threatening and politically unreliable. Children of intermarried couples were considered "certain victims' and sent to death camps, along with German Jews whose non-Jewish spouses died or divorced.

While in Berlin I had spoken to some soldiers on leave from Poland. They told me with grim satisfaction that the Jews were being prepared for *starke Dezimierung* (widespread decimation) by being starved and shot. The enormous Jewish ghettos in Lódz and Warsaw were being turned into enormous Jewish cemeteries. The many thousands of Jews still in Germany were under a collective sentence of death.

In spite of the fact that this was a time of triumph for Germany I noticed a distinct change in morale. If the reality of war was remote for Berliners earlier in the year it was not so now. The British started their retaliatory bombing of Berlin in mid-August, and people were stunned. Göring had told them it couldn't happen. And now guns all over the city fired wildly into the night sky, and buildings were going up in flames. Every night five million people ran to their cellars. There was no talk now of Britain giving up. The only question was, "Could she be conquered?"

⌘ ⌘ ⌘

I gave my report to Brian when I returned to Bern. More than 30 firms, all of them contributing to Germany's war effort, had made alternative arrangements in the conquered territories, should Göring's campaign to achieve air supremacy prove abortive. The assignment had not been difficult or dangerous. I had been helped by Hitler's victory in France. Everyone I spoke to, production managers, chemists, and engineers was confident that the war would soon be over and saw no reason to keep their plans secret. I told Brian about Marian. He said he could get her a passport, but that it would take a few days. That was the good news. The bad news was that I had to leave almost immediately for France.

The unexpected collapse of France in the spring of 1940 caught SOE off guard. The speed with which the Allied armies were defeated by the German Blitzkrieg left the British Secret Service without a cadre of local contacts and other "stay behind" personnel who would normally have been in place in any defeated country of such importance. In spite of "Operation North Pole" (a plan to send Dutch agents from London in planes by night to France) there was not a single agent in place between the Balkans and the English Channel. If the Dutch agents were captured and made to radio back false messages to England they were to substitute one vowel for another, indicating that the message was sent under compulsion. As soon as "Operation North Pole" started, the agents fell into the hands of the Germans. They transmitted the agreed false signals, but London disregarded them. The Dutch kept on dispatching agents who were captured as soon as they were dropped.

German intelligence must have been amazed that so many spies were dropped into their laps. Out of 54 agents, 50 fell into German hands, 47 of whom were sent to Mauthausen, where they were executed. After the war this grim tragedy was the subject of a parliamentary inquiry in Holland. The blame was ascribed to the gross blunders of the SOE, caused by "the lack of experience, utter inefficiency, and the disregard of elementary security rules."

I knew nothing of this awful misadventure at the time. In spite of wanting to return to Berlin, I set off for France in the hope I would not be away for more than a few months. I was to gather intelligence about the preparations for *Operation Sealion* (the code name for the invasion of England). Aerial reconnaissance had shown that Hitler was massing divisions and shipping at the Channel ports. If he planned to invade England it would have to be before winter set in. As it was already July, I thought I would be back by the end of the year.

But things did not work out as I had imagined. I would stay in France till June 1941, almost 11 months.

I called Marian and told her that everything was on hold until I got back. She must have been as disappointed as I was, although her voice did not betray it. Later she told me how ashamed she felt for feeling upset when she thought of what the people in concentration camps had to endure. It was the rarest thing for one of them to escape and cross a frontier.

But every day that passed, the more dangerous it became. Sometimes I woke up in the middle of the night to find myself shouting, "No, No," as Marian was being taken away.

Brian suggested I base myself in Calais, midway between Boulogne and Dunkirk, the most likely area where Hitler would mount his invasion.

⌘⌘⌘

My time in Calais was almost over before it began. Our luggage was subject to a spot check at Calais by a women auxiliary of the Gestapo, one of the so-called "gray mice," named aptly so because of their uniforms.

I had two suitcases. In one was a Marconi Mark.11 radio transmitter. It was in its own leather case, but its weight (10 kg) meant the suitcase could not be passed off as empty. A shortwave transmitter was a weapon of war, strictly outlawed, and its illegal possession brought one before a firing squad.

A hundred things raced through my mind, but there were uniformed police all over the platform. It was my good luck that the Frenchman in front of me was deliberately uncooperative, protesting and bad-mouthing the women searching our luggage. Although he was speaking French, the woman searching him knew she was being abused. I thought she might lose her temper at any moment and have us arrested.

I stepped forward. I told her that I would not tolerate a Frenchmen talking to a woman of the Reich in this way and to leave it to me. I turned on the man and told him that if he didn't shut up, he would find himself behind bars where the Gestapo would cut off his balls.

He changed his manner immediately.

I caught the woman's eye, and she acknowledged my help with a smile. When I put my luggage on the table, I opened the case that contained only my clothes and told her I had come from Berlin. She gave my clothes a cursory look and checked it. Before opening the second case I told her that it only carried more of the same, and she waved me through.

Finding a safehouse was easier than I had thought. In the summer of 1940, before the Germans were able to organize trains to take their prisoners to Germany, most of Calais had seen long columns of prisoners winding their way to a temporary camp behind the Porte de Bologna. The sight of these men had hardened the people of Calais against the Germans, and they refused to accommodate them. There were a number of houses with rooms to let. I chose one in Rue Mollien near St. Pierre Park. The house belonged to Jeanne Lévy, a woman in her late twenties. Her husband had been killed six months earlier flying a reconnaissance mission over Germany, leaving her widowed with two small sons. Given her circumstances, she was unlikely to inform on me, whatever her suspicions.

Everything I knew suggested that Hitler was against a Channel invasion. His armed forces had been developed and equipped for a continental war. His ambitions lay in the East. He could not afford to wage war against Britain until he had absolute security in Eastern Europe. In fact he was so keen to avoid a war on two fronts that he offered to make a pact with the British, asking for nothing more than the return of the former German colonies and the recognition of his conquests in Western Europe.

When this overture reached London through the agency of the Papal Nuncio in Bern, Churchill sent a note to the Foreign Secretary (Lord Halifax) saying, "We do not desire to make any inquires as to terms of peace with Hitler, and that all our agents are strictly forbidden to entertain such suggestions."

This rebuff left Hitler no choice but to attack Britain since England had to be defeated before he could turn his forces against Russia.

The invasion called for the German army to sail from Rotterdam, Calais, Boulogne, and Le Havre. After securing southeast England it was to march north as far as Gloucester, taking London on the way. Since the navy would be unable to protect a crossing on so broad a front, the responsibility for the success of *Operation Sealion* rested on the Luftwaffe. It had to gain and hold command not only of the sky but of the Channel as well.

It was obvious after my first trip up the coast to Rotterdam that preparations were well underway. French, Dutch, and Belgian airfields were extended to take the Junkers 52s, which had been converted into troop carriers. More than 200,000 German soldiers were concentrated around various Dutch, Belgian, and French ports. Every dockyard and slipway from Gdynia to Cherbourg had been requisitioned. Armies of workmen were altering the bows of self-propelled barges to enable tanks and guns to be more easily carried. On top of this the ports were choked with hundreds of motorboats and tugs. I counted 36 small warships in the Rhine estuary and the Kiel Canal, and 45 merchant ships at Le Havre. But even this flotilla could not transport more than 50,000 men at a time, which must have worried the German General Staff.

On August 13 Göring launched the "Battle of Britain" to prepare the way for the amphibious and airborne landings to follow. A thousand fighter aircraft and 1,500 bombers crossed the channel. Waves of Dornier, Heinkels, and Stuka bombers, protected by swarms of Messerschmitt fighters, passed overhead. The Luftwaffe was ill-served by its lack of intelligence about the British air defenses (in 1940 there were few if any German agents operating in the UK). This failure was compounded by Hitler's demand for an immediate reprisal for a bombing raid over Berlin. By switching from bombing air bases to attacking London, the Luftwaffe left the fighting power of the Air Force almost intact. Fighter Command inflicted on Hitler the first decisive defeat of the war, and English bombing put an end to the plan of using French and Belgium harbors as anchorages for an invasion fleet.

10

I remained in France until the end of May, by which time it was clear that Hitler had abandoned *Sealion*, at least for the time being. Soldiers and equipment from the embarkation ports were moving northwards towards Russia and the harbors opened up for commercial shipping. I doubt if Hitler saw it as a major setback. Britain was still not in a position to cause him any real damage.

When I got word that I could return to Switzerland, I dropped everything and made my way back to Berne. I had been able to pinpoint coastal targets and tell SOE about German troop movements. One never knew at the time the extent of one's contribution, and it was rare for an agent to be mentioned by name when the facts of engagement were disclosed. Most agents preferred it this way. Few of us thought we were doing anything exceptional.

Brian had obtained Marian a Swiss passport. Meanwhile Himmler had given orders that any Jew caught hiding was to be punished by death. The net was tightening daily. I called Marian and told her to meet me in Berlin as planned.

I spent the day before returning to Germany decorating my apartment. I bought a few prints and a Persian carpet, rearranged the furniture, put flowers in every room. On the morning I left I put a bottle of champagne in a silver bucket on the hall table with a card, *Marian, welcome home. All my love.*

The day after I returned to Berlin Herr Nagel dropped Marian off in a side street behind the Belle-Alliancew Platz.

After the war I wrote to the Nagels, asking after Alex and Karl. Both boys had been killed: Alex early on in the war in Russia, and Karl soon after D-Day in Normandy. From the very first the Nagels had felt nothing but contempt for the Nazis. It was a tragedy that their sons died defending a Germany they both disowned.

Neither Marian nor I could believe that we were together again. After so many sleepless nights, so many dreams, and so many unspoken thoughts, it was as if the reality of it had taken us by surprise. We just looked at one another, holding hands. Tears came into our eyes, and we started to laugh.

That evening Marian took me to the Tiergarten to meet her mother. She was in her early forties, attractive and shyly silent. She worked for an anti-Nazi organization that helped Jewish refugees. She took both my hands and kissed me when Marian told her that we were going to Switzerland.

We did not talk long. Neighbors, her mother said, reported any change in her movements to the Gestapo and she had to get home. "Even friends," she said, "betray each other in order to survive" (nearly three-fifths of the Gestapo case files were initiated by tips from informants).

Neither of us saw her again. She was a casualty of the final days of Berlin when the Russians turned their guns on what was left of the city and razed it to the ground.

I held Marian in my arms all night, but we did not make love. Few people can live with fear, as she had for the last three years, and not be affected by it. As soon as we lay down together, I felt that she would not be at ease until we left Germany. We talked for a long time. Eventually she fell asleep in my arms. I was too keyed up to sleep. I went over every detail of our journey, asking myself "what if," trying to anticipate every possible intervention by the Gestapo.

We caught the 9.00 a.m. train to Switzerland. The ride was uneventful until we got to Ravensburg, when two Gestapo boarded the train to check passports and papers. The next stop was Friedrichshafen on Lake Bodensee, where the ferry would take us to Romanshorn in Switzerland. When the Gestapo entered the compartment, one of them held out his hand and I gave him our passports. Marian turned her face towards the window. The lieutenant who checked our passports asked me if we were travelling together. I said we were.

He studied Marian's passport, turning the pages, frowning. He asked me why her passport did not carry an entry stamp into Germany. I shrugged and said that the border police must have slipped up. It sometimes happened. But I knew that the only person who had slipped up was me. My heart stopped beating. It is just such silly mistakes that wreck the most carefully thought-out plans. I said that next time I would make sure her passport was stamped.

But he ignored my outstretched hand and said we could make our excuses to the *Grenzpolizei* in Friedrichshafen.

At Friedrichshafen we were escorted off the train with half a dozen others and made to wait outside the Station Master's office. As time dragged on, I felt Marian's confidence start to wane. I had never felt so angry with myself. I was so happy to get her passport that I had completely forgotten about the entry stamp. I was in a dead fear of the consequences. If Marian was interrogated, it was all over. I held her hand and tried to look calm.

We must have waited an hour before we heard a car pull up and shouts of *"Heil Hitler."* A few minutes later a uniformed guard ushered Marian and I into the station master's office.

Sitting behind a desk, dressed in the uniform of an SS major, was Karl's friend Claus Buchheim.

"Claus," I cried, "thank God it's you." I walked over to shake his hand, but he didn't move a muscle.

Marian, who had allowed herself a smile when she saw Claus, had gone as white as a sheet.

Claus picked up my passport. He examined it and asked with feigned astonishment if it was mine. I told him because of my feelings for Germany I wanted nothing to do with the war. Rather than be conscripted I had left Australia for a neutral country and changed my name to Albert Oeri to avoid embarrassing my family.

It was an unlikely story, and he clearly didn't believe it. Turning to Marian, he asked her if she had changed her name too, "to avoid embarrassing her family." Marian didn't say anything but held his eyes. "Mariam, isn't it...after Moses' sister?" She did not correct him.

I cut in, asking if he had heard from Karl, but he ignored me. Claus held all the cards and he knew it. I told Claus that if he would return our passports, he would not see us again.

"That, at least, I can promise you," he said, nodding to the guard who marched us back into the waiting room.

A man sitting opposite us looked at Marian and said "Jewish?"

I nodded.

He asked if I knew where we were going.

I told him Berlin.

He shook his head. "For you, Dachau. For the girl…who knows?"

Nothing in the ordinary pain of human living comes anywhere near what I felt at that moment.

11

When we arrived in Berlin we were pushed into a van and driven to Police Headquarters on Prinz-Albrecht Strasse, which was used by the Gestapo as an interrogation center. We were led to the basement, where we were photographed and had our fingerprints taken. Marian and two other women were then led away by the Gestapo for interrogation.

I did not see her again until she was transferred to Auschwitz. I wanted to cry out that I loved her and that if we were ever together again I would spend the rest of my life making up for this moment. As she was led away she turned to me and smiled, as if to say she regretted nothing.

As soon as the door closed behind her, I was marched down a long tunnel-like corridor illuminated by single bulbs hung on cords with cells on either side. From some of the cells came low moans, the subdued cry of pain, or perhaps despair. At the end of the corridor I was led upstairs and ushered into a room, one of perhaps 20 or 30, available for simultaneous interrogations. The guard pointed to a small four-legged stool in front of the desk and said, "Sit."

My interrogator wore civilian clothes. He was middle-aged, his eyes set closely together with a full-lipped mouth that seemed only partially to widen when he spoke. He looked at the charge sheet in front of him. "So you like Jewish women?"

My passport was not on the table. Was it an oversight, or had Claus withheld it? Either way I was not being charged with spying. I had expected to be taken out and shot. I felt a surge of relief.

"Your name?"

I gave the first German name that entered my head. "Claus Buchheim."

"You can't *have* Jews in Germany, so you take them to

Switzerland?" He said the word with a sadistic relish. He must have read from the documents in front of him that I had been travelling with Marian. I was going to be charged for having sex with a Jew, a punishable crime called *Rassenschande* (racial shame, indicating racial pollution).

The only way to face such people is to humor them. "German girls are better," I said. "It was a mistake."

He grunted.

The interview was over. I was charged under "Article One of the Decree of the Reich President for the Protection of People and State" for consorting with a Jew and sentenced to six months in prison.

Marian did not get off so lightly. They had her passport. She was questioned by two men, one after the other, until she lost count of the time. Seated on a low backless stool, her interrogators stood over her, alternatively threatening and cajoling her. They wanted to know how she had got a Swiss passport. At first she said she'd bought it on the black-market, then finally admitted her brother had given it to her. The Gestapo took down his name, not knowing that her brother was dead.

The next morning she was transferred to Ravensbrück concentration camp.

The day after my interrogation I was taken to a remand prison in Moabit, pending transfer to Münich. I was kept in solitary confinement for eight days. When the door was shut and the latch fell into place, I experienced that loss of freedom that comes with incarceration. Time and space dissolve into a dark ennui that envelops you. The cell had stone walls, a small barred window, and a peephole in the door. From side to side I could manage three short strides. Each moment passed more slowly than the next.

But the real torment was my fears for Marian. Where was she? What would happen to her? What hell had I led her into?

I was transferred from Moabit with other "protective custody" prisoners to Münich on June 21, 1941. The date is easy to remember. On that morning the Germans army invaded Russia.

When we arrived in Münich, we were marched to Gestapo Headquarters. Calls for water and food went unanswered. Instead we were pushed into a cell and left to our own devices. Most of the prisoners in our group were communists—serving three and a half years for printing anti-Nazi leaflets and handing out propaganda coins (they looked like real coins but carried an anti-Nazi inscription and a smashed swastika). Among the others was a professor from Humboldt University who had been caught listening to the BBC and a Catholic teacher who failed to join the Nazi Teachers' Association.

Next morning we were assembled in the prison yard in front of a Gestapo officer who checked off our names. The man looked civil, so I asked him where we were going.

"It is not for me to say. It is not wise to ask questions." Then he reeled off the regulations: conversations during the march with one's neighbor, or any other prisoner, was prohibited; so was to make signs to each other, to exchange written messages, or to step out of the line; any disregard of the regulations would be punished immediately.

I closed my mouth.

As soon as we turned north I knew it was to Dachau. Two years earlier I had driven along the same road with Alex admiring the vast marshy area to the south, the *Dachauer Moos,* which was the inspiration for the "Dachau school" of painters. It looked very different now that I was a prisoner. Denied access to a world I could not inhabit anymore, the landscape seemed to have no real presence or meaning.

My heart tightened as soon as I saw Dachau with its three-metre-high concrete walls and guard towers. Even from the outside the camp looked like a closed universe, a colony of terror hidden behind walls. We were lined up outside the *Jourhaus,* a two-story guard house crowned by a watchtower. In front of us was a large iron gate carrying the inscription *Arbeit Macht Frei* (Work makes you free), a totally meaningless slogan since no one was ever released because of hard work.

After waiting several hours an SS officer strode through the gate and took command. We were marched through the gate to the *Appellplatz* or roll call square. It gave me my first good look at the camp. It covered an area of about a square mile. Between the concrete wall and an almost vertical ditch was a two-metre-high voltage fence. In front of the ditch lay an eight-metre-wide verge, the "death strip," covered with white gravel to make shadows visible at night. Anyone who stepped on it was shot without warning. Guard towers were placed at 20-yard intervals. Each carried four machine guns, their barrels directed at the camp. Patrols with leashed dogs moved in the area between the wall and the electrified fence. No one was allowed to enter or leave the camp unless accompanied by an SS officer known to the guards at the gate.

The prisoner's quarters consisted of 34 huts constructed of thin wooden boards arranged in two rows on either side of the *Lagerstrasse*. The administrative offices were on the south side of the camp, the disinfection barracks on the north. The crematorium was in the camp's northwest corner, behind the wire fence. There were no curves, arches, or blind spots. Nothing eluded visible control.

After more counting and name-calling we lined up in front of a row of rapport scribes sitting at wooden desks waiting to take down our details. One by one we were summoned forward. The man in front of me had a yellow Star of David pinned to his jacket. When he reached the *schreiber's* desk, the German looked up and said, "The name of the whore that shitted you out?" Other questions began with, "Filthy Jew..." or "Trash Jew...."

When I stepped forward, the *schreiber* looked up and said, *"Die Juden sind unser Ungluck"* (The Jews are our misfortune). When asked my name, date, and place of birth, I said I was from Berghausen, ten miles from Braunnau, "where the Führer was born." It was rather silly, but there was something emotionally satisfying in even useless lying.

After these formalities, we were marched to the shower room. It was then that I saw the 200 prisoners standing to attention at the end of the *Lagerstrasse*. They had already been standing for 24 hours, a punishment for some infraction or other, their ranks broken every few yards by those who had collapsed.

During roll call that evening, the whole camp would watch as two SS officers walked over and shot those who had fallen in the back of the neck. It was a sickening and frightening introduction to the camp.

After we had showered, our heads were shaved and scrubbed with rags soaked in disinfectant. We were given a striped blue-gray prison uniform, a shirt and cap, and wooden clogs. The uniforms were blood stained, ill-fitting, and handed out without thought to our size or height. The clogs were different sizes, practically worn out and more for the left foot than the right. Dressed in our prison clothes, we all looked much alike, the first step in our depersonalization. Our names were called, and we were given a number—our sole form of identification from that moment on. Reduced to a cipher among thousands of others, we became *Nummermenschen* (number-men)— men with no name. Our transformation into the serial society of the nameless was complete. Few of us emerged feeling that we were the same person we had been the day before.

The admission procedures were too traumatic for some prisoners. They forgot their numbers or refused to be identified by them and didn't respond when shouted at. The *Kapos* pounced on them with a vengeance, smashing their heads against the stone floor.

I was stunned by the violence, but it was another lesson: the only attitude permissible towards those in power was submission. In Dachau there would be no assistance in times of distress. Removed from the protective sight of public domain the SS could do with us what they liked. Violence, omnipresent, demanded presence of mind right from the start.

We were lined up again and marched to our hut. The huts were divided into two parts, each with their own entrance leading to a small "living room" and dormitory. The dormitories had three lines of wooden beds, one row against each wall and one down the center. By stacking one bed on top of another, three beds high, each hut could accommodate 170 prisoners. But by the simple measure of sleeping three, sometimes four, prisoners to a bunk, the SS were able to pack 1500 men into a hut. The struggle to find a place among the nameless called for certain toughness. In order to live you had to engage in a grinding tussle, frequently at the expense of others. No tie of friendship or sympathy was strong enough to survive life in Dachau. If tragedy and need brought people together and gave birth to friendship, then the need was not extreme and the tragedy not great.

I peered into the dormitory and saw a room full of half-starved glaring faces, each one with its head shaven, looking like a row of death masks. These were our bunkmates. But for the poor souls standing motionless in the *Lagerstrasse* and our bunkmates, who had arrived earlier that day from Sachsenhausen, the camp was virtually empty. The *Kommandos* (labor gangs) did not return until after sunset. The only other inmates in the camp were the prisoner-functionaries who worked in the administrative building, which also contained the kitchen, laundry, showers, and workshops.

At seven o'clock that evening the loudspeakers jumped into action. We lined up on the *Appellplatz*, where the dreaded morning and evening roll calls took place, staring rigidly in front of us, listening to a penetrating acoustic barrage of radio music, an overture for the returning work squads. The columns of returning men looked like the remnants of a broken army. They limped forward, emaciated and footsore, dragging their bodies into the square. As they passed through the gate a *Kapo* shouted, "Hats off! Eyes right!" Mechanically the shaven heads snapped to the right, saluting the SS's arch of triumph. Anyone who didn't respond was immediately pulled from the column and thrashed. The last to arrive were the cart bearers, dragging the bodies of the dead. Seventy-three corpses were laid out on the parade ground for counting.

Counting began when the *Arbeitseinsatzführer*, the SS non-com responsible for organizing prison labor, appeared on the Parade Ground. The evening roll call had no time limit. It could be extended at will. If a single prisoner among thousands failed to answer or make himself heard, the whole lengthy procedure was repeated. If an escape was suspected, search parties were sent out and we were left standing, sometimes for hours. It was always a false alarm. The missing person had collapsed or died.

Immediately after roll call we queued up for the evening meal. I had not eaten for three days. Those of us who had arrived that day were told to wait. The camp leader and commandant had a few words to say to us. More time passed. Finally SS *Hauptsturmführer* Krüger and the Commandant, Egon Zill, deigned to appear. Krüger told us that we had to maintain absolute obedience. Every transgression was associated with a graded series of punishments. These extended from solitary confinement to flogging and death. To touch the fences was considered sabotage and was punished by death. Anyone caught smuggling messages out of the camp was hanged. One could expect no mercy from the guards. (They killed when it suited them and were rewarded for doing so. Of the more than 31,000 deaths that occurred in Dachau, a quarter were "bounty" killings).

Then it was the turn of the Commandant, Egon Zill. His speech was short and sadistic. "I'm letting you live. The Great Reich has shown unprecedented mercy. You anti-socials are leprosy on the body of Germany. You offenders have insulted the Führer and German society. You have been allowed to live. It is a pity. But I submit to it. You must do the same. Those who try to resist the discipline of this camp will come to me on their knees, I tell you, to ask for it to be enforced on them. SS discipline is a steamroller, and nothing grows again where it has been. Dismiss!"

Zill was a sadist and a murderer. One evening after roll call he ordered some Russian POWs to strip naked in front of him. He watched them for a long time while he amused himself with his riding whip. Finally he took his revolver from its holster and shot them one by one in the nape of the neck. Zill liked his victims naked. If he made you undress, you knew it was the end.

After the war a court in München sentenced him to life imprisonment but later accepted his appeal, reducing his sentence to fifteen years. He died in 1974 at home in Dachau, a mile from the camp where he buried his dead.

After Zill finished speaking, it was too late for our evening meal. We were marched straight to our hut. Because of the prisoners from Sachsenhausen the dormitory was hopelessly overcrowded. Although many of them had dysentery, they were forbidden to go to the latrine at night. The sacks of straw that served as mattresses and the woolen blankets were sodden with excrement and swarming with lice and fleas. I forced myself to lie on the edge of a bunk, ignoring cries of "No space." A turn here, a move there, and your bunkmates spread out immediately. You had to flex your body before moving so as not to lose a centimetre of space. There were few regrets in the morning for those who died during the night. If you bunkmate died, it meant a little more room for one's self.

⌘ ⌘ ⌘

We were awakened at 4.00 a.m. by the block-leader who ran through the hut shouting *"Aufstehen! Raus! Raus!"* In the space of 40 minutes 12,000 prisoners lined up to go to the latrines, queued for a piece of bread and a cup of ersatz coffee, and assembled for roll call. I was in the meal line when I realized that I had no utensils. It was a moment of panic. Other than the water I had gulped down when under the shower I had not anything to eat or drink since leaving Moabit. The only drinking water you got was at meal times. A mug was the most precious commodity a prisoner could have and he guarded it with his life. Hunger can be temporarily offset by pain or fear; not so with thirst. I traded my bread for a gulp of coffee from someone's mug.

Dawn was still an hour away when we were called to attention. Illuminated by searchlights we waited for our camp lords to appear. Roll call was always a time of harassment, of shouting and waiting. When everyone was finally assembled, the *Kapo* in charge of each barrack gave the number present to the *Blockführer*. Everyone had to be present, including the dead. The dead had to be physically present, standing upright, naked, supported by two prisoners. After the SS had checked and rechecked the numbers reported to them, the command was given to form up in work squads. Those of us not assigned to a *Kommando* were told to remain where we were.

New arrivals, such as ourselves, were assigned to work in the gravel pit behind the Dachau marshes. The citizens of Prittlbach and Dachau did not give us a second look, not even those who stood a few feet from us as we marched through the gates. They saw what was happening, they saw what we looked like, but no one uttered a single word of encouragement or threw us an apple or a piece of bread.

Were we really so invisible with our picks and shovels and death carts? The evasive answer given after the war to the question, "How could you have allowed it?" was, *"Ja- wir wussten uberhaupt nichts was passiert da draussen!"* (We really didn't know what was going on there!). But they knew very well. On the few occasions one caught someone's eye they pretended not to see you, their face frozen in that "wooden" unseeing expression familiar to so many photographs of confrontation.

Kapos and SS prodded us to march in double-quick time. Dogs trained to snap at our heels ran up and down barking. Those of us wearing the ill-fitting clogs for the first time walked barefoot to stop the bleeding. My one lucky break happened when the SS went berserk and flayed into us for not marching quickly enough. When they ran into us with their whips, I stumbled to the ground, falling against a rubbish bin. As the contents spilled out, I seized a tin can and a handful of potato peelings. I had found a mug and a source of food.

The gravel pit was a large open-air excavation of rock and shale. When we reached it I was assigned to a *Kommando* charged with breaking up the rock dislodged by blasting. A second group separated the gravel from the sand. A third group shovelled the gravel into a heavy wagon and a fourth *Kommando* hauled the wagon back and forth to a dumping ground a mile away. Guards stood all round the edge of the pit shouting at us to work faster, *"Los! Los! Bewegt euch, schneller!"* (Faster! Faster! Get going!). It didn't matter how hard you worked; it was never hard enough.

After ten days it was all I could do to lift the iron hammer above my head. My back ached from the continuous stooping. I had blisters on the palms of my hand, and my fingers bled. I soon learned to "put on the breaks," conserving my energy while pretending to work normally. The first hour from six to seven was the worst. The next hour was very long, so was the next, and all the remaining hours till midday when we were given a bowl of watery soup. An hour later we were back in the pit, counting the hours till darkness called a halt.

I got to know the tricks that made time pass: going to the latrine, thinking of your next meal, counting the blows to break a rock. Time passed when an SS-man jabbed you with his rifle butt, and time passed when you looked into the face of a *Kapo* and thought what you would like to do to him. And so one got through the day, counting and scheming, trying to ignore the insults and ward off the kicks and rifle butt in the ribs. The average life span of those who worked in the pits was less than 12 weeks. No one could survive very long on the sparsely allocated rations and the grueling marches to and from work. Exhaustion and harassment took its toll. Work was not a means of survival, but a temporary reprieve until death.

The first prerequisite for survival was to set aside any preconceived ideas about human values. In Dachau there were none. The overriding reality of life was death. It could occur at any moment, at work, in the camp, on the paths, in the huts. There was a practical maxim in the camp: remain inconspicuous! This had to be a conscious decision: a necessary active achievement in the art of self-protection. I became anonymous. I worked in the center of the gravel *Kommando*, hidden from the armed guards who surrounded us. During roll calls I disappeared into the middle rows, suppressing any urge to cough or sneeze. I never loitered at the corner of a barrack or wandered aimlessly across the *Appellplatzl*. If I had to walk near an SS-man or cross his field of vision I always moved at normal speed, not too fast, not too slow.

After my first week I did not live from day to day, but from one meal to another. I was plagued by obsessive thoughts of food. Hunger became a permanent state so that it was no longer a sensation but an ever-present hollowness. After a few weeks of nothing but camp rations the body wasted away, metabolizing fat, then muscle, to fuel the unceasing energy demands. The stumble into a rubbish bin was my salvation. Impatient to get back to camp at the end of the day the guards walked ahead of the death carts at the rear of the column. Because I was always among the last to line up, I was "punished" by being made to drag one of the barrows back to camp. Whenever I passed a rubbish bin I let a corpse slip from the cart and while retrieving the body rifled the bin. The extra rations kept me alive. Not everyone was prepared to take this risk. But since death could strike at any moment, I had nothing to lose.

Because I had committed "an error of judgment" in sleeping with a Jew, I had to attend classes three evenings a week on Nazi ideology. The classes took place almost immediately after roll call, leaving very little time to collect our scrap of bread and, if lucky, a thin slice of German sausage. Since food took priority over everything else, we were often late, which gave the *Kapos* another excuse for exercising their clubs. To make sure we did not doze off during the lectures, the *Kapos* walked up and down the benches, hitting anyone who dropped his head. To stop ourselves from falling asleep, we sat on sharp stones, bloody bottoms being preferable to bloody heads.

During the last lecture, a few weeks before my release, the political officer, Karl Eissle, dragged a Jewish prisoner on to the platform. Eissle humiliated the man by forcing him to spit on some Torah scrolls. When he ran out of spittle, Eissle supplied him with more by spitting into his mouth. The man was on his last legs, ravaged by diarrhea and starvation. His cheeks were sunken, his eyes lustreless, his clothes covered in excrement and blood.

Eissle pointed to him. "From a biological point of view the Jew seems completely normal. He has hands and feet and a sort of brain. He has eyes and a mouth. But, in fact, he is a completely different creature. He only looks human, with a human face, but his spirit is lower than that of an animal. A terrible chaos runs through this creature, an awful urge for destruction, primitive desires, unparalleled evil, a monster subhuman." Eissle made it clear that Jews were *geborene Welt-und Reichsfeinde* (born enemies of the world and of Germany) and fit only to be trampled on. He spat in the man's face and ordered us to do the same as we filed out of the room. When my turn came, I walked past Eissle's victim without turning my head, an action I was to pay dearly for.

⌘ ⌘ ⌘

After six months in Dachau, I counted myself lucky to be alive. Many others who had arrived in Dachau with me had died, killed by violence, starvation, or labor. The night before my release I succumbed to certain euphoria. By craft and cunning I had cheated the crematorium. By avoiding contact with the SS, I had steered clear of the punitive jungle of offenses that called for retribution. I had lost weight, been beaten, had lice, but kept body and soul together.

I tried to imagine sitting down to a full meal, looking in shop windows, behaving normally, but could not. Life before Dachau had disappeared altogether, fading from view and from memory, hidden by the psychological strategies for survival that called for the abandonment of everything that might distract one from the *Kapos* and

SS.

On the morning of my release I was marched with several other prisoners to the *Jourhaus* to get our discharge papers. The upper floor was occupied by the camp leader, his deputies, and the offices of the Gestapo trial commissioner. We were summoned upstairs one at a time. The two men in front of me came back waving their papers excitedly, shouting their freedom. A guard beckoned, and I followed him upstairs into the commissioner's office. I had been waiting for this moment for six months.

Heart beating loudly, I stood in front of the Gestapo commissioner while he read my file. I looked out the window. I could see the tops of the poplar trees beyond the camp wall. For a moment I imagined myself outside, the camp behind me, free again.

After a minute the commissioner put down my file. *"Hauptsturmführer* Eissle has noted that your political instincts have remained unchanged. Today you will be transferred to the *Strafkompanie* (the "punishment" barracks). Your detention has been extended for another six months."

I don't remember feeling anything—not frustration, not despair, not even anger. Just a numbness that left no room for thought or feeling.

12

There was a dusting of snow on the ground and a bitter wind. Dachau is not far from the Alps, almost 1,900 feet above sea level. Winters are very severe. As I followed the guard down the *Lagerstrasse*, the wind picked up and I started to shiver. I was not the only one. Prisoners in the snow *Kommando* swept up the snow with hunched shoulders, their heads bent forward against the cold.

The prisoners in the *Strafkompanie* were mainly Jews, but also prisoners who had violated camp regulations. It was fenced off from the rest of the camp and out of bounds to all SS but the *Blockführer* and the guards under his command. When we reached the gate I was handed over to SS *Untersturmführer* Karl Phol.

Phol would have been hung a hundred times over if inmates had not killed him when Dachau was liberated. He walked like a gorilla and had a body to match. He packed such a punch behind his powerful shoulders that a slap with his open hand could knock you unconscious. Phol carried an iron bar rather than customary whip. He killed without warning, hitting his victim across the back of the neck as if striking a rabbit.

Phol wasted no time in introducing me to the mistreatment that befell everyone under his charge. He pushed me into a hut where a dozen other prisoners, on all fours, were scraping the feces, urine, and dirt from the floor. Phol gave me a rag and told me to get busy. Nearly everyone had diarrhea from typhus or drinking polluted water. Feces dripped down through the cracks in the bunks covering the floor in excrement several inches thick. Defilement was inevitable, because Phol had forbidden anyone to leave the hut after the evening meal till roll call the next morning. Pleas to visit the single latrine were met with an order to squat in deep knee bends, forcing you to evacuate on the spot. His ruthless impulse to humiliate showed itself by destroying whatever human dignity was left by making his victim mop up his excrement with his clothes.

Without water and a hard broom it was impossible to wash the fetid mess off the floor. We scraped the boards with our nails, mopping up the slimy half frozen dirt as best we could. Like Sisyphus, we were doomed from the start. Phol inspected our efforts after evening roll call and flew into a rage. After working all day, the floorboards were still dirty. He made us "swim" up and down the floor till our clothes and bodies were covered in filth. Although we were fouled already, the stench from this exercise left one gasping for air. The *Strafkompanie* had a single latrine (an open bucket) for nine hundred men. Lack of water, soap, and a change of clothing meant that we were permanently covered in our own dirt. We were being systematically subjected to filth. It was a deliberate excremental assault to induce a state of profound dehumanization. Phol wanted us to die in our own shit.

It was an iron law in the camps that those who did not wash soon died. Veteran prisoners could tell after a few days whether new arrivals would succumb to dirt, decay, and rot. Anyone who became negligent about cleanliness soon lost the will to live—not because washing protected you against illness, but because it helped maintain your self-respect. Every evening I followed the example of those who wiped themselves down with a rag soaked in their own urine. It was just one of the daily never-finished battles to remain visibly human.

The customary roll call was followed by the evening meal after which we returned to our huts. Crammed against my bunkmates whose bodies were as soiled as mine, I lay awake wondering what act of vengeance Phol had in store for us. Having been beaten up repeatedly, I had learned that almost every physical pain was bearable—if one knew beforehand exactly what was going to happen.

The unexpected act of terror was always the most difficult to deal with: it gave one no chance to foresee one's reactions and no scale to calculate one's capacity of resistance. I knew we would be punished for not cleaning the floor to his satisfaction. That, after all, had been the purpose of the exercise. The standard punishment for disobeying an order was death by hanging—an event beyond all normal experience for which nothing can prepare you.

We were awakened the next morning at 4 a.m., an hour earlier than other prisoners (in winter reveille was an hour later). It was bitterly cold, the temperature well below freezing. We stood in our prison clothes for an hour, waiting for Phol to take roll call.

As dawn broke, we saw the outline of the gallows. From everything I knew about Phol, we were doomed. My fear was confirmed after roll call when Phol ordered those of us who had worked on the floor to step forward. Two of our number had died during the night, cheating the hangman. Phol was furious. He double-checked the dead to make sure the block staff had not made a mistake. Wanting to take his revenge, I was sure he would not spare the rope.

Death on the gallows did not occur from a broken neck—the rope and distance of the fall were too short—but from suffocation. Death was painful. It was drawn out and lasted several excruciating minutes. After each hanging, the whole camp was marched past the gallows in formation, not to show respect for the dead, but to the gallows, the symbol of SS of power. I did not want to die. None of us did. Together we might have done something—overpowered Phol, taken his gun and shot him before we ourselves were gunned down. But in the freezing cold, our bodies half numb, surrounded by SS with their guns at the ready, any action—even if we were capable of it—would have ended before it began.

Phol glared at us, heavy, menacing, his feet spread apart. *"Volkschädling*, you think I've forgotten...?" he screamed. He barked out an order, and half a dozen guards came running.

We were marched, not to the gallows, but out of the gate to the woods near the crematorium, where six prisoners were strung up on poles. They had been left hanging all night. All but one was frozen stiff. The surviving prisoner, whose body weight had sprung his shoulder balls from its sockets, leaving him hanging by his dislocated arms, was semi-conscious. How he had lived through the night was a mystery. Enraged that the man was still alive, Phol hit him across the face, body, and genitals with his whip. When the man's head dropped, Phol pulled out his revolver and shot him.

Still holding his pistol, Phol ordered us to undress. Guards fastened our hands behind our backs with a heavy rope threaded through a pulley set three meters off the ground on a wooden stake. On Phol's order the guards pulled on the ropes, and we were yanked off the ground. My arms and shoulders felt as if they were being torn apart. Sweat broke out in my forehead and lips. My breath was reduced to short gasps. All the pain was concentrated in a single, limited area of the body, my shoulder joints. I tried not to give Phol the satisfaction of hearing me scream but couldn't help it. As if this was the cue that Phol had been waiting for, he began beating one of the prisoners. He used a whip made of thin wire and cord. The first few blows lacerated the skin. Each new lash bit deeper. The more blood Phol drew, the more excited he became. After 50 lashes the man's back was raw. By 100 the bones were exposed. The man slumped, motionless. Phol, his strength exhausted, passed his blood-clotted whip to a guard. Before returning to camp, he gave instructions that we were to get a similar thrashing.

After Phol walked off, the guards gave us 25 lashes each. This was meek punishment compared to what Phol had inflicted. Even so, the first couple of strokes seemed to split my body in two. I had never imagined that flesh could experience such pain and survive to feel it. After the fourth stroke the pain seemed to shift from my back to my brain. I heard myself scream, felt my bladder empty itself, my stomach turn and throw up its contents. Then as suddenly as it started, it stopped. The guards had had enough.

While the SS smoked their cigarettes, we struggled to stand upright. One man was still screaming, his upper lip bitten clean through. My body was so numb that I scarcely felt anything at all. Such was the relief of being alive that I almost thanked the guards for not killing us. But expressions of this kind provoked an adverse effect. The more one managed to touch the SS, the more dangerous they became.

We shuffled back to camp, leaving seven bodies lying on the ground beneath the birch trees. Once inside the camp we had to remain standing until the *Kommandos* returned that evening. The cold was intense. Standing upright was an added torture. Pain, pride, and humiliation ran through my body in hot and cold shivers. Hate kept some prisoners alive; others thought of revenge. But I never saw hatred hold out against death. The only sure way to stay alive was to grit one's teeth and refuse to die.

By the time we got back to our block, it was dark and had started to snow. When I removed my sodden shirt one of the prisoners bathed my back with urine and staunched the bleeding with strips of cloth torn from his own shirt. In a world of cruelty and horror where any conception of humanity had almost been destroyed, there were unexpected acts of kindness and even selflessness that restored one's faith in human goodness. We had nothing to share, but when an exchange did take place it revealed the paradox of extremity: that life persists in a world ruled by death.

As the pain wore off, hunger returned with its customary pangs. Hunger was ubiquitous and pervasive. You encountered hunger in the first few days after admission to the camp, and it never left you. The hours are filled with imagining how you will taste each crumb of bread, savor each mouthful of soup. But at meal time I gulped down the spoonful of watery soup and few grams of bread like everyone else.

One of Phol's cruelest tricks was to bait us with bread. Knowing that food to a starving man was synonymous with life, he would appear, like a savior holding a loaf of bread. As soon as he entered the block, 900 starving men rushed towards him, calling for bread in a dozen languages. Holding everyone at bay, he pointed to several men who stumbled forward, hands outstretched. Before giving them anything, he made them get on all fours and bark like a dog before they could pick up with their mouths what he had tossed them. I would have done the same. Whoever thinks that he would have behaved differently has never touched the rock bottom of life: he has never known the thin line between survival and death. Another game was to offer someone a sausage. Told to close his eyes and open his mouth, Phol urinated down the man's throat, roaring with laughter as the prisoner retched all over himself. I doubt if Phol ever reflected on the morality of his actions or knew what his buried motives were.

Although I had already outlived my time, thanks to scavenging on the road to the worksite, I knew this meager supplement would not hold body and soul together for another six months. I did not want to die, but I did not fear death. It is not difficult, after all, to bring life to an end. The inevitability of it took away the dread. One lived every hour knowing that life was not only finite but in danger of ending unexpectedly. It undermined everything one was taught to believe in. How to combat it was a question each had to answer for himself. Failure to do so encouraged an inner sclerosis that hastened one's vulnerability to every mishap.

13

The day after our ordeal in the forest Phol assigned me to the transport *Kommando*. Although considered among the worst assignments, it had its compensations. One sometimes found scraps of food in the transports that brought the POWs to Dachau. Survival was often a matter of chance. One lived by chance and one died by chance; your good luck was commonly at the expense of someone else's bad luck. For the Russian POWs their turn never came. If they did not die in the freight cars, they died very soon after.

I learned my first news of the war from the Russians. Germany had invaded Russia, the Japanese had attacked Pearl Harbor, and Hitler had declared war on the United States. What was a "European conflict" in the summer had, in the space of six months, become a World War. Another surprise was that Russia, in spite of its indifference to the elimination of France and British suffering under the Blitz, had been welcomed by the Allies as a brother-in-arms. The brutality of Stalin's regime and his alliance with Nazism was forgotten. With a wave of the wand an enemy had became an ally.

In Dachau, meanwhile, the transports arrived with their cargo of Russian POWs. Typically the SS kept their distance, not because they were horrified by what they saw, but in order to take action if the need arose. But the need never arose. The few survivors were too weak to understand what was happening, let alone react by fleeing or trying to resist. Each transport carried as many as 2,000 Russian prisoners, a third of whom died on the journey. The prisoners were so tightly packed the dead stood upright. When we opened the doors we saw half-eaten bodies.

After six months of concubinage with death, a corpse was no novelty. The sheer will to survive triggers defense mechanisms. You tell yourself that the death of the other person is not your own death; that the dead are no longer living and are therefore beyond suffering and pity. But the dead Russians made a deep impression on me. Some of them were little more than boys, their lives prematurely cut short. The youthful legions lost to war were doubly dead for having died so young.

We loaded the bodies onto wagons, stacking them like logs, and dragged them to the burial pits in Leitenberg. Those who were capable of walking were force-marched to the SS rifle range at Hebertshauen. When they got to Hebertshauen they were lined up against a concrete wall and used for target practice. The sound of firing could be heard all day.

By evening the earth in front of the wall was crimson with blood. Terrible as the work was, it was preferable to the gravel pit. It was less backbreaking, and the guards kept their distance. On rare occasions we found scraps of food left behind. Without these scraps it would have been impossible to survive.

The transports stopped suddenly in April. Zill had complained to the *Sichereitshauptamt* (The Central Security Department of the SS) that Dachau's burial pits were overflowing. He was also worried by the number of POWs who "collapsed dead or half dead from exhaustion" during the march to Hebertshauen. "They have to be picked up by a vehicle following behind. One cannot prevent the German inhabitants from taking notice of these events..."

When the transports were rerouted, I was afraid that Phol would send me back to the gravel pit. It would have been a death sentence. My body had begun to feed off itself, hastening the progress of starvation. With just a few months before my release, the gravel pit would become my graveyard. But when the transport detail was disbanded, Phol assigned me to the snow *Kommando*.

The SS would not tolerate snow within the camp. If flakes fell during the day they had to be removed immediately. But often at daybreak, a quilt of snow one or two feet deep covered the ground. I was paired with a Catholic priest, Father Schefler. We used shovels and boards nailed to wooden planks to pile the snow into huge heaps, which we loaded into a large barrow or onto tables that were carried to the Würmbach, a river beyond the camp perimeter. According to custom, everything was done at a running pace. SS stood or walked behind us, hitting us with sticks and shouting at us if we slackened for a second.

After the last snow in mid-April Father Schefler and I returned our shovels and were pointed in the direction of the crematorium. Using the dump cart that we used to haul snow we collected the dead from around the camp and took them to be cremated. Collecting the dead was the only unsupervised task in the camp. We were able to approach the kitchens without being questioned; there a friend of Father Schefler's gave us leftovers from the SS mess. These scraps of food were a godsend.

There were always bodies to collect from outside the barracks after morning roll call. Each night saw its harvest of dead. After making the rounds of the camp there remained the Bunker, disinfection barracks, and the infirmary. The Bunker, in addition to serving as a prison, was the camp's torture center. On the walls in the two rooms used as torture chambers were hooks on which the SS hung their victims when they wished to flog or torture them. The Bunker yard was graveyard in its own right, with corpses dragged from the "standing cells" (cubicles 2'6" square without light or air) and those who had not survived being flogged on the "trestle" (a slatted table not much bigger than a butcher's block). The SS used especially finished leather whips, which they soaked in water before using. The usual number of strokes was 25, but we saw bodies that had been lashed more than a hundred times. The SS were never obliged to torment and murder, but they always could if they wished, in passing or on impulse, with purpose or without.

While one can harden one's self to most things to the point that behavior becomes mechanical, I never approached the contorted bodies and faces of the dead outside the infirmary without feeling pity and anger. While illness and starvation was the most common cause of death in the infirmary, there were always some who had died as a result of Dr. Rascher's experiments.

Rascher's experiments for the Luftwaffe included freezing prisoners to simulate the conditions faced by pilots shot down over the Channel. His guinea pigs were young healthy Jews or Russians. They were put in a vat of icy water or left to freeze in sub-zero temperatures with an insulated probe inserted into their rectum to measure the drop in body temperature. Most victims lost consciousness and died when their body temperature fell below 25 C. Rascher tried to resuscitate his victims when they lost consciousness by injecting boiling water into their stomach, bladder, and intestines. To spice up his experiments, he brought in a bus load of gypsy women from Ravensbrück to copulate with the ice-cold bodies.

Rascher reported directly to Himmler, who took it upon himself to suggest various modifications. He proposed the use of a sauna to revive the dying rather than live bodies since "women did not produce enough heat," and approved Rasher's request to learn how much salt water could be ingested before death.

In spite of Rascher's friendship with Himmler, it did not save him from the gallows. Himmler had Rascher arrested, not for his murderous experiments, but for deceiving him about his children. When Himmler learned that Rascher's three children were "rescued" from among 80 Jewish orphans sent to Hartheim to be gassed, he declared that Rascher had acted in violation of Nazi race laws and sentenced him to death. Rascher was executed in the Bunker yard in April 1945, just before the Americans liberated the camp.

In normal circumstance death belongs to the dying and those who love them; in the camps death belonged to the SS, the *Kapos,* and the doctors. When I first started working with Father Schefler, he told me, "The camps have taught me that the dignity we seek in dying must be found in the dignity with which we have lived our lives. The honesty and grace of the years of life that have been brought to an end is the real measure of how we die."

Father Schefler was a causality of Hitler's drive to exterminate all opponents, real or imagined. Although Hitler had concluded a concordant with the Pope, he considered the agreement worthless. He told von Papen on his return from the Vatican that "the evil that is gnawing our vitals is our priests... The time will come when I'll settle my account with them.... They'll hear from me alright...," And hear they did.

A party song sung by the Brownshirts as they rounded on the clergy left nothing to the imagination:

"Sharpen the long knives on the pavements,
so they'll cut the bodies of priests more easily!
And when the hour of retribution strikes,
We'll be ready for every sort of mass murder."

Under the pretext of "incitement of the people," priests were rounded up and sent to Dachau and other camps in their thousands. Nazi logic followed the edict of Deuteronomy: "All dreamers of dreams, prophets, and givers of signs shall be put to death."

The clergy were isolated from the rest of the camp to prevent them from giving comfort to the dying. The chapel, a corrugated iron hut built by the priests while Dachau was still a detention center, was left standing because the SS got a kick out of the notice they nailed to the door: "Here, God is Adolph Hitler." The clergy were forced to give up their breviaries and rosaries and were punished if caught celebrating mass or giving the sacrament. Father Schefler was in the *Strafkompanie* because he had been caught giving General Absolution to a dying prisoner.

Jesus for me was never more than a Zadik, a Jewish rabbi, a man who lived off his past like everyone else. He had never become the human being in whom God had incarnated himself and allowed himself to be sacrificed for our sakes. But when the Father spoke about the Passion, I listened. It was not Christ, externally existent outside time who faced the terror of the cross, died and was resurrected, but we ourselves. If the Mass has any meaning at all it must be our Mass, our fate, our transfiguration.

It was one of the unwritten laws of camp life to avoid topics that could evoke sadness, pain, or despair. Remembering the past made all too clear what our real situation was. All that was permitted was sifted fragments of the past devoid of any emotional value. Father Schefler never spoke about himself, his family, or his past life, and neither did I. But I was drawn to him like a son to a father. His belief in deliverance, the healing power of prayer, the prospect of better things to come, made life more bearable.

If we finished the day's work before evening roll call, I returned to the hut to sleep. There was never enough time for rest. It was a constant temptation, imposed by exhaustion, to close one's eyes and sink into oblivion.

Father Schefler, however, went to the infirmary. "If you want proof of God's existence," he told me, "you need go no further. Among the dying there remains enough humanity to divine that the will to live is not animal, but sacred." His compassion had nothing to do with his office, but everything to do with grace, in the sense of love freely given. He and the other priests helped the sick with no possibility of immunizing themselves against disease. They took the sick in their arms, helped them to turn over, comforted them when dying. Nothing I said could undermine the integrity that was sure to doom him.

A few weeks before my discharge Father Schefler came down with typhus. I tried cooling his body with water I collected from the ditch near the crematorium. As hopeless and ineffective as this measure was, it kept him out of the clutches of the SS till almost the very last day. Just before he died, he said, "I have a little journey to make…"

I took his body in a wheelbarrow to the crematorium, where it was thrown by an SS-man on to a pile of corpses waiting to be incinerated. I think at that moment I learned to pray. If the camps posed the supreme riddle for the religious spirit, it was no less true for nonbelievers like myself. Father Schefler's acts of love and self-sacrifice were derived from spirituality greater than our own. He believed that even the SS, alienated from God, hostile to the truth, in the grip of dark powers, helplessly culpable of trespasses and sins, had a dignity because of the personal being that God has given to each of them.

A few days before my release, against all camp wisdom, I thought about Marian and our moments together. Memories I had dared not recall flooded into my heart and mind. "The only thing that counts is faith expressing itself through love," the Father said. And I understood for the first time how a man who has nothing may still know happiness.

At the end of my six-month term I was marched to the *Jourhaus* to receive my discharge papers. Once again I dared look at the trees beyond the camp. It awakened vistas that I had long forgotten. As we approached the guard house, I saw several hundred Jewish prisoners lined up in front of the gate. We were ordered to fall in behind them. A few minutes later the *Largerführer* gave the order to march and we set off for the station. When we reached the station, the doors of the waiting boxcars were slid open, and we were pushed inside. Things had moved so quickly that I had no time to think about what was happening. Before the doors slammed shut, I heard someone say, *"Folgender anschlag, Auschwitz."*

14

uards walked up and down the train slamming their rifle butts against the doors, shouting, *"Schweigen! Schweigen!"* (Silence! Silence!) but to no effect. When the doors were slid open, they released a wave of putrid air and cries for food and water. Hysterical men and women, clamoring to reach a child or spouse, pressed forward, only to fall back under the whips and curses of the SS.

The men and women in the boxcars were the latest victims of Eichmann's "resettlement operation" of Austria's 80,000 Jews. They had been given a little bread at Vienna's Aspang station but no water and not been told where they were going. They had traveled for three days; it would take them a further four to reach Auschwitz.

As the crow flies, Auschwitz is only 350 miles from Dachau, but the train stopped repeatedly for no apparent reason and for hours at a time. During the day the sun turned the boxcars into an oven. At night it was desperately cold. Even our huddled bodies did not prevent us from shivering. People had vomited on the floor, overcome by the stifling atmosphere and the foul odor of excrement.

Every time the train stopped we beat our fists and hands against the wooden boards, calling desperately, "Water! Air!"

The guards replied by banging the doors with their rifle butts and firing warning shots in the air. By the third day (the sixth for those from Vienna) our car was a mortuary. Overcome by the fetid air and stench of urine and feces, a child died every few hours. Distraught mothers cried hysterically, groping for their children's bodies. As time went on, more and more prayers were said for the dead.

⌘ ⌘ ⌘

By the fourth day I found myself slipping in and out of consciousness, my tongue swollen from lack of water. I kept myself wedged against the side of the car, knowing that if I slipped to my knees I would suffocate. Nothing stretches the minutes more than fear. I told myself, as I had many times before, that I was still alive. It was little enough, but in a system whose end point is killing, this affirmation was an act of resistance in itself.

It was not clear to me why I was being sent to Auschwitz. Only later did I learn that it was the destination for anyone who lived out their term in the *Strafkompanie*. No one was expected to survive.

I knew we had arrived at Auschwitz as soon as I heard the crazed barking of half-wild German shepherds. It is a noise one can never forget. Heavy footsteps crunched on the gavel, the seal on the cars were broken, and the doors pushed open to shouts of "Out! Out!"

In front of us stood SS men, whips in hand, dogs pulling against leather leads. "Everyone out. Leave all baggage in the cars." We stumbled over bodies towards the open door, gulping the air, blinded by the lights bearing down on us.

SS doctors quickly made their selection—a wave here, a gesture there—as they walked down the columns that extended for hundreds of yards. The sick and men over 40 were sent to the left. Most women also went to the left, along with children under 12.

A man asked if he could stay with his wife.

"Later," came the reply.

A woman held onto her child.

"Good, stay with child."

Another woman held onto her case. A guard shouted, *"Verboten!"* and it was snatched from her hand.

Anyone who crossed the line from one side to the other was brutally pushed back.

The SS carried out the selections so quickly that no one had time to come to their senses. The speed of events generated a shocklike rupture. There was no time to think clearly, even if one was in a fit state to do so. In just a few minutes Eichmann's victims were separated from everything that had constituted their former lives: their personal possessions, then their closest family.

Resistance was virtually impossible. Guards armed with machine guns and fixed bayonets were posted every few yards. Blinding searchlights covered every move. Although regulations prescribed "correct" treatment for new arrivals in order to avoid panic and maintain deception, we were driven forwards with rifle butts and whips. Cries of pain, despair, misery, and grief could be heard above the noise of barking and shouting.

Auschwitz is a chilling sight at night. The floodlights, which were never extinguished, revealed a dense prison of brick buildings, watch towers, concrete posts, and barb wire. In the distance a stout brick chimney belched out fire and smoke, giving the air a peculiar sweetish odor, one which I recognized from Dachau. The smell was permanently in the air at Auschwitz, no matter which way the wind blew.

On the way to the registration barrack we passed the *Kleine Posstenkette* (small cordon). Hundreds of women, draped in tattered clothes, ravaged by illness or hunger or both, rushed towards us, thrusting their arms through the barb wire begging for food. The women in our column gasped with horror, unaware that in a matter of days they too would be reduced to the same pitiful state.

Men and women were usually registered separately, but that morning we were herded into the reception building together. SS guards, some still drunk from a night's carousing, tore the clothes off anyone who hesitated. Any man who tried to protect his wife was beaten to the ground. Letters and photographs were torn from people's hands, denying them the last memorabilia of their lives.

As soon as we had undressed, we were made to climb onto a table to be examined: oral and rectal for men; oral, rectal and vaginal for women. The guards who reached into our private parts did not lubricate their gloved fingers, but used the same finger for all three intrusions, laughing obscenely, comparing penises, breasts, and buttocks. This sado-sexual behavior was too much for some women. Moral disgust, if it arises too suddenly, creates an emotional trauma undermining the will to live. Those who had poison capsules took their own lives: others collapsed in a dead faint. Torn from the anchorage of the outside world, it took time to find a new center of gravity. It was only later that you realized that the choice of death in order to resolve a moral conflict was pointless in a world where dying contributes to the success of evil.

After being prodded and pushed, we were shaved by functionaries who cared little for the pain they inflicted. First the hair on our head, face, and body was shaven; then the closely shaven areas were scrubbed with dirty rags that had been soaked in disinfectant. When Auschwitz was liberated, the Russians found seven tons of hair awaiting shipment to Germany. It was used to fill cushions and mattresses. The families of the Third Reich slept on the hair of its victims.

While we were being attacked with scissors and razors, an SS officer walked up and down, pulling aside the prettiest girls. To see them better he lifted their chins with the handle of his whip. If a girl pleased him, he asked her if she was a virgin: *"Jungfrau?"* If the answer was "yes," he gave a nod, and the girl was spared. Girls who passed this inspection were visibly relieved. No one told them they were earmarked for the SS brothel.

Degraded to our naked bodies, we were driven into the shower room, men and women together. Faucets sprinkled us with drops of water. Like everyone else I held my mouth under the pipe. *"Verboten! Verboten!"* shouted the guards, rushing at us with their arms raised. The water smelt foul. It tasted of rust (the SS were prohibited for using it even for washing). I got severe diarrhea as a result, but thirst had left my throat raw. Dripping wet, we were smeared with a solution of calcium chloride from head to toe. The chloride seared the body, causing a fresh outburst of screams and cries. Still dripping, we were given our prison clothes. I got a pair of broken-down shoes with wooden soles and a pair of ill-fitting blue-and-white prison overalls. The overalls were crawling with lice blood-stained.

The next rite of passage was a tattoo by a female *Lagerältester*. Men were tattooed on the outside of the left forearm and women on the inside. Because I did not have enough flesh on my bones I was tattooed on the thigh. For Jews, this was a galling experience. Mosaic Law forbids being marked. We were tattooed with a metal-tipped stylus and indelible ink; a number of small, bluish spots appeared almost instantly in the form of a number. The number made each person identifiable. Mine was 175,389. Henceforth in the eyes of the SS I was a cipher among hundreds of thousands of others.

After being numbered we lined up in front of a row of *Rapportschreibers* waiting to take down our particulars. Although it had been no help to me in Dachau, I knew the *Arbeitseinsatzführer* kept a card index of all prisoners. Since survival could depend on what was written on your card, it was essential to claim Aryan descent and a profession that might realize a material advantage.

Therefore, when asked my name, date, and place of birth, I recognized the Bavarian accent and replied in the same inflection. The clerk looked up. I told him I was a Technical-Sergeant with the XX11 Army Corps and that while on leave in Berlin I had been arrested by the Gestapo for sleeping with a Jewish girl. The SS cared little for Himmler's instructions about sexual intercourse with women of other races. Two of their generals, Kruger and von dem Bach, had gone so far as to say that no punishment should be inflicted for disobedience to this order. I hoped the scribe felt the same way and would pass my card to the SS non-com responsible for organizing prisoners' labor.

The admission procedures over, we were marched through the camp gate. Like the *Jourhaus* in Dachau, it carried the cynical inscription *Arbeit Macht Frei*. After standing for most of the afternoon, the women were ordered to fall out and taken to their barracks. The men were ordered to Block 37, one of the sixty or so red brick buildings that made up the camp. The barracks were appallingly overcrowded and even filthier than those in the *Strafkompanie*. At that time there was only one latrine in the entire camp, a shed with an open sewer about 30 yards long without seats. Immediately after morning roll call 7,000 inmates suffering from diarrhea and dysentery raced to find a place at the latrine. The time allocated by the camp's regulations to this necessity was just 10 minutes. The sewer was supplied with such an anemic supply of water that it could not flush the discharge of 10 prisoners, let alone 7,000. The result was an excretory catastrophe, worse and more chaotic than anything in Dachau.

That evening after roll call I had my first meal for four days, a cup of watery soup made from nettles and weeds, and a piece of gray bread. Unlike the arrivals from Vienna, I knew that in order to get by it was necessary to locate illegal food, dodge work, and find influential friends. The first requisite was to find a bartering partner or intermediary who was willing to sell whatever food they had managed to save. But I had nothing to barter and nothing to sell. In these circumstances the only way to ward off starvation was sleep.

Overcrowding in Auschwitz resulted in a constant struggle of all against all: at the latrine, in the meal line, and especially the dormitory. There was little feeling of camaraderie, especially with regard to newcomers, because they took up space and time and did not know the unspoken but ironclad rules of coexistence and survival. When we were directed to our living quarters, those of us from Dachau brushed aside the protests and made space for ourselves: one did not ask to share a bunk, you appropriated space where you found it. We were crammed seven to a bunk, close enough to hear each other's heartbeat. The nights were filled with the sounds of groaning and cries of hunger. Sometimes a skeletal prisoner jumped up screaming: his bedfellow had just died, and the lice were emigrating on to him.

Shortly after midnight the *Blockältester* and a swarm of *Kapos* stormed through the hut shouting, *"Selekcja!" "Selekcja!"* (Selection! Selection!). Instinctively I jumped to the floor. Anyone slow to respond was dragged from his bunk and beaten. We tumbled out into the night, pushed into line by truncheons and whips. Huge spotlights illuminated the camp. In front of us stood SS doctor Franz Bodmann.

Selections took place at roll call or during work, in the barracks and the infirmary, during the day or night, suddenly and without warning. To make room for arrivals the SS liquidated exhausted inmates, exchanging them for fresh prisoners. Selections were a murderous means for system maintenance. Bodmann, wearing a doctor's white housecoat, began his inspection. He nodded at one man, pointed at another, passing down judgments in an instant. Anyone who did not stand upright, who did not look strong enough for hard labor or whose looks did not please him, had his number taken. The man next to me, a Viennese, asked why we were having a medical examination in the middle of the night. No one had told him that selections were not for the infirmary but for the gas chamber.

I was never quite sure how to act at the critical moment. Was it safer to look the SS in the eye or drop your head? To beg for mercy or say nothing? One thing was certain. You could not look at an SS officer in the face as if he were another human being. Acknowledging your common humanity was fatal. I was acutely conscious of the bones sticking through my skin. I braced my shoulders, took a deep breath, filling out my chest.

Bodmann approached. It was an agonizing moment, a time of tormenting uncertainty. I glanced briefly at his eyes, then at the ground, then at the SS men accompanying him. It was always the same fear at this moment. The consciousness of death was known not by death's certainty, but rather its uncertainty, creating abrupt changes between hope and fear. Would you hold together or fall apart?

Then the moment of deadly confrontation passed. Bodmann and his retinue moved on. The *Kapos* did not grab me by the arms, yank me from the row, take down my number. I breathed again.

In a few minutes it was all over. A block with three or four hundred prisoners had been sorted out, the selection completed. To reach a verdict, Bodmann needed neither reflection nor time. It rested on his proficiency in assaying the human body, his familiarity with death. A flick of the finger, a slight turn of the head, was all that was needed. The arbitrary will of the SS determined who was one too many.

The condemned had until morning roll call before being taken away. Their fate was met with understanding but not sympathy. Selection was a series of death sentences. There was only a single disjunction: to the left—death; to the right—life. Each person hoped he would not be chosen, that selection would fall on the next person. To oppose one's fate one it was necessary to distance yourself from those the SS had written off—in order not to write yourself off.

I lay awake listening to one of the condemned intone a mournful chant. He sang in Yiddish, but I knew the words.

The man prayed for his soul. He asked God not to hide his face from him or put him away in anger. "Hear my prayer, O Lord, and give ear unto my cry; hold not thy peace at my tears: for I am a stranger with thee, and a sojourner. O spare me a little, that I may recover strength: before I go hence, and be no more seen." His waiting was almost over. Before the day was out, he would know the truth about everything, and all his missing years would be pieced together.

Others reminded God of the cry of his chosen—"For thy sake we are being killed all the day long; we are regarded as sheep to be slaughtered," with, of course the same implication: "Rise up and come to our help! Deliver us for the sake of thy steadfast love."

But in Auschwitz the gas chambers were evidence that God was under no obligation to Israel.

⌘ ⌘ ⌘

Dawn arrived too early. We were awakened again by whistles and shouts of *"Aufstehen! Raus! Raus!" Kapos* stormed into the barrack, rubber truncheons flying. Chosen because of their criminal records, the *Kapos* were given almost unlimited power. If a prisoner died, no questions were asked. Although they played the executioner's game, they died as victims, either at the hands of the SS or the prisoners themselves.

I tried not to think about my condition, although I could barely stand upright. Physically and mentally, this was the low point of my life. Officially we were to get enough food to keep us alive, but we never received the minimum. The bread was made largely of sawdust: the soup with thistles or anything else that was at hand—offal, old rags, even bits of string. I found myself clawing on the ground for any scraps I could find. All I could think of was food. I was slipping into the no-man's land of the *Muselmänner.*

The *Muselmänner* embodied the irretrievable hopelessness that affected us all. They were everywhere in the camp. Their skin was encrusted with dirt, their gaze gone, their eyes hollowed out, their clothes threadbare and soiled, moving with slow, hesitating steps, dragging their fleshless feet along the ground in a decrepit slouch and talking incessantly about food. A large number died under the truncheon of a *Kapo* or from the blow of an SS rifle butt. They dropped dead at roll call, in the latrine, or on their pallets without their bunkmates even noticing. The SS called them *Figuren* (puppets) and their death *ungestorbener Tode* (deaths that have not died).

Their pathetic appearance and dejected air with their head bowed reminded me forcefully that we were just like them, a non-person without any rights. With all meaning drained from their lives, it might seem that they had no reason to go on; but most were too weak to seize the chance that came from time to time to end their lives in a way they had chosen. Spectacles of human ruin, broken by hunger and cold, they moved insensibly to a senseless death. The need to protect ourselves from the sight of our own fate made us avoid them, even ignore them. Very few *Muselmänner* survived. Death claimed them before they died.

The *Zugänge*, or newcomers, were placed in a *Kommando* that would most rapidly break them bodily and spiritually. For those of us from Dachau it was a double penalty. We were marched to the new camp at Birkenau. Waiting for us was a massive road-roller weighing several tons. It required 60 prisoners to pull it. With bent backs and lowered heads we dragged the roller up and down the *Lagerstrasse*. Those of us who were too weak to exert much effort depended on others to provide the momentum. Anyone who stumbled or collapsed under the strain was crushed under its weight. The *Kapos* never let up for a minute, shouting "Faster! Faster!" driving us on until the axle rumbled and groaned.

The noon break was followed by another round of numbing labor until 6:00 p.m. One never knew how much time had passed or how much remained. I counted the seconds. I counted them again, just as I had in Dachau: 60 in a minute, 3,600 in an hour, 180,000 in five hours, trying to arrest the nightmare of timeless time.

At the end of the day we picked up the dead and placed them on carts. The SS had an uncanny knack of knowing who was most likely to falter on the way back to camp. What happened to Barszewski, a Polish Jew, was typical.

Barszewski, who had struggled to keep his head up all day, was told to pull one of the laden carts. He had almost made it back to camp when Schätzle, the senior guard, made him run at the double. The Pole stumbled, lost his balance, and let go of the handles.

"You stupid Jew," shouted Schätzle. "How long have you been working for?"

The Pole raised his hands and spread out his fingers.

"Five months!" shouted Schätzle. "You've lived too long. A decent

Jew would have died three months ago." Schätzle lifted his cudgel and brought it down on the Pole's head, killing him instantly. Barszewski's body was added to those in the barrow. Drowning in daily episodes of atrocity, we had neither tongue nor spirit to protest.

⌘ ⌘ ⌘

After 10 days I could take no more. Death comes with organ failure and starvation and the departure of the spirit, all at once. I had seen it many times, and now felt it within myself. We know nothing about death beyond the single fact that we have to die, but what does it mean, to die? Is it the final limit of all that we are able to imagine, a locus of emptiness so that nothing remains? In Colossians the hymnic language is high-flown, suggesting exciting possibilities in the supernatural world. Resurrection is not a day of assembly but the bestowal of a new form to our spirit. In some sense we are both ourselves and distinct from ourselves, "a new creation," in Paul's words. But whether death be blunt or thrilling, a slide into darkness or an incubatory flash tearing the bonds of our material being, dying itself is remarkably easy. I felt myself slipping into a twilight zone, surrendering to a great lassitude and desire to sleep.

When I did collapse, my final thoughts were of Marian. *"Was Du erlebst, kann keine Macht der Welt Dir rauben."* (What you have experienced, no power on earth can take from you.) Father Schefler, who told me this, was speaking of the people one loves. In some corner of my brain I knew that if I died, I would not see her again. The SS would have succeeded in erasing the roots and ties of my life. I would be another anonymous death, swept up the crematory flu. I cannot explain from where it came, but I found the strength to struggle to my feet. I knew my life was nearing its end, but until that moment I had to appear that I still had the right to live.

My breakdown happened on the afternoon of my second Sunday in Auschwitz. If it had been a work day, I would have died. Towards evening Vacek, one of the senior *Kapos* and deputy to the *Rapportführer,* ordered an unscheduled roll call. I lined up in the back row, hidden from Vacek and the *Rapportführer*. Vacek had a red triangle on his jacket, the sign of a professional criminal. The fear of being lynched by the inmates drove him ever deeper into the clutches of the SS. In order not to be killed he curried favor with the SS by intensifying the level of violence he meted out to those below him.

Because we did not immediately jump to his orders, he made us lie down and then, on command, jump up again. Because we did not all jump up together, the exercise was repeated. After we jumped up and down 15 or 20 times, the purpose of the drill became clear. His first victim's feet and legs were swollen with edema, which prevented him from jumping in double-quick time.

Vacek pounced on the man, knocked him senseless, and dragged him across the yard to the latrine. His second victim had received a blow to the head during an earlier roll call and had lost his hearing. Slow to his feet, he was also set upon and dragged to the latrine. The drill continued. The longer it went on, the more difficult it was to jump up and down. This was what Vacek wanted. By now we were all potential victims. I could not keep up with the others but bobbed up and down, shielded by the prisoners in front.

After 20 minutes Vacek had 12 or more victims lined up against the open sewer. He faced them, mimicking his SS masters, legs apart, arms akimbo, issuing one command after another: "Lie down! Get up! Crawl! Roll over! On your feet!" till they were covered in muck.

Vacek harried and chased them from one end of the yard to other, making them crawl on their bellies and jump to attention. They tripped and fell, blood streaming down their faces. Anyone who couldn't get up was dispatched with his truncheon. Remorseless command followed remorseless command until they had all succumbed. Vacek's bloodthirsty gaze surveyed the harvest of dead, visibly pleased with himself, sweat dripping from his face. For this carnage he would be rewarded with a voucher to the SS brothel or given one of the young Poles with a pink triangle on his jacket.

While Vacek was bludgeoning men to death, Schlage, the *Rapportführer*, looked on approvingly. The slaughter over, Schlage took out his notebook. At that moment, a lawyer from Zilina, unable to contain his anger, cried out, "My God, what is going on here! Have we all gone mad! Prisoners are being killed by prisoners...!"

It was a suicidal remonstrance. Furious, Vacek lunged forward, swinging his truncheon, until another half-dozen men lay sprawled on the ground.

But the voice was not silenced. "This is terrible! Innocent people being beaten to death...."

Luckily, neither Schlage nor Vacek heard this last remark, and we were told to close ranks.

Suddenly, accompanied by a wave of whispering, the lawyer pushed himself forward. He looked Schlage in the eye and said with indignation, "Herr Commandant, I must report that the *Blockältester,*" pointing at Vacek, "has killed innocent men. I am sure that he took the lives of these people without your consent. I therefore ask you to investigate these killings and see that he is punished."

You could hear a pin drop. No prisoner addressed an SS officer. It was tantamount to a death sentence. I could not believe the man's courage. The lawyer must be a *Zugänge*, someone who did not know that we were all expendable.

Stunned by the lawyer's unexpected outburst Schlage stood rooted to the spot. Hardly able to control his rage he bellowed, "Vacek, come here!"

Vacek ran to his master's side.

"Did you hear what this Jew said?"

"I did, Herr *Rapportführer,*" said Vacek, his eyes glinting with anticipation.

"Then give him what he deserves!"

Vacek swung his club, crushing the man's skull with one blow. Splattered in blood, Vacek dragged the lawyer's body across the yard to the pile of corpses. If the lawyer thought his refusal to live among men voluntarily blind to injustice would move Schlage, he had been fatally wrong. To the SS the man was nothing, a Jew. Whether he went up the chimney or perished on the *Appellplatz,* it was all the same.

Schlage, who had watched the killing with satisfaction, returned to his notebook, noting the number of dead. Then he raised his head and began to call out some names. Mine was among them. I was sure we were destined to share the same fate as Vacek's victims. I stepped forward, expecting the end. Schlage gave each man an order. Then it was my turn. "Report to the *Transport Abteilung.*"

It took a moment or two for his words to sink in. I was being transferred to the motor pool. When death looks the other way, it is felt as a gift from God.

15

Aquinas said that fate is the action of God's providence. As I
followed Vacek to the motor pool, it certainly felt that way.
The *Transport Abteilung* was attached to the northern
perimeter of the camp facing the Birkenau slip road. Enclosed by barb
wire, it consisted of a couple of huts converted into workshops and
garages, the prisoner's barrack and the *Kommandeur's* office. Parked
between the perimeter fence and the workshops was a fleet of SS staff
cars, trucks, and ambulances.

Vacek handed me over to the gate guard, who pointed in the
direction of the barrack. I crossed the yard, stumbled against the door,
and fell into the world of the *Prominenten*, the senior camp prisoners.
Although the Prominents lived in close proximity to other inmates,
they lived in a different universe. The veteran inmates had everything
the other prisoners lacked: clean clothing, their own beds, kitchen,
shower room, and lavatory. There was even a "day room" with chairs,
books, and a radio.

I could not believe what I saw. In the middle of the room was a
cast-iron pot-bellied stove, around which half a dozen men were seated
reading and talking. Behind them a man was ironing his clothes, while
another was lying on a daybed with his feet up. I asked for the
Blockältester and someone called for Helmut. One man got up and
helped me into a chair, while another went into the kitchen. The smell
of food nearly made me faint.

⌘⌘⌘

I spent the next two weeks in bed looked after by Helmut and Poletz.
At first they would not give me any food, but tea and some flour mixed

with a little skim milk. Poletz had worked in the Excelsior in Berlin before the war and was a first-rate chef. He spoon-fed me every few hours for the first few days until he was sure I wouldn't swallow everything in one mouthful. Even so it was not until the fourth or fifth day that my hunger subsided, and some strength returned to my body. After a fortnight I felt well enough to do light work around the hut, and by the end of the month to take my place in the machine shop.

The *Transport Abteilung* was a reprieve from hell. There were no selections, no violence, and no roll call (a necessary concession since drivers were employed round the clock). Having my own bed was an extraordinary luxury. One of the worst features of camp life was the overcrowding. The barracks were a cell of human bodies. Maintaining distance was impossible; territorial violations unavoidable.

The men in the *Transport Abteilung* were German. Elsewhere in the camp they were largely Polish and the language little more than a gesticulated, abbreviated code designating threats and warnings. There were no words to describe feelings and few words that pointed to the future. Conversation was limited to food, illness, and warnings necessary for survival. It was an emergency language for an extreme situation and did nothing to strengthen the bonds of human relations. Fraternization was never more than an alliance of fleeting coalitions. Being able to speak again and be spoken to in words of more than one syllable, in sentences not predicated by hunger and fear, was the first step towards regaining a sense of normality.

The Auschwitz that arose out of the swamps and wastelands of the Vistula and which grew into a prison empire was made possible by the *"befristete Vorbeugehäfltinge,"* or BVs, German criminals like Helmut. Helmut was at the apex of prisoner hierarchy. He had been a *Quartiermeister* in the SS before being convicted of theft. His SS background and rank put him in a good light with the senior General Staff Officers. The most important of these was Ziegler, the *Arbeitseinsatz* in charge of labor deployment, and Spittler, Head of Department IV, responsible for building maintenance, camp vehicles, food supply, and clothing.

Because the camps were chronically understaffed, and there was a constant drain of its personnel to the front, the SS was forced to delegate more and more responsibility to the senior prisoners for the daily operations of the camp. All the German BVs had positions of authority. Their ties to the SS and internal coalitions were inscrutable to prisoners in the rest of the camp. What those prisoners could see and experience directly was the Prominents' authority. Many of the BVs abandoned the norms of reasonable behavior, making public displays of power that did not stop short of intimidation and even murder. Helmut was an exception. He was one of the few *Funktionshäftlings* who did not indulge in sadistic violence.

The place that gave its name to the camp was the small Polish town of Oswiecim, 50 kilometers southwest of Krakow. Following the occupation of Poland in 1939, Oswiecim was incorporated into Germany and renamed Auschwitz. In the early days of its existence only Polish dissidents were sent to Auschwitz.

But in 1941 Himmler seized upon the idea of transforming the dilapidated barracks into a concentration camp. Auschwitz was situated on major railroad lines. Its surrounding area was rich in natural resources, making it an excellent location as a source of labor for factories that would manufacture war materials. The man Himmler chose to transform the camp and construct Birkenau, which was to become Auschwitz 11, was Rudolph Höss. Höss took up his appointment in April 1940, a month before the arrival of 30 German criminals from Sachsenhausen, where he had been commandant. To one of these men, Bruno Brodniewicz, belongs the dubious distinction of being given the first Auschwitz camp serial number. Helmut, our *Blockältester*, was number 5. These 30 men made up the network of functionary-prisoners holding official posts in the prisoner hierarchy.

But concentration camps are not death factories. Auschwitz and Birkenau could accommodate more than 200,000 prisoners between them but did not answer the question of eliminating a large number of human beings. The answer was found almost by accident. Karl Fritzch, Höss' deputy, experimented using Zyklon-B on 600 Russian prisoners in the bunker of Block 11, the punishment block. Zyklon-B (the German trade name for hydrogen cyanide or prussic acid) was a commercial form of hydrocyanic acid used as an insecticide. Within a few minutes of hurling in a couple of canisters of Zyklon, the Russians were dead.

"Those who were propped up against the door leaned with a curious stiffness and then fell right at our feet, striking their faces hard against the concrete floor," recalled one of the Polish prisoners assigned to clear the bunker "Corpses! Corpses standing bolt upright and filling the entire corridor, till they were packed so tightly it was impossible for more to fall."

Fritzch had found the answer to the "final solution" of the Jewish question.

In the span of just five years, Auschwitz metamorphosed from a locus of terror into a universe of horror.

16

The omnipresence of death shuffled time's order, shifting the present to center stage. But in the *Transport Abteilung* the threat of imminent death was greatly reduced. It was always there, waiting and ready but had broken ranks with the arbitrary and inescapable. Time regained some normality. The present admitted to a future and with it the possibility of escape.

People had escaped from Auschwitz, but it required extensive organization and collective assistance. I had no outside contacts, nor did I have an introduction to the camp's underground or Polish Resistance who could secure escape routes through a network of liaisons. On first sight it seemed an impossible idea. But Auschwitz was a world in which the impossible was always possible. As luck would have it, help was near at hand in the unlikely person of the Transport Chief himself, *Hauptsturmführer* Hans Jost.

Hans Jost came to see me while I still convalescing. When I saw his black uniform my body stiffened. I thought I would be yanked out of bed and beaten. SS officers did not visit sick prisoners, unless it was to shoot them. But Hans pulled up a chair, asked my name, and how old I was. While we were talking, his eyes never left my face. I reminded him of someone. Then he told me that his son, Wilhelm, was also 23. Wilhelm had been killed a few months after the start of the Russian campaign when his regiment ran into a division of the Mongolian infantry. Hans showed me a photograph of his son wearing an SS camouflage tunic. The boy was more thickset than me, but I saw the resemblance.

Hans was a big man, over six feet tall, the impression of bulk increased by a peculiar bending of the knees when he walked. He almost seemed to be retaining his balance by moving forward, yet his step was firm. His face was large, his nose big, fleshy, arched. His thick dark-brown hair was brushed back from the forehead and over the crown of his head, adding to its massiveness. His eyes were brown, prominent, heavy lidded. His hands seemed out of keeping with the strength of his body. They were plump, like those of a baby and dimpled at the knuckles. His teeth were large and strong, deeply stained from smoking. He struck me as someone who would not find it difficult to do his share of the world's work.

Hans came to see me nearly every other day. He had an eye and a memory for things which recalled his life in Münich: the householder's duty of sweeping away the snow from the footpaths in front of the door; the selling of live fish which used to be brought to the fishmonger's in a barrel and let out through a trap-door into a tub; the food and the beer and what he called a "real German sandwich"—a large slice of rye bread and a thick cut of roast veal.

He was born in Ebersberg, about fifteen miles east of Münich, an area I knew, which gave us something in common to talk about. After completing elementary schooling he took his father's advice and joined the army. Although the officer corps in those days was limited almost exclusively to the sons of the aristocracy, military service was a jumping-off point for those born into the middle or lower-middle classes without a diploma.

In 1914 Hans was one of the cheering, singing crowd that gathered in the Odeons Platz to listen to the proclamation of war. He was just 20. Assigned to an Infantry unit he was sent to the Western Front. His regiment came within a few miles of Paris before an Allied counterattack at Marne drove it back to the Aisne River. He took part in the German attack at Verdun, was wounded in the neck, and sent back to Germany. After his release from the military hospital in the spring of 1917 he was promoted to sergeant and returned to the Front in time to take part in the decisive engagement at Amiens, which marked the launch of the Allied offensive.

When the Germans capitulated a few months later, Hans returned to Münich with his regiment and joined the *Freikorps*, a paramilitary group of right-wing ex-soldiers convinced that they had not lost the war, but been "stabbed in the back" by their own politicians and the Jews (ignoring the fact that Jewish causalities in the German army had been disproportionately high). Hans' war continued: but the enemy had changed. It was now the Communists and any democratic movement that threatened the fledgling Weimar Republic.

One of the many political parties that sprang up during this chaotic period was a right-wing anti-Semitic group called *Deutsche Arbeiter Partei* or German Worker's Party. Among its earliest members was Corporal Adolph Hitler. Hans saw Hitler for the first time in 1920 at a "German Day" rally in München. The force and immediacy of Hitler's passions and the violence of his denunciations held him spellbound. His message was reduced to terse formulas: all Germans were to be united in a Greater Germany; the peace treaties were to be abrogated; and the Jews were to be expelled from Germany:

> When I am in power the annihilation of the Jews will be my first and most important task. I shall have gallows erected in Marienplatz in München, as many as can be fitted without stopping the traffic. Then the Jews will be hanged, one after the other, and they will stay hanging until they stink and the last Jew in München has been destroyed.

World trade and finance, in difficulty since the 1920s because of war debts, collapsed in the 1930s. The Nazis blamed the economic difficulties on the Treaty of Versailles, the politicians who signed it, and the Jews, because of their supposed extra-national loyalties. Hitler's solution to Germany's troubles was unequivocal: Nazi leadership. By 1933 the Nazis had secured sufficient votes to win enough seats in the Reichstag for Hitler to be named Chancellor.

Hitler's first act was to summon his Reich governors and tell them, "We now must eliminate the last remnants of democracy." The police, the army, and the civil service were made part of the Nazi apparatus. Judges and clerks swore allegiance to Hitler and as a symbol of their subservience wore an eagle and swastika badge on the breast of the traditional judge's robe. The church was similarly browbeaten into submission. *"Heil Hitler"* replaced *"Gelobt sei Jesus Christus"* in Catholic schools, and Protestants were placed under the supervision of a Nazi bishop. On July 14, 1933 the *Official Gazette* contained the brief announcement: "The German Government has enacted the following law, which is herewith promulgated: The National Socialist German Workers' Party constitutes the only political Party in Germany."

Reality in the new Reich was the political dominance of the party. Its end justified all means, and its means included not only every technique of propaganda and indoctrination, every device for breaking down the moral conscience, but also the terrorism of the SS and Gestapo, prisons and torture, transported minorities, and concentration camps. Hitler's Germany was a cul-de-sac for human progress: a reign of terror, despotism and darkness, and men were its slaves.

Facing dissolution by demand of the Versailles treaty, many of the *Freikorps*, including Hans, joined the *Sturmabteilung*, (SA), a paramilitary organization of the Nazi party commanded by Ernst Röhm, a homosexual thug, and like Hitler an early member of the Nazi Party. By the autumn of 1933 Hitler had put his stamp on Germany and the SA clamored for its share of the spoils. Hundreds of its members had been killed in brawls with opponents of the Nazi Party and now that Hitler was Chancellor, Röhm had visions of himself heading a National Socialist army incorporating the German armed forces.

To remove the threat posed by the SA, Göebbels and Göring spread the rumor that the SA was planning a coup, giving Hitler the excuse for a bloody purge; the "Night of the Long Knives." In three days more than a thousand leading SA men were murdered. Only Röhm was given the privilege of committing suicide and so establishing his guilt in the eyes of the world. He was given a loaded pistol and told to take "the honorable way out." After 10 minutes, not hearing a shot, Theodor Eicke (commandant of Dachau) returned to Röhm's cell, picked up the revolver and shot the SA leader in the head. Eicke was rewarded for this act by being promoted to Inspector of Concentration Camps.

Without its leaders the SA was an emasculated force and ceased to exist. After this drastic disowning, the German army paid its dues. Every member of the German Armed Forces swore an oath of allegiance which Hitler himself had drafted on a slip of paper—an oath not to the Constitution, not to the Fatherland, but to Hitler personally: "I swear by God this holy oath: that I will render unconditional obedience to the Führer of the German Reich and People, Adolph

Hitler, the Supreme Commander of the Armed Forces, and will be ready, as a brave soldier, to stake my life at any time for this oath."

With this oath the *Wehrmacht* and, through it, the German people became bound body and soul to the person of Adolph Hitler and his policies. From that oath there was no divorce until Hitler took his own life 11 years later.

After Röhm's execution Hans was quick to see that real power lay with the SS and joined its ranks. The SS recognized Hans' service with the Army and promoted him to *Untersturmführer* (Lieutenant), a rank that he would not have enjoyed in the German army. In 1935, when Hitler announced the reintroduction of conscription he amalgamated the various SS squads used for semi-police tasks into a full-scale fighting division, the Waffen SS. Thanks to his service record Hans was made an instructor in the SS officer training school in Braunschweig and later at Bad Tölz. In 1938 he applied for a transfer to one of the newly formed *Einsatzgruppen* units.

Three months before the start of Operation Barbarossa Hans was ordered to report to the police academy at Pretzsch (Silesia) where the *Einsatzgruppen* units destined for Russia were being formed. Each *Einsatzgruppe* was made up of between 800 and 1,200 men operating just behind the advancing German troops. At Pretzsch he and the other officers were told that on Hitler's orders the *Einsatzgruppen* were to shoot all Jews, gypsies, communist officials, and Soviet prisoners of war. They were to be killed without trace, without investigation, and without tears. Women were to be executed along with the men and the children in case they grew up "to oppose National Socialism and nurture a desire to avenge their parents' slayers."

Until his transfer to Auschwitz Hans led "search and destroy" missions in the occupied territories. The *Einsatzgruppen* regarded these genocidal patrols as sport and their quarry, irrespective of age or sex, were hunted down like animals with bloodhounds. *Völkermordkohorte* (killing teams) competed with each other to see who could slaughter the greatest number of Jews. After a successful operation the dogs were rewarded by being fed breasts and penises. In little over a year, the *Einsatzgruppen* killed 1.4 million Jews in Russia alone.

At the start of the campaign Hans and the other officers were unsure if their men had the stomach for killing women and children. But they need not have worried. The *Einsatzgruppen* accepted Himmler's word that killing Jews was not the same as killing people ("They and we are not the same"). By making the personal will of their superior the guiding principle of their actions, rank, and file, SS saved themselves the burden of having to judge their own actions. This was the basis for the unwavering execution of criminal orders. But to be on the safe side, Hans introduced his men to murder by a step-by-step escalation, beginning with the killing of adult males before exposing them to the shock of having to murder women and children. Like much else, killing was something one could get used to.

The more Hans drank, the more he remembered. He traced his Group's progress through the Ukraine beginning in Upper Silesia, reaching Lvov in July after organizing large-scale murder operations in Krakow, Zamosc, and Sokal. After the Babi-Yar massacre, the unit traveled south to Kharkov and then to Belgorod and Kalach in the direction of Stalingrad. By this time murder and routine had become one.

It was at Reschety, a small village on the road to Belgorod, that Hans came face to face with himself as never before. It was as sudden and compacted as the moment when a blinded Saul fell from his horse on the way to Damascus. Hans had killed one to one before Reschety, men and women, but had shot them in the SS manner, in the back of the neck. In Reschety he stood in front of his victims, face to face. The murder of the Reschety Jews was a reprisal against the death of an *Einsatzkommando* by partisans a few days earlier. Although Hans' Group was complicit in the killing of thousands of Russians by this time, and the death of one of his men was the first casuality the Group had suffered, he was ordered to take 100 lives in reprisal: the entire female population of Reschety, all the men having been drafted into the Russian army.

Hans told his men to clear the village, to shoot the elderly and infirm and to march the women and children to the edge of the nearby woods. The line of naked women and children stretched for 40 yards. Hans remembered one woman pointing to the sky, reassuring her 10-year-old son, who was fighting to hold back his tears. Many said prayers, others recited the *"Barauch Dayam Emmeth"* (Blessed be the true Judge), usually spoken on hearing about someone's death but now uttered for themselves.

The cries got too much for Hans. He nodded to his men, and they started to fire at point-blank range. Terrible screams, accompanied by the crackle of pistol fire, filled the air. Hans had not ordered the women to turn their backs, a command it was now too late to give. Blood from the shattered skulls splattered his tunic and face.

The man on his left was amusing himself with two sisters. "Which of you Jews shall I shoot first....?"

The line was broken now, with bodies lying everywhere.

Hans' last victim was a young woman, slim with dark hair, holding a baby in her arms. She stood patiently, knowing her fate, not weeping or pleading for mercy. Hans stood in front of her, reloading his revolver. When he looked up, their eyes met.

"Why are you doing this?" she asked.

There was a moment of silence. Hans did not speak Russian but understood the question. For a second he faltered. He knew that he had no right to take the life of this woman who faced him, with plaits in her hair holding a baby. The confrontation, so unexpected, filled him with confusion. Steeling himself he raised his revolver to her forehead and pulled the trigger. The baby fell from the woman's arms and lay at Han's feet. He shot the infant with his eyes closed.

When the killing was over, he did not share in the celebrations that followed these occasions. He walked into the woods, vomited, and sat down.

That night he had his first nightmare. He was not alone. One of the men awoke, firing his gun into the air. A couple of days later he asked for a transfer. Hans thought he would be sent to the front. Instead he was given leave, promoted to *Hauptsturmführer,* and sent to Auschwitz as Head of the *Transport Abteilung.* The transfer was easier than expected because Himmler had issued an order giving dispensation for men who suffered a "breakdown."

As Hans was one of the very few who asked for a transfer one must assume that most of the men in the *Einsatzgruppen* endorsed, individually and voluntarily, the killing of Jews.

17

Marian had always been the quiet yet passionate center of my life. Now, with a visible improvement in my situation, she was at the center of my desire to live. I felt a real but imperceptible tie with her. Such feelings may sound silly, but they are experienced as events of absolute certainty. It gave me the courage to believe the impossible: that there was life after Auschwitz.

I began to think seriously about escaping. Sooner or later we would all die. Killing was rank normality, routine, and there were no exceptions. We would be gassed, we would be burned, we would be hanged, or we would be shot. This much we knew. The smoke of human remains never let us forget it. My one hope lay with becoming a driver. When a driver left the camp, he was always accompanied by a guard. Greed often got the better of the SS when the transports arrived. Although it was strictly forbidden, they left their vehicles to pick up anything of value dropped by the arrivals. At night, given the noise and confusion, I imagined it would be possible to drive off without being noticed. The scenario was attractive, but improbable. Even if one was not gunned down, there would be no escape without permits and passes.

Although the motor pool offered the best chance of escape, it was the most dangerous in terms of seeking inside help. If it became known that someone was planning to run, the individual concerned was likely to suffer a fatal "accident." The *protekcja* enjoyed by BVs depended on preserving their loyalty to the SS; deviants were eliminated before they could disturb the status quo. The battle for power and privilege was a life and death struggle, and no one was allowed to get in the way.

Unlike other prisoners, the Prominents were quite content with their lives. In a society where death was the norm, they had survived through their astuteness in successfully organizing themselves and gaining the indulgence and respect of the SS. They had everything they wanted—clothes, food, and young boys or prostitutes to attend to their sexual needs. It was a bizarre world situated between the SS and prisoner society, but one which gave them a relatively secure living standard. If they escaped and were caught, they would be shot or sent to the front. Until the Day of Judgment arrived, and it would, Auschwitz was the better option.

For the first five months I worked in the machine shop making engine parts and items to trade. We bartered tools and cutlery for bread, potatoes, and cigarettes from the kitchens and storerooms. Our monopoly of scarce but essential items made the *Transport Abteilung* a source of economic power in the camp "market." Barter was prohibited, but absolutely essential if one was to stay alive. No one could live on the allocated rations. Prisoners hacked out their gold fillings in order to trade them for three or four rations of bread. Whoever did not want to die had to "organize" or find someone who would "organize" on their behalf. To "organize" meant to procure illegally. It was the most important word in the Auschwitz language. The only way around economic exchange was theft, which was endemic.

The storehouse of all wealth was the *Effektenlager*, 30 barracks filled with prisoners' belongings in Birkenau, nicknamed "Canada" because it was a place of abundance. It held not just foodstuffs and clothing, but diamonds, tapestries, silk underwear, cognac, rare books, and even paintings. The more items new arrivals brought with them, the better life was in the camp. The transports were the most important material foundation for daily survival. Prisoners working in Canada to sort out confiscated goods had their own way of smuggling things out. Before returning to camp, the prisoners were searched and anyone found hiding money or valuables was severely beaten or shot. But the risk was worth taking, especially if a guard could be bribed. The SS were not averse to personal enrichment and black racketeering. Deals could be struck.

Twenty train cars per day were loaded with confiscated property at the Auschwitz railroad ramps and sent to Berlin. According to calculations made by the Nazis themselves, the total average profit from one prisoner, not including the value of the victim's bones, after the

94

cost of burning the body had been deducted, totalled 1,631 RM, about $150. A plaque currently on display at Auschwitz notes that 1.5 million people died in the camp between 1940 and 1945.

18

It was clear to everyone that Hans liked me. He had visited me while I was convalescing and when I was on my feet he asked me into his office most nights to drink with him. It was unheard of for someone in his position to take an interest in a prisoner, and it raised a few eyebrows.

Hans was the only SS officer who spent all his time within the precincts of the camp. Senior SS had comfortable barracks near the old Polish tobacco company and for the most part worked in the administrative area outside the fence. Because Hans kept to himself, he was on the fringe of the narrow circle of *Kameraden* who ran the camp. But as long as the motor pool ran smoothly, checks and monitoring were ignored, and Hans was left to do as he pleased.

Hans knew we were involved in countless acts of "organizing" and that our cooperation with the camp administration was less than total. But Hans himself was less than conscientious when it came to the execution of his orders. He had little patience for administrative work and pushed most of the paperwork that flowed across his desk to Helmut. Industrially organized murder rests on a substructure of painstaking registration and exhaustive bookkeeping. Changes had to be carefully recorded, daily work slips filled out for all prisoners, deaths and transgressions noted. By delegating the mechanism of bureaucratic control Hans effectively gave Helmut control of our lives.

When I got to know Hans better I risked asking him how he felt when on a *Sonderaktion,* a euphemism for a liquidation operation. "Did you ever think of your wife and family when you were shooting women and children?"

"No, I can't say I did. I didn't see them as people. I can't explain it…. They were naked, packed together, and after the killing, the pits of bloody corpses… It had nothing to do with humanity."

Indifference is more powerful than hatred or anger as a driving force of violence. Death was not a victory over dangerous enemies, but a slaughter of innocents. Hans changed my perception of murder from an inexplicable nightmare for which there was no answer to an eminently human event that demonstrated those extremes that only man is capable of doing.

Hans' office was a wooden hut detached from the barrack facing the main gate. Beside the usual office furniture, there was a camp stretcher that Hans slept on when he was too drunk to walk to his quarters. As winter set in, Hans became more maudlin, drinking heavily and talking endlessly about the "operations' he took part in. It was only when drunk that he talked about Reschety and his confrontation with the young mother with the baby. He put his arms round me, called me "Wilhelm," and shook his head. Listening to Hans I felt neither anger nor revulsion, neither hate nor pity. After two years in the camps I had developed a paralyzing cynicism, even about murder and death. I listened to his horror stories while memorizing the map on the wall behind his back. It was a large ordinance survey map of Central Europe covering Poland, Czechoslovakia, East Germany, and Austria. It showed minor and major roads and pinpointed Nazi camps and fuel depots. It was priceless information.

Because I used the familiar *"du"* when speaking to Hans and he used the diminutives, *"Ach mein Willy,"* when talking to me, Helmut and the others thought I was his boyfriend. I didn't deny it. It gave me a certain status. One's position vis-à-vis others was always a question of standing. Although status must be ascribed by others one must also ascribe that status to one's self, expressing it in personal behavior. The reward for status was material advantage, but it was by no means the only one.

There was a lot of homosexuality in the camp, particularly among the older SS officers. It had its start in the *Wandervogel* (Wandering Youth), an organization similar to the Boy Scouts. After World War 1 many of these ex-*Wandervogels* joined a homosexual *Freikorps* under Ernst Röhm. Röhm's ambition was to create a social order in which homosexuality would be the model for human behavior. Homosexuality was so rife in the Nazi Party that Himmler complained to Hitler that too many of its leaders were chosen for sexual reasons. Himmler did not object to homosexuality (he had given orders that no homosexual was to be arrested, even if they repeatedly engaged in sodomy, without his express permission) but was alarmed at the number of nonqualified people receiving senior positions on the basis of their relations with Röhm and his cohorts. Karl Ernst, a militant homosexual who had been a doorman and a waiter, was given the rank of Colonel General and a command of 250,000 men when he joined the SA.

Hitler, whose own stunted sex life was neither completely heterosexual nor completely homosexual, believed that the job of "liquidating" his enemies was best undertaken by homosexuals "despite all the slanders." But whatever his personal proclivities he could not accept that between 7 and 8 percent of men in Germany were homosexual, "depriving the Fatherland of the children they owed her." The police stepped up their raids on homosexuals, arresting 90,000 between 1936-45, 15,000 of whom were sent to concentration camps.

Towards the end of the war, when the Nazis were in a frantic rush to exterminate everyone in the camps the "Butch" homosexuals were released and drafted into the Army. The "Femmes" suffered the same fate as the Jews. After the war homosexual concentration camp prisoners were not acknowledged as victims of Nazi persecution. They were refused reparations and under the Allied Military Government of Germany forced to serve out their terms of imprisonment regardless of the time spent in the camps.

19

The first snow flurries drifted across the camp early in November. By December the temperature stayed below zero throughout the day. Auschwitz became a frozen landscape of barb wire, hunched figures, and silent barracks. I had suffered one winter in Dachau, and knew that there was no worse time in the camp. Polish winters are harsh, with temperatures regularly falling below—20C. The thin cotton garments and wooden clogs were no defense against the biting cold. The dawn *Appel* (which we did not attend) in biting winds and sub-zero temperatures killed off anyone unable to keep awake. Those who broke ranks or stamped their feet were doused with water until they froze into blocks of ice. After each roll call there were standing corpses, kept upright by frozen limbs.

Deliverance in Auschwitz took only two forms, escape or death. As my health improved, so did my will to live. Because the prospect of escaping from within the camp was well nigh impossible, I asked Helmut to add my name to the driver's roster. Only BVs or senior camp prisoners were permitted to leave the camp and meet the transports at the ramp. The only other way out was to be assigned to the *Fortschaffung Kommando* (pick-up squad), a euphemism for collecting the dead. Because no one volunteered for this task, Helmut offered it to me.

Although it would not take me to the ramp, it was a first step. It took me outside the camp, albeit only as far as Birkenau. But it would allow me to map the immediate environs. I told Helmut I had done the rounds in Dachau and had seen the worst; but what I saw was unlike anything I had experienced.

I was given the keys to a flatbed truck and two Polish "corpse-gatherers"—neither of whom spoke German. We started work before dawn, immediately after *Appell*.

The first stop was the electric fence that surrounded the camp. During registration we were told that if we didn't like Auschwitz we could "hang ourselves on the wires." Every night 20 or 30 prisoners, usually young girls, found the courage to do so, drawn to the grave because there seemed no other alternative. We pried their twisted bodies off the wire with hooked sticks, not looking at their faces. I could not help thinking how I would feel if Marian was among them. It was not a question that words could answer.

Prisoners who died during the night from exhaustion, injury, or illness were laid out in front of the huts. I had lived with the dead for 20 months, but I had not handled the bodies of women and children before. Women prisoners made up about 30 percent of the Auschwitz population. Supervised by female *Kapos* with longstanding criminal records, their cruelty was appalling even by Auschwitz standards. In August 1942, under the pretext of suppressing an alleged revolt, they killed 90 French Jewish women with poles and axes. Until August 1942 female prisoners were placed in the main camp, separated from the men by a wall of iron sheets and concrete posts. After this they were moved to Birkenau, and it was in Birkenau that most all prisoners were ultimately killed.

When I first saw Birkenau, I thought it cold and forbidding; a place of eternal displacement. Even when I got to know the camp it never lost its air of wretchedness and misery. It covered an area of 440 acres enclosed by two rows of electrified fences 10 miles long. The wooden barracks were little more than open stables, built hastily on swampy ground without any insulation. Prisoners walked on dirt floors which raised clouds of dust in summer and became a quagmire in winter.

Because the huts were infested with fleas and lice, women were regularly stripped, doused with insecticide, and made to stand for hours while their clothes were fumigated. Not all the clothes were returned. Those with nothing to wear were beaten for being shameless and became candidates for selection.

Dead bodies were everywhere in the women's camp. We had to use sticks to drive off the rats. These rodents, fattening on the flesh of human remains, were the real heirs of Auschwitz

But you could not permit yourself to think about the things you saw. The acceptance of death was the precondition for being able to resist it. As powerful as the pressure of the present was, the only way to realize any kind of equilibrium was to become emotionally numb. There were times when I thought to pray, but more often than not, the words did not come, or I could not find them. The incomprehensibility of so much violence and suffering discredited language. Auschwitz put an end even to prayer.

20

The Christian church sanctifies suffering. If we suffer, we shall reign with Christ: *Christus factus est obediens usque ad mortem crucis.* That, for Christians, is the way of the cross: to suffer patiently until death and accept everything in the spirit of love. But in the camps suffering was completely without value as suffering. Nothing demonstrated this more than the wrongs perpetrated against children.

During the war children lost their lives in many ways and in many places, but the largest number of them perished in Hitler's camps. Children who escaped selection on the ramp were harnessed to wagons, put to work laying roads, sentenced to penal squads, incarcerated in the bunkers of Block 11, tortured, and shot. Hardly a day went by when one didn't see a boy or girl being beaten to death for approaching a fence to exchange words in the hope of hearing about his or her family.

Non Jewish children over the age of three escaped the gas chamber. They were torn from their parents and dispatched to *Lebensborn* centers to be "Germanized." Everything was done in these centers to make the children reject and forget their background. Children who resisted being "re-educated" were shipped off to concentration camps (usually to Kalish in Poland) and exterminated. Children waiting to be re-educated were kept in Block B1a. Most of them were skin and bone. Disease and starvation had first claim on their lives, and if they were not transferred soon after their arrival, succumbed to Dr. Josef Mengele's experiments.

Mengele wanted children of a certain height for his guinea pigs. Although he preferred Jews and gypsies, he was not overly particular. When he wanted a new batch of "volunteers," the most recent arrivals (since they were usually in better health) were made to undress and stand against a line drawn across a wall. All those whose heads were below the line were sent to Birkenau. As the children climbed into the back of our trucks, they called out their names to whoever was in earshot so their parents might hear what had happened to them.

One of the German drivers told me that he heard one boy, a little older than the others, telling his friends as he was being hoisted onto the truck, "Climb into the car; don't scream. You saw how our mothers and our fathers, our brothers and sisters were taken away. Now it is our turn, and we'll see them again up there." Before the truck took them away, he turned to the SS and called to them in German, "But don't think you'll get away with it. Very soon it will be your turn too."

Of the 228,000 children who entered Auschwitz, only 435 survived. Most were Jewish and had been subjected to medical experiments and macabre surgical procedures performed without anesthetic. They left the camp in states of physical and psychological distress. Innocence was no protection against evil.

Nearly all the Auschwitz doctors were engaged in sterilization experiments. Himmler, who masterminded these projects, planned to sterilize all non-Germans after the war. He estimated that the neutered population would live long enough to build the new Reich, after which they would perish without descendants. Although I got to know many of the doctors by name, I had most contact with Clauberg, Schumann, and Mengele. Because they thought I was German, they talked to me. The only thing that counted was belonging to the "master race."

Doyen of the doctors was Carl Clauberg. Before coming to Auschwitz, Clauberg ran a clinic for the treatment of sterile women in Königsberg University. Himmler asked him to reverse his research and devise a technique for mass sterilization. Delighted with the prospect of an unlimited number of human guinea pigs, Clauberg left Königsberg and after a year in Ravensbrück came to Auschwitz. He had a preference for young women. I often saw six or seven of them lined up outside his office, chatting nervously, not knowing what to expect.

He injected caustic substances into their cervix during gynaecological examinations to see what effect it had on their reproductive organs. Using the methods he developed, he claimed that one doctor and ten assistants could sterilize a thousand women a day. His injections totally destroyed the membranes in the womb and the ovaries.

One of his victims, a Polish girl from Lecknia, told me that after she had been sterilized, she looked down and saw blood pouring out of her belly which Clauberg had cut open to observe the lesions. "We are like trees without fruit," she said. "They took us because they didn't have rabbits."

Clauberg was captured by the Russians after the war. He was tried in 1948, sentenced to 25 years' imprisonment but was released after just seven years. He resumed practice under his own name and proudly advertised that he had "perfected an absolutely new method of sterilization which would be of great use today."

An outcry by survivors resulted in his arrest in 1955. He died mysteriously in his cell in Kiel two years later.

Schumann was a sadistic little man who spoke in monosyllables. He exposed his female patients to X-rays and then removed their ovaries to see if they were still fertile. His male patients fared just as badly. They were made to put their penis and scrotum on a metal plate that was bombarded with high frequency X-rays. Their prostrates were then brutally massaged with a piece of wood inserted into the rectum to release the sperm that was sent to Breslau for examination. If his victims survived, they were dispatched with intracardiac injections of benzene, because the radiation burns made them unfit for work.

Schumann opened his own consulting practice after the war and was not recognized as a war-criminal until 1951. He left Germany before he could be arrested, working in the Sudan and later in Ghana, where he was detained and repatriated. He stood trial and was imprisoned. Released in 1972, he spent the rest of his life in Frankfurt and died in 1983.

Of all the doctors who made up the murderous ecology of Auschwitz, Mengele was the one I was most wary of. He was quite capable of taking you into his confidence at one minute and sending you to the gas chamber the next. He was a good-looking man, tall, with short-cropped dark hair. He was fastidious in his dress and hated any imperfection in his victims. If anyone he examined had a blemish on their skin, a birthmark or tattoo, or a scar or wound, he or she was sent to the ovens. When he spoke about his experiments, he referred to his subjects as if they were insects with human bodies. He had absolutely no regard for human life. Although it was contrary to SS practice to shoot anyone on the ramp (because of the commotion it might cause), I saw him shoot a mother and child who had just come off a transport at point-blank range because the child was lame. When someone nearby protested, he sent everyone who had traveled in the same freight car to the gas chamber with the remark, "Away with this shit!"

Mengele's experiments to refine the master race led him to some extraordinary conclusions. Studying the racial differences in the structure of the lower jaw he told me that he had proved that non-Aryans had descended from the great apes, but that God created the Nordic races with no evolutionary ancestors. If this finding guaranteed immunity from killing, his God was the devil. In order to satisfy Mengele's mania, guards scouted the ramps for twins and dwarfs for his experiments. As the unsuspecting arrivals were herded off the transports, SS would shout *"Zwillinge!"* (Twins!)

Parents were forced to make a quick decision. Was it good or bad to be a twin? Many mothers, hoping for special treatment for their twins, pushed them forward.

The twins never knew what Mengele injected into them or why. Because they were kept alive during the experiments, their suffering was extreme. Miklos Nyiszli, Mengele's prisoner pathologist, told me of an experiment that he said was not untypical.

A pair of Hungarian twins were made to sit in a vat of almost boiling water. Just before losing consciousness, they were strapped to a table and given several two-liter enemas after which their rectums were distended for a gastric intestinal examination without anesthesia. The two boys screamed so loudly that Mengele ordered them to be gagged. They were then given a urological examination during which tissues were taken from the kidneys, prostrate, and testicles. When considered too weak for further experiments, they were given a phenol injection to the heart. The bodies were then dissected, and their organs sent to the "Institute of Biological Racial and Evolutionary Research" in Berlin.

Mengele was a law unto himself. Nobody ever questioned him. "Why did this one die?" "Why did that one perish?" was not in the SS vocabulary. Murder of Jews had been expressly stated to be both necessary and noncriminal. Mengele professed to do what he did in the name of science, but there was too strong an element of sadism in his experiments not to suspect other motives.

If the mother of the twins was still alive, she was brought into the dissecting room and made to look while he examined her children. One woman went mad when she saw her twins lying next to each other on the dissecting table with pins through their heads and their testicles cut open.

Another woman told me that she had looked on while Mengele collected blood samples from her twins in such quantity that both children died in front of her eyes. The blood that Mengele didn't use was sent to the front, along with blood "donated" from other victims. Jewish blood, its "inferior quality" notwithstanding, saved the lives of German soldiers.

Most inmates in Auschwitz came across Mengele only during selections. They provided him with a constant supply of research material. Mengele and his retinue could show up at any time, day or night, and order the prisoners to undress and line up. Polished boots slightly apart, his thumb resting on his pistol belt, Mengele surveyed his prey with dead gimlet eyes, passing judgment with a wave of his cane. Death to the left, life to the right, *"links oder rechts,"* to the gas chamber or the dissecting room. The memory of this slightly built man, not a hair out of place, his Death's Head SS cap tilted rakishly to one side, remains vivid for all who survived his scrutiny.

The only time I saw Mengele show emotion was when he found an interesting "test case." Otherwise he was utterly unfeeling and cold-blooded. In February 1944 he sent an entire Jewish block of 600 women to the gas chamber because some of them had typhus. Five months later, under the pretext of combating a spotted fever epidemic, he ordered the liquidation of 4,000 prisoners from Terezin. For these "extraordinary achievements" Mengele was promoted to the post of First Physician and awarded the War Cross of Merit.

Mengele fled Auschwitz on January 18, 1945, disguised as a member of the regular German infantry just hours before the Russians liberated the camp. He was captured as a POW but released because the Allies had no idea who he was. After hiding as a farm laborer in Upper

Bavaria, he sailed to Argentina in 1949 with the help of the "Edelweiss Group," an organization of former Nazi officers. The German Government issued a warrant for his arrest in 1959 and offered a reward of £250,000 for information about his whereabouts. He remained undetected until his death in 1979, when he suffered a stroke while swimming at a beach near Bertioga in Brazil and drowned.

Mengele never expressed any regrets about the experiments he performed on twins or the hundreds, if not thousands, of deportees he sent to the gas chamber. He told his son Rolf, when they met for the last time, that he did not feel personally responsible for what had happened in Auschwitz and not to believe what was written about him. In common with many other Nazis, Mengele was incapable of self-reflection.

Although most of the SS doctors fled before Auschwitz was liberated, 40 were arrested and handed over to the Poles. Their trial in Krakow ended on December 22, 1947, with 23 of the accused sentenced to death, six to life imprisonment, and 10 to prison for between three and 15 years. Only one was acquitted. It was the Nazi doctors, more than the camp administration, who were most implicated in mass murder in Auschwitz. There has never been a period in human history in which doctors have been so guilty of abrogating their pledge to save lives.

21

In Auschwitz, the ultimate wish—not to know—was ineffective. Sound travels. One heard cries. One heard screams. One heard the moans of the dying. And if this was not enough, the wind carried the burnt offerings from the crematoria across the camp. Drowning in daily episodes of atrocity and human misery sapped the spirit of hope. To be human one must feel human, and for much of the time one felt anything but human. But there were people who did not allow their compassion to suffer, or let their humanity be destroyed.

One such person was Eva. At one time she must have been quite beautiful. She had deep brown eyes, finely chiseled features, and full lips. Three years in Auschwitz had taken their toll, but she refused to be cowed by the overlapping series of horrors around her. Eva was one of the prisoner doctors who worked in the *Revier* or infirmary. As soon as she saw me, she knew that I was a *die Prominenten*. I had flesh on my bones. I was wearing civilian clothing, and my head was not shaved. I was aware of my status but did nothing to hide it. It was my only defense against a random assault by the SS. But every time I saw Eva, I was conscious of the gulf between us, and how far I had sealed myself off from the rest of the camp.

The *Revier* was a vestibule of death. Incredible as it sounds, it suited the SS to have an infirmary in the camp. It facilitated selection by grouping those unfit to work in one place. Because killing was the simplest means to combat disease, sickness meant immediate and mortal danger. Selections of the sick occurred daily. Packed in overcrowded rooms, infested with fleas and lice, their shirts soiled, often naked, the sick lay on paper pallets filled with wood shavings or straw that had been ground to dust. Anyone with paratyphoid fever or diphtheria was sent to the gas chamber without being given the chance of recovery.

Because anyone not fit to work suffered the same fate, Eva

temporarily discharged, but readmitted the following day, those who suffered from bodily punishment (broken arms and legs and skull fractures, ulcers and abscesses from gunshot wounds) in an effort to save them. Although keeping infection a secret was a limited life-saving act, she occasionally succeeded in switching patients who had been selected by the SS doctors for those who were critically ill or already dead. It was a dangerous stratagem, heightened by irregular inspections by the SS seeking more bodies for selection.

A permanent feature of the camp scene was the numerous piles of bodies outside the infirmary barracks. Less conspicuous, but more heart rendering, were the little shoe boxes tied with string. Women who gave birth in the camp were automatically sent with their babies to the gas chamber. Mengele was very strict about this ("This camp is not a maternity ward!") and encouraged those who were pregnant to declare themselves by promising them larger rations and transfer to a maternity hospital when the time came.

In spite of the warnings, many women revealed themselves, not realizing the final horror of their action until it was too late. Only when a baby was stillborn or unlikely to survive was the mother spared and allowed to return to her barrack. This ruling placed a terrible burden on Eva and the prisoner doctors. Were they to kill the baby and save the mother, or deliver the baby, and send mother and child to their deaths? This awful dilemma had only one outcome: to pinch the baby's nostril when it opened its mouth to breathe. Every day, among the dead, were three or four shoe boxes, their lids tied with string.

Eva died during one of the many typhus epidemics that swept through the camp. I saw many deaths, but only two affected me deeply—Eva's and Father Schefler's. Her courage and pity and readiness to sacrifice to help those only a little worse off than herself was a ray of light in an otherwise dark universe. Eva has no obituary, but she will live in the minds of those who knew her and owe her their lives.

22

In the Spring of 1943 the *Fortschaffung Kommando* was given to a Jewish *Kapo*. This was no goodwill gesture on Helmut's part. The growing number of death trains to Auschwitz meant that every driver was needed to carry the arrivals from the ramp to Birkenau. My name was added to the roster. I was not unhappy. The *Kommando* had been a daily descent into a world that undermined God, religiosity, morality and hope.

Released from the *Kommando,* my thoughts turned again to escape. Resistance in the camp centered round the infirmary. Many hundreds of prisoners converged on it, bringing with them and taking away information. I asked Eva before she died to put me in touch with the underground. But her only contact was a young Zionist whose group was devoted exclusively to saving Jews. The only other group with contacts outside the camp was Polish. But they were hostile to Austrian and German prisoners because they spoke the language of their killers. These avenues closed, I was unsure where to turn next.

Meanwhile I carried the weak, the invalid, and the sick to Birkenau. After March 1943, when the four giant crematoria in Birkenau became operational, no one was taken to the Auschwitz infirmary or the quarantine barracks. We worked in shifts, around the clock. Throughout the summer the death trains brought their cargo of human fuel for the crematoria: from Rumania, from Holland, from France, from Croatia, from Greece, from Macedonia.

Selection on the ramp was a cleverly constructed hoax made to look as if everyone was being singled out for his or her own good, unaware that under the guise of a medical diagnosis death sentences were being passed. When the women were separated from the men, there was a flurry of agitation. Parents screamed for lost children, shrieking their names. The two columns stood only meters apart.

Anyone who crossed the line or dared to reach out to wife or daughter was roughly pushed back. At this point almost everyone realized that they had been misled. But there was no resistance. Overwhelmed by the speed with which everything happened, phases of waiting or thinking were radically suppressed. What was relevant contracted to one's immediate world: baggage, breathing space in the crowd, family. From the start victims had no chance to work out even the rudiments of a plan for action. They were too confused to do anything but follow instructions. From such confusion there easily follows disorientation and surrender.

Although the crematorium was hidden from view by trees and bushes the clouds of smoke and pillars of fire belching from the squat brick chimneys left little to the imagination. Even so, few arrivals would have believed that those black clouds were all that remained of the thousands of prisoners who had arrived just hours before them. But even if they had their suspicions, there was little they could do. Most of us, at one time or another, were prompted to do something heroic—like standing up to the Germans or calling attention to what was going on. But one look at the SS with their hands on their guns made you realize the futility of any such gesture. Individual acts of counter violence would have triggered extreme mass reprisals.

If the entire transport was destined for the gas chamber, *Lagerführer* Fritz, the man who tried out Zyklon-B on Russian prisoners, was devastingly blunt. "You have come to a concentration camp, not a sanatorium, and there is only one way out—through the chimney. Anyone who does not like it can try hanging themselves on the wires (the electrified fence that carried 6,000 volts). You Jews have no right to live longer than a fortnight; if there are priests among you, the period is one month; the rest, three months." Realistically three months in Birkenau was an eternity, and few made it that long.

Not every SS officer was as callous as Fritz, and for good reason: it created a good deal of unrest and put the guards on edge. But the murmurs soon quietened. Resignation culminates more often in apathy than in resistance.

After selection on the ramp, we took those unable to walk directly to the gas chambers in Birkenau.

Here they were welcomed in a manner that allayed suspicion. "Now listen carefully. In your own interest—I repeat, in your own interest—before taking up residence in the camp we ask you to take a shower and be disinfected. In this building (pointing to the crematorium) is a large bathhouse. As soon as you enter the changing room, please get undressed as quickly as possible. After taking a shower, everyone will get a bowl of soup. This is a necessary precaution that we are taking for your own benefit."

The deception did not end there. Pointing to someone in front of him, the SS officer asked, "What's your profession?"

"I"m a tailor," came the reply.

"Men or women's?"

"Both."

"That's excellent! You are precisely the sort of person we want. When you have had your shower, come and see me."

There was more in this vein. "We need craftsman of all kinds, fitters, mechanics, welders, bricklayers, and the like. Of course, the men have to work, but the women won't have to, unless they volunteer. They can help in the household or the kitchen. Everybody is going to get well paid here. Now go and take your shower quickly, otherwise your soup will get cold."

Life flooded back into the upturned faces. The SS man's words had the desired effect. People dropped their belongings and followed a cinder path edged with grass to an iron ramp from which 10 or 12 concrete steps led underground to a large room dominated by a signs in German, French, and Greek: *To the Baths* and *To Disinfection.* While walking five abreast down the staircase to the dressing room in the basement, they were each given a piece of soap and a towel. As a rule, women and children went first, followed by the men.

The whitewashed walls were brightly lit. Along the walls were numerous benches above which were numbered coat hangers. Signs in several languages drew everyone's attention to the necessity of tying their shoes together (so that the thousands of pairs of shoes needed by the Third Reich would not get mixed up).

Guards stationed in the dressing room told everyone to undress. This was not a popular command and had to be repeated, often several times, and more menacingly on each occasion. *Sonderkommandos* (Jewish corpse workers) were on hand to help the elderly and the lame. In ten minutes they were all naked, their clothes hanging neatly on pegs, their shoes tied together, the number of each hanger carefully noted. As soon as an SS man opened the heavy oak doors at the end of the room, the crowd was pushed into another equally well-lit room with rows of columns at thirty-yard intervals. These were not structural pillars but perforated sheet-iron pipes fastened to the floor that passed through openings in the ceiling, ending outside as little chimneys. When the last person entered the room, the doors were shut tight. As the SS man slid the bolts into place, he looked through the circular peephole made of two thick glass plates sealed with rubber gaskets, gave an approving nod, and waited for the "disinfector."

The disinfector (holding a gas mask with a special filter and four canisters) in the company of an SS doctor arrived in an ambulance donated by the International Red Cross. The doctor was necessary because the small amount of irritant gas normally added to Zyklon-B to warn of the presence of a dangerous substance was removed to hasten the killing process. Although the cans carried the warning *Attention! No Irritant!* a doctor was always on hand to do what was necessary if the *Desinfektoren* became exposed to the gas. On the roof above the "shower room" the disinfector put on his gas mask, opened the *Zykon*-B cans, and poured their contents into the vent down the induction shafts. In a matter of seconds the poisonous gas had spread like a mist through the room. Within several minutes, 20 at most, everybody was dead.

Before the victims entered the gas chambers an SS doctor (usually Mengele or König) performed one last gruesome task for Hitler's Germany. He walked among the naked men and women, feeling their thighs and calves, selecting "the best pieces." After gassing, the marked bodies were laid out on wooden tables. The doctor then proceeded to cut off the pieces of flesh, which they threw into enamel buckets. The muscles of the still warm corpse expanded and contracted, making the buckets jump up and down. This butchery was necessary because the doctors sold the meat they used for culture media to the butchers in Oscwein. König was overheard saying, "Horseflesh would do, but in war time it is too valuable for that sort of thing."

Among König's other gruesome duties was to select corpses for the Danzig Anatomical Medical Institute, where special facilities had been built to manufacture soap and leather from human bodies.

When the Red Army captured the city, they found 148 corpses stored in metal containers and eight-nine human heads waiting to be processed. Soap was actually being produced until late 1944. The most surprising aspect of this appalling story is that the Head of the Institute, Professor Spanner, never faced charges after the war even though the whole ghastly enterprise was revealed at Nuremburg. The processing of corpses was not a crime.

23

The graveyard shift proved abortive. The guard never left my side. Other then telling me he was from Odessa, he was taciturn and surly, rarely speaking. Nearly all the guards were Ukrainian. Because the Germans did not trust them completely they were given non-military police jobs. Most of them detested the Germans, and the Germans knew it. But they shared the Germans hatred of Jews, which made them suitable for guard duty and taking up positions as sentries at the ramp After enlisting they were taken to the SS training camp in Travniki, where they took an oath of loyalty to Germany. After six weeks 'training they were awarded the title of SS *Oberwachman* and issued identification, rifle, and live ammunition. Knowing our relationship with their SS masters, they treated us with caution, but showed no mercy to rank and file prisoners.

Early in October I was given an ambulance to drive. The large red cross painted on both sides gave legitimacy to the exercise on the ramp. To add to the charade my guard and I wore Red Cross armbands and white tunics. The *Deutsche Rotes Kreuz* was another ruse to deceive the unwary.

The quarry for an agent is, for the main part, not human life but information. But circumstances change. The virtues of nonviolence can only be tested when set against violence and certain death. Not killing when killing offers the only chance to live is to seek self-destruction. I was prepared to kill my Lithuanian escort, if need be. I could be clear of the station and railroad in just a few minutes. But once the alarm was raised, things would move swiftly. Hartenstien, head of the SS unit responsible for security, would telegraph details of my escape to Gestapo Headquarters in Berlin. Copies of the telegram would be sent to the administrative headquarters in Sachsenhausen, to all commanders of Gestapo and SD units in the east, and to all frontier police posts. But I knew where the danger spots were from the map behind Hans's desk. Escape was possible.

But when night fell, my resolve to violence collapsed. My failure to act shook my self confidence. If ever I believed that I could kill indiscriminately, I was wrong. Escape maintained the fiction of a future, nothing more.

During my time as a driver the deadly sequence of steps that led from the ramp to the gas chamber was interrupted only once. In midsummer, 97 men, women and children arrived from Berlin in regular carriages, not cattle trucks or boxcars. Families were not broken up on the ramp and there was no selection. Guards stood well in the background, the dogs held in check. But for the Star of David on their jackets there was nothing to identify them from any other group of Germans travelling by train. After a short welcome address by an SS officer, unheard of in Auschwitz, Eberhard (another driver) and I took them to a specially prepared hut behind the commandant's house. In the hut were tables laden with food and drink. Neither of us could believe what we saw. It was a reversal of everything that Auschwitz stood for.

It was not until the SS began handing out postcards that the reason for their VIP treatment became clear. They were asked to write short positive messages about their trip and arrival. The cards were sent unfranked to Berlin, where the Gestapo read them to make sure that they did not contain any information that would identify the location of the camp. The postcards were then posted normally. As well as the date stamp, the Berlin Post Office added its public service slogan: "Speak briefly on the telephone."

A few months later the recipients of these cards started arriving at Auschwitz. The cards had revealed the addresses of friends and relatives to the Gestapo.

As soon as the newcomers had filled in their cards, the SS ordered them back onto the trucks, and we took them to Block 11. At the far end of the long narrow courtyard between Block 10 and Block 11 is a brick wall joining the two buildings. In front of it the SS had prefabricated another wall, erected to protect the one behind it from bullets and deaden the sound, made out of logs covered with black painted cork. Originally a place of execution for political prisoners and Resistance fighters the "black wall" had become a place of general execution.

The Berlin Jews were made to line up, five deep, facing the wall, and told to undress. The command was so unexpected that they stood in stunned silence. Suddenly all hell broke loose. *Kapos* rushed at them, truncheons flying, knocking women and children to the ground. When the terrorized victims picked themselves up, they began to shed their clothes to avoid more blows and abuse. Demoralized by the violence, they were completely cowed. *Kapos* forced the first five victims to kneel down in a row. An SS officer stepped forward and shot each person in the nape of the neck. As soon as the bodies were dragged away the next line was pushed forward, kneeling in the blood of those who had just been killed.

The murder of these Jews affected me deeply. They had reminded me of a world now gone: the coffee shops in the Unter den Linden, the crowds on the Kurfüstendamm, the scents and sounds of the Tiergarten. I turned to look at Eberhard. His face was a mask. He had seen it before.

Later he told me about the last execution he watched. After the order to undress was given, a girl asked her mother why she had to take off her clothes.

"Because we have to" came the reply.

"Is the doctor going to examine us?"

"Yes, my darling. He will make you well, and soon we'll be happy."

It took all the woman's self-control to hold back her tears. When the command was given to step forward, the woman picked up her daughter and held her close to her chest. Unable to kill mother and child with one bullet, the SS officer walked around the woman, looking for a spot on the child's body to fire at.

Suddenly a shot rang out. Blood spurted from the little girl's neck and her head slumped forward. The woman felt her daughter's blood run down her body and lost control. She flung the child at the SS officer as he was pointing his revolver at her.

The man dropped his gun. He raised his hands very slowly to his face to wipe away the blood. After several seconds without moving, one of the guards realized that his commanding officer was in a state of shock. He picked up the murder weapon, looking up at the officer as he did so.

"Carry on, *Sturmmann*," stammered his unnerved chief. "I've had enough."

The Corporal raised the gun to the woman's head and pulled the trigger.

"In Auschwitz," Eberhard said, "there are only victims and executioners."

24

Helmut told me that someone answering Marian's description had been seen in the SS brothel. Because there was a continuous exchange of prisoners between camps, there was a possibility that she had been transferred to Auschwitz. I was excited but would not let myself believe it was her. If it was Marian, her life was even more precarious than that of an ordinary prisoner. The SS had an unlimited supply of girls to choose from. If they wanted a change of face, or if a girl failed to please or became pregnant, she was sent to the gas chamber. There was no reprieve.

I asked Helmut to find out more. The next 48 hours seemed like 48 days. Two days later he gave me a scrap of paper with the name *Marian Adel* on it. From that moment I thought of nothing but how we might save ourselves.

⌘⌘⌘

The following morning I led the convoy of trucks to the ramp to meet a transport from Bochnia. Families had been assembled in the town's main church, where they were confined without food or sanitary facilities for several days. We carried those on the point of dying to Birkenau, which raised the hopes of the arrivals on the platform— which was the intended purpose.

When we reached the crematorium, my Ukrainian escort began pulling out the sick by whatever part of their clothing he could get hold of. I remained in the ambulance, watching my guard's efforts in the rear view mirror. Suddenly my door was flung open, and I felt a blinding blow on the side of my head. I was dimly aware of being dragged to the ground, kicked, and cursed. Through a bloody haze I could just make out a pair of polished jackboots and instinctively tried to stand up. Anyone who did not get to his feet immediately was a candidate for a bullet in the back of the neck. I struggled to my feet, my head spinning.

In front of me was an SS officer, revolver in hand. "Who do you think you are? Why aren't you working your arse off like everyone else? The ovens are overflowing! Get in there and start dragging out the corpses!" It was SS *Hauptsturmführer* Jüttner.

Jüttner was in a rage because he had been ordered to clear the backlog of bodies and was making little progress. Any attempt to answer Jüttner or remind him that we were to stay with our vehicles would have brought my life to an end. In Auschwitz the truncheon or a bullet replaced communication. When he told me to move, I didn't argue but ran stumbling towards the crematorium.

Jüttner was unable to dispose of the dead because the ovens could not keep up with the numbers being gassed. About 2,500 corpses could be cremated in 24 hours in each crematorium, but this number was insufficient. The corpse storage rooms were overflowing. Although the capacity of the pyres in the birch forest behind the camp was virtually unlimited there were no spare trucks for Jüttner to transport the dead. The strident whistle of the death trains could be heard every few hours. Every vehicle was busy carrying the children of Israel to Birkenau.

Above the entrance of crematorium 11 was a black wrought-iron lantern. In the morning mist its yellow light cast a pale shadow on the ivy leaves growing against the red brick wall. If one had not known better one might have assumed that the heavy doors led to a walled garden or courtyard. In reality it was the entrance to hell. Nothing on God's earth could prepare one for the sight of those huge ovens spitting out flames. I had stepped into Dante's Inferno. The force of the flames and the heat was so strong that everything trembled from the roar. *Sonderkommando,* scraping a glowing white substance from the ovens, their bodies streaked with sweat and soot, looked as if they had emerged from the bowels of the earth. It was Sheol, Hades, and Hell all in one.

A *Kapo* pounced on me when I entered the crematorium, pushing me towards the elevator at the far end that carried the bodies up from the gas chamber. The furnace room, about 30 meters long, had five furnaces housed in a rectangular brick structure. The mass of flames and gases leaped down, passing through underground flu channels that connected the ovens to a single brick chimney. The noise of the ventilators was deafening, adding to the cacophony of shouts and curses. I was so intent on dodging the *Sonder* men and piles of corpses that I did not see the *Kapo* behind me. When we reached the elevator, he gave me a violent shove that flung me headlong onto the floor. *Jüttner* had got to him as well. Unless he was seen swinging his truncheon and urging everyone to work faster, his life was not worth a candle.

I had watched the Bochnia arrivals disappear down the underground viaduct to the shower room. An SS officer tried to reassure them. "Nothing terrible is going to happen to you. All you have to do is breath in deeply. Inhaling is a means of preventing infectious diseases. It's a good method of disinfecting…"

Then I lost sight of them. Now, separated only by a door with a circular peephole, I saw them again. When the lights went out and the shower heads remained dry, they realized that the showers were sham.

Someone began to recite the Shema. "Hear O Israel, the Lord our God is one God…" Voices joined in: "My God, before ever I was created I signified nothing, and now that I am created I am as if I had not been created. I am dust in life, and how much more so in death. I will praise you everlastingly, Lord, God everlasting. Amen. Amen. Amen." Another man said the Vidui, the final confession. His voice faded, replaced by muffled sounds of coughing and cries for help. After a few minutes the cries changed to a death rattle, and the banging against the walls and doors subsided.

The giant ventilators were turned on. *Sonder* men crowded against the door, ready to drag out the dead. When the air was sufficiently pure the iron bolts were slid open, Jüttner, revolver in hand, was first in, looking for survivors.

Corpses were piled high, one on top of the other. Zyklon B develops its deadly fumes from the ground up, spreading gradually to higher levels, forcing its victims to claw and trample on one another in the struggle to find air. Infants and children lay at the bottom, adults on top of them, their skin colored pink with occasional red or green spots.

Some foamed at the mouth; others bled from the ears.

Sonder men ran into the chamber wearing rubber boots and hosed down the bodies with powerful jets of water to wash away the feces (involuntary defecation is the final act of those who die by gas). Under Jüttner's watchful eye they pulled apart the entangled bodies, tied leather straps around the wrists of the dead, and dragged them outside. I followed them into the chamber but hardly knew where to start.

Jüttner was on me in a second. "Start dragging out those corpses!"

In front of me lay the body of a woman. She was so thin that her ribs and hip bones almost punctured her skin. I reached down and lifted her up. Her eyes were dull and glassy, as if overlaid with a thin cloud of film. As I looked into her unseeing face, so young and pale, I felt an inexplicable feeling of tenderness towards her and picked her up as one might a sick child.

Jüttner, who was watching, exploded with rage. "What do you think you're doing?" He pulled the woman out of my arms by her legs and dragged her, head bumping across the concrete floor, to the chamber's anteroom.

I didn't wait to be told again. I closed my mind to what I was doing. "Groan quietly; do not mourn for the dead," advised Ezekiel, and this is what I did.

The *Kapos* were as assiduous below ground as they were above, hitting anyone who slackened for a minute. The exertions opened the cut on my head made by the butt of Jüttner's revolver. The cut was not deep, but blood ran down my face and shirt. Fearful that Jüttner would think I was as good as dead and get rid of me, I worked with my head down, which encouraged the bleeding.

It took four hours to clear the chamber, but there was no respite. While *Sonder* men relieved the 2,000 corpses of their spectacles, artificial limbs, and probed the bodies' private parts for hidden gems, the "tooth pullers' opened the mouths of the dead with crowbars, removed any gold teeth, and placed them in a solution of hydrochloric acid to remove the flesh and bone. When Jüttner was satisfied that the bodies had been picked clean, we dragged the naked corpses into the freight elevator and into the furnace room.

Bodies lay everywhere: on the floor, in the passageways, even beside the ovens. Some Slovak Jews who had been dragged in to help the *Sonder* men became so distraught when they recognized their kin among the dead that they collapsed. Unable to dodge Jüttner's blows, they begged him to finish them off with a bullet. Jüttner kicked them to their feet, shouting at them to get back to work. But they threw themselves at his feet again, overcome by what they had seen. Jüttner, purple with rage, ordered them thrown into the ovens.

Several more gassings were scheduled that day and Jüttner was at his wit's end, shouting at everyone to work faster. Convinced the ovens could take more bodies, he ordered an extra corpse onto each pallet. Each furnace was designed to take a pallet holding three bodies, two lying face to face, the third wedged between them, not the four or five that Jüttner insisted. The extra corpses fell off when the pallets were pushed into the furnace and had to be thrown in by hand or held with a pitchfork so that they stayed inside. Tongues of flame shot out of the ovens every time a door was opened.

The ash bins quickly filled with a glowing white substance, all that remained of those who had been alive a few hours before. The burning fat started to pour over the collection trays into the grooves cut in the concrete base under the oven grill, threatening to start a fire. A heavy iron scraper was thrust in my hand, and I was told to start clearing the channels that carried the residue to the outside vats. The ovens had become so hot that it was impossible to use the scraper for more than a minute at a time before drawing back.

As I bent over to scoop up a handful of water from the bucket in front of the furnace I felt a *Kapo's* whip cut into my back. "You lazy.... Get back to work."

The force of the blow made me lose my balance. I fell against the oven door, turning as I did to save my face. I felt a searing pain across my back and shoulders and passed out. Someone threw a bucket of water over me.

As I came to, I heard Jüttner shouting an order. I knew I was done for. At that moment, as far as Jüttner was concerned, I was already dead. My only thought was to stay alive.

I forced myself to my feet. I knew I had only seconds. A word from Jüttner, and I would be thrown into the first open oven. I picked up the scraper and began clawing at the ducts again.

At dusk my guard plucked up courage to tell Jüttner that we were expected back at the depot. Jüttner looked at him for a moment, then dismissed us with a wave of his hand. The SS man's energy was indefatigable. Before we left, he had hijacked another truck from somewhere and was berating the driver for not pulling his weight.

Hans was first to see me when we got back to camp. He was visibly shocked. My face and arms were covered in blood and the exposed skin on my back was badly blistered. He did not have to ask where I had been. I stank of death. He must have realized at that moment that his *protejka* did not guarantee my survival. I was in Auschwitz to die, like everyone else.

25

Until my confrontation with Jüttner, I was able to maintain a certain perspective on the future. Its loss constituted a deep cleft in the consciousness of existence. I was here to die, and so was Marian. To ask why was meaningless. *"Hier ist kein warum"* (There is no why here). Questions had no answers, so it was useless to ask any. For a few days, when I looked at someone, I saw two bodies, their live body and their corpse body. Jüttner had reduced the human to the state of objects good for the fire. At its worst, human life is not tragic but unmeaning: Auschwitz denied man his spirit.

Helmut dressed the burns on my back and told me that Hans wanted to see me. I did not want to come between Hans and Jüttner. It was fatal to become involved in a row between SS officers. If Hans pulled rank on Jüttner and asked for an explanation, it was tantamount to a death sentence. Rather than risk falling out among themselves, the SS eliminated the cause of the infraction.

But Hans did not want to hear about Jüttner. As soon as I entered his office he stood up and asked me, almost aggressivelyhow long I could count on staying alive. It was a question we asked ourselves every minute of the day. I didn't answer. There was no answer. Then to my astonishment he said, *"Lieber sohn, ich hole dich heraus!"*

"What?"

"I'm taking you out!"

Hans had planned everything down to the last detail. He would take me to the station in Krakow in time to catch the morning train to Berlin. He handed me an envelope with the necessary passes and permits and enough money to last two or three weeks.

The question of my disappearance would not arise. I would be numbered among the thousands of prisoners that died every day. Whether Hans was doing this for me, his son, or as retribution for past sins I had no idea. It didn't matter. I put my arms around him and we embraced each other briefly. It was a gesture that for one moment broke through our differences and united us as human beings.

As soon as I left Hans I wrote a note to Marian, which I gave to Helmut. I said that loved her and not to give up hope. There was no space for more. The chit had to be anonymous and small enough to be swallowed. The penalty for carrying mail was death, and one took fearful risks delivering these scraps of paper. But it was one of the very few ways that prisoners in different barracks could contact one another, and no one ever refused to carry a message if they had access to another part of the camp.

⌘ ⌘ ⌘

At 3.00 a.m. the next morning Hans backed a staff car into the workshop, and I climbed into the boot. A few minutes later we were clear of the camp. The road to Krakow has a number of twists and turns, but we got to the station in less than an hour. Hans wished me good luck. I thanked him and said I would not forget him. If Hans had not disappeared after the war and been brought to trial, I would have spoken in his defense. But we both knew that there was nothing one could do or say that would remove the stain of Cain from his forehead.

While waiting for the train I tried to accustom myself to being free. It was not easy to shed the feeling of vulnerability. It took several days before I felt confident enough to walk about, to be looked at and spoken to. What I saw through the window of the train was an unreal world: people walking in the streets, entering shops, talking in groups. Life had become so displaced that it was difficult to adjust to ordinary living, especially the human feeling that finds expression in laughter.

The train was full, mostly with troops. All looked extremely weary, which made me think that Germany's morale was breaking at last. I had to show my papers three times, twice to the Gestapo and once to the *Bahnschutzpolizei*. Hans had made out my pass in the name of Fritz Siegel, *Unterscharführer*, on leave from Auschwitz. No one asked any questions.

126

Much of Berlin was in ruins. Between the Reich Bank and the University, the houses were nothing but empty shells. The Adlon Hotel where my father had stayed was bombed and so were many of the buildings in the diplomatic quarter on the edge of the Tiergarten. Every road had its gang of women, *"Trümmerfrauen,"* wearing kerchiefs round their hair and clearing the rubble with their bare hands.

When I reached my apartment building, I was glad to see that it was still standing. Steel doors had been put in the basement but apart from that, there were just sandbags piled up against the windows. I heard no one say *"Krieg ist schon gewonnen"* (the war is already won) as they did a few years ago. Now it had become, "When will it end?" Berliners have a motto: *"Berlin bleibt noch Berlin"* (Berlin is still Berlin). But people were not so sure anymore. Too much had been laid waste by bombing.

I could not stop thinking about Marian. Many of the women who were returned to the barracks after working in the brothel either threw themselves against the electrified fence or lost the will to live. A woman selected for the brothel would be "tried out" in what can only be called gang rape. Once selected for the brothel her life was no longer her own. She was simply a body to satisfy the needs of the SS. The suffering these women endured is one of the least-acknowledged aspects of the history of Auschwitz.

The common element in all successful escapes was help from outside. I was outside, and although escape was always problematic and uncertain, I had a plan that with Max's help would get me back into Auschwitz. I had not seen Max since I first went to Berlin, and hoped that he was still working for the Ministry of the Interior. I posted a note for Max in the personal column of the *Gross-Berliner Ärzteblatt.*

The next night we met in a bar we both knew near the Comic Opera. A Richard Tauber song from the 1930s recalled the times when the Brownshirts were everywhere in Berlin. But the days of victory parades and goose-stepping was over. The reality now was British aircraft humming overhead, and the nightly frightened rush to the cellars.

Max saw the cut on my head and asked what happened. I told him about Auschwitz. It was all news to Max, and it affected him deeply. He knew about the work camps, the so-called *Arbeitslager* and *Ausenstationens* (external stations), most Germans did, but not about the *Todeslager* (death camps). Because Nazi ideology and policy cut forcefully against the grain of social traditions the Germans would never give up, Hitler imposed a fetish of secrecy on any program he knew that people would reject. This was formalized in an order prohibiting anyone who worked for the government or military agency to be "informed or seek to know more about secret matters than was required for the enactment of his or her duties." It was posted on the walls of every government office and communicated to all guards, troops, Party and government officials. The penalty for breaching this secrecy rule was the concentration camp. No one dared ask what his neighbor was doing. Hitler not only persuaded the Germans that wrong was right, but that they should accept the legitimacy of forbidden knowledge.

I told Max about Marian and my plan to return to Auschwitz as a chemist from Degesch, one of the two companies that had acquired the patent for Zyklon B. I had a fair knowledge of pharmaceuticals, thanks to Lloytron, and given the right help was sure that I could enter the camp without arousing suspicion. Degesch chemists frequently visited the camp to study the "effectiveness' of their insecticide. Because drivers in the Transport section rarely visited the VIP quarters it was unlikely that I would be recognized: and if I was it would not be reported for fear of incriminating Hans.

Forty-eight hours later Max handed me a heavy manila envelope with a set of car keys, a permit from the WVHA (a branch of the SS Central Office responsible for Concentration camps), a letter of identification from Degesch, and a forged pass signed by Richard Glücks, Inspector of Concentration Camps. Although Max could hold his own in an outlaw work where tact, toughness, and vigilance had to be constantly on the draw, neither his courage nor sharpness would save him from the gallows, if he had been searched.

⌘⌘⌘

I returned to Auschwitz after five days, a long time in the life of a prisoner. Roadblocks and random stops by uniformed *Sicherheitspolizei* interrupted the drive, but I made good time reaching the camp in 16 hours. Nothing on the approach road suggested that it led to a place of mass murder. The dull gray landscape, unbroken but for a farmhouse or two, was so nondescript that the ordinary traveler would have passed by without noticing anything unusual.

As I approached Oswiecim, I saw the telltale clouds of black smoke, the residue of another round of human dead. Passing the station I saw columns of men and women who during selection had been earmarked for Birkenau. My heart went out to them: huddled shapes, barely able to stand up any more and climb out; thin clothing, mostly in tatters, a few blankets over hunched shoulders; gray, hollow faces. I knew the road they were taking, and what awaited them. By nightfall their ashes would be floating on the Vistula.

I drove past the Block commander's barracks to the main gate. The barb wire, the electric fence, the Iron Gate with its ridiculous inscription, brought me back to Auschwitz with a start. Up until then I had not thought about the consequences of my return if I were identified, or the feelings that might surface when I entered the camp. My hands trembled, my pulse quickened.

My composure might have wavered if Höss himself had not appeared at that moment. He had received a call from Max (ostensibly from the office of the WVHA) and was expecting me. We did not give the Hitler salute but shook hands. He introduced me to Otto Moll, head of the crematoria, then left us, saying that we were both expected for dinner. I had heard about Moll. He liked to set his German shepherd loose on young, attractive Jewish women after they had undressed.

He was captured after the war and hanged after being found guilty of "horrendous" crimes by the Krakow High Tribunal. Listed among the crimes was his practice of lining up four people in a row, one behind the other, and shooting them with a single bullet.

Moll spoke with a sharp voice that put me on edge. I did not feel comfortable with Höss, either. Höss had a high forehead, eyes that gave little away, and a prissy mouth.

Later Höss told the court in Nuremberg that he never had any friends, or any real intimacy with his parents and with the exception of a black pony felt no real affection for anything—which I could believe. Although he was friendly, there was little warmth in his manner. He didn't look like the greatest mass murderer in history, but then murderers don't carry the mark of the beast.

Moll suggested I park in front of Block 24 beside the main gate. Block 24 was a Sonderbauten or "special barrack." Since the brothel was on the first floor, it could not have been more convenient. Moll led me to my quarters, complaining that he had few able colleagues and that most of them were unsuited for "this type of work." The extermination program, he said, needed at least a Commissar and three secretaries, whereas he had to oversee the entire operation on his own.

I told Moll that I was taking part in an ongoing program to learn what factors affected the toxicity of the crystals when they were released. Moll had carried out a few experiments of his own. He said that Zyklon was more effective on warm-blooded animals, including humans, than it was on insects and that the exposure period was longer when used for delousing than homicidal gassing. For delousing, concentrations of up to 16,000 parts per million were necessary and exposure time as long as 72 hours, whereas 300 parts per million was all that it took to kill humans in just 15 minutes.

I asked Moll if he was worried that the Allies might find out about the gas chambers after the war. He shook his head. "None of them," he said, pointing towards the prisoner barracks, "will be alive to tell what happened, but even if someone did survive, no one would believe them. There will be suspicions, a little evidence might be uncovered, but it will not amount to much; we will destroy everything.... Who will listen to the few who get away? The events they describe are too monstrous to be believed."

That evening Moll and I made our way to the tree-shaded stucco house known as Villa Höss. It stood near the northeastern corner of the camp separated from the barracks by a high concrete wall covered by a rose hedge. Höss introduced me to his wife, Hedwig, and their four children. After a few drinks Höss started talking about himself.

Moll had evidently heard Höss' life story before and tried not to look bored.

Hedwig smiled and nodded, clearly in awe of her husband.

Höss said that his father was a devout Catholic and that when his second child survived a difficult birth he took an oath dedicating his three-year-old son (Höss) to God and the priesthood. Young Höss was taken to Lourdes and attended church regularly. Had his confessor not told his father about a fight he had with another boy, a betrayal that undermined his belief in God and the church, he said he would have entered the priesthood.

After his father's death in 1917 Höss lied about his age and persuaded a cavalry officer in his father's old regiment to take him to the front. Recalling the war, he said there were two experiences he would never forget. The first was the shared intimacy among men in combat ("We were closer to each other than I had been to my father"). The second was his first kill. "My first kill!" he said with emotion. "A barrier went down. From then on I continued to kill and kill just as they taught me."

When the war ended he returned home to find his mother dead and Germany on the verge of collapse. He joined the East Prussian *Freikorps* and took part in a political murder for which he was sentenced to 10 years' imprisonment. Höss and the other defendants said they were unable to explain their actions because they were drunk but insisted that the killing was an "execution" and not murder because the victim was a communist. Hitler sent an open telegram to the killers expressing his "unbounded admiration" for them.

The following year, when Hitler became Chancellor, he had them released.

After his release Höss got a job on a farm and joined a right-wing group called the "League of Artamanen" (part of the Hitler *Jugend*). He met and married Hedwig and became friendly with one of the League's founders, a failed chicken farmer called Heinrich Himmler. Attracted by the elitism of the SS ("I could not resist the temptation") Höss abandoned the League. After six months' training in Dachau, Höss became a camp guard, the first step on his path to Auschwitz.

Höss said that he found the violence practiced in Dachau unacceptable. "I felt too much sympathy for the prisoners and should have told Himmler that I was not suited to concentration camp service."

Moll smiled, Hedwig nodded. I hope she did not read his written testimony (which he wrote in Nuremberg) in which he openly boasts of the satisfaction he felt in being able to whip a prisoner to the bone. "When the man began to scream I went hot and cold all over...I am unable to give an explanation for this." An explanation was at hand if he had cared to admit it. Höss was a sadist. It is the creed of the psychical cripple. The experience of absolute control over another gives the illusion of absolute power, an exhilarating feeling for someone whose life is without happiness or meaning.

His sons evidently had more insight into their father's character than his wife did. Prisoners working in the garden of Villa Höss saw the boys play a game that involved the older one, sword in hand, mimicking his father, shouting at his brother to run at the double "*Schnell! Schneller!*" (Fast! Faster!) The younger boy ran a few yards, staggers, spun round and fell to the ground, exhausted. His brother stood over the crumpled figure. White with rage he whipped the prostrate body repeatedly. As his fury subsided he gave his brother a contemptuous kick. The younger boy rolled over, mouth open, eyes glazed. The game was almost over. The elder brother turned to an imaginary *Kapo: "Zum Krematorium!"* he commanded and walked away, satisfied.

After dinner I asked Frau Höss what she thought of Auschwitz. *"Hier will ich leben und sterbem"* (I want to live here till I die). I don't think she realized that Auschwitz was a killing center and that the chimney behind their house was belching out human remains. But her brother, a frequent visitor to Vila Höss, was under no illusion. In an interview given after the war he remembered asking Höss how he was able to condone the brutality and the killing.

Höss replied, "You always ask and ask. Look—you can see for yourself. They are not like you and me. They are different. They look different. They do not behave like human beings. They have numbers on their arms. They are here in order to die. Here you are on another planet. Don't forget that."

Early in 1945 when the Third Reich was collapsing, Himmler helped Höss arrange a false identity for himself as a sailor with the name of Fritz Lang. Höss went into hiding but was captured and extradited to Poland. The Supreme National Tribunal tried Höss for taking the lives of 300,000 prisoners, a million citizens, and 12,000 Soviet prisoners of war. He justified his crimes by saying, "The thought of refusing an order just didn't enter one's head, regardless of what kind of order it was... So I didn't think I would ever have to answer for myself." This was the stock Nazi answer, uttered in the belief that there are no norms above authority by which power can be judged.

Höss was sentenced to death on April 2, 1947. He asked only for permission to send a farewell letter to his family and to return his wedding ring to his wife.

On the morning of April 16 he was brought back to Auschwitz and hanged on wooden gallows a few yards from his villa near Crematorium 1 in the main camp. In his last letter to Hedwig he wrote that he believed in everything he had done. She lived many years after him, managing a pastry shop in Fulda. His two sons left Germany to start new lives—one in America, the other in Australia.

26

After dinner Moll took me to the SS mess for a nightcap. The mess was crowded, full of smoke and very noisy. In one corner there was a small stage where women were auctioned off to the highest bidder, and girls were made to have sex with bull mastiffs and rottweilers. Moll said that we had missed the "entertainment," but if I wanted a woman, they were in Block 24.

We drank until midnight. No small part in generating aggression among the SS was boredom. Nothing in the camps really brought these men to life. Essentially they remained untouched, filling the emptiness in their lives by drinking, sex, and violence. It is only one short step from the passive enjoyment of cruelty to the act itself—and most SS had crossed the threshold.

Moll finally got to his feet. After saying good night, we left for our quarters.

Time had moved unbearably slowly at Höss's dinner table. I had to stop myself from glancing at my watch every few minutes. Never has time been so frustratingly chained to inactivity.

I waited in my room till 1:00 a.m, the latest I could allow if we were to be clear of the camp before *Appel*. I left a note for Moll, saying that I had an urgent call to return to Berlin. Then I walked back along the gravel path to the brothel. It was illuminated by a single light above the door.

I climbed the stairs to the first floor and entered a large room, lit by a single overhead light. Thirty or more girls sat on benches. Some were sleeping, their heads bent; others stared unseeing in front of them. A couple of girls glanced at me when I came in, then looked away. Several girls could not have been much older than twelve or thirteen. Their lives were spared because there were German officers who liked to have sex with girls that age. At the far end of the room a door opened into a corridor with rooms on either side. I looked around for Marian but did not see her. My heart sank. I walked down the rows of benches, looking at each girl in turn—and then I saw her. She was thin and bloodless, as if made of ivory. I tapped her on the shoulder. "You," I said, in a voice I could hardly control from breaking, "come with me."

I turned and led the way towards the door before she could recognize me. She got up and followed me. The SS did not usually take girls to their quarters. I was in civilian clothes, a VIP, and would not be questioned if stopped. I paused just long enough to see that no one was coming and walked quickly to the car. I told Marian to get in and lie down. At that moment it dawned upon her that something was awry. She looked at me, her mouth opened, and her eyes filled with tears. It was the wrong time and the wrong place to take her in my arms, but I couldn't help it. I held her closely and kissed her.

The Lithuanian guard scarcely glanced at my VIP pass. At that time of night it was unheard of for anyone but senior camp personnel to either enter or leave the camp. Ninety minutes later we were in Czechoslovakia.

Prostitutes were usually spared the 4.00 a.m. roll call, giving us 15 hours at most before Marian's absence was noticed. After checking the electrified fences the guards would report her escape to the Gestapo. But by that time we would be halfway to Switzerland. If Moll connected my absence with Marian's disappearance he would keep it to himself. Someone had always to be a scapegoat when a prisoner escaped.

When we reached Liechtenstein we made for Schaan, north of Vaduz near the Swiss border. Max had given me the name of a shopkeeper, Jacques Coulondre, whom he said would help us. We spent the day sleeping on sacks of flour in his storeroom behind the shop. Later that night he took us across the Rhine in a fishing boat. We saw some lights, which Jacques said was the village of Buchs.

We waited till daybreak, then walked along the road, hoping to catch a ride. We had gone only a few hundred yards when we were stopped by a soldier who shouted to us in German. Then I saw that he was wearing a Swiss uniform. I told him we had escaped from a German prison camp and were making for Bern. He said that we must come with him as there were some formalities that had to be "complied" with. As soon as we got to the military post I called Brian. It would have taken weeks using the normal channels to convince the Swiss that we were not refugees.

A few hours later we were on the train to Bern.

Marian and I had scarcely said a word to each other since leaving Auschwitz. Although this was one of the great moments of our lives, it didn't feel that way. We didn't embrace one another, burst into tears, or thank God. She was too exhausted, and I wanted to get us to safety.

It took Marian a long time to accept that she was free and the worst was over. I had been a BV, one of the upper class of the prisoner elite for most of my time in Auschwitz. I had been fed, clothed, and was psychologically unscathed. The return to normality was relatively painless.

Marian had no access to privileges. Her time was marked by hunger, humiliation, cruelty. She had been saved from the gas chamber by her face and figure but carried the scars of her confinement. For Marian the adjustment to civilized society would never be fully realized.

As soon as we arrived in Bern, I took Marian to a private hospital used by the Legation. She remained there for five weeks. I visited her for two or three hours every day, sometimes just holding her hand. Her doctor told me that she could no longer have children. Marian never told me what happened, other than that she had been ill treated. Her psychological scars were just as severe, although they remained hidden until we were married.

⌘ ⌘ ⌘

My apartment was exactly as I had left it so many years before. The champagne was still in the silver bucket. My note to Marian lay on the table, unopened. Only the withered petals of the roses and fallen leaves pointed to the passing of time. Everything was familiar, but unfamiliar. The oval mirror, the Monet above the bed, and my books belonged to a past I could scarcely acknowledge. After Auschwitz, nothing was the same again.

Brian guessed that I had been caught and sent to a concentration camp. Until he heard from Max, he had given up hope of seeing me until after the war. Like Max, he found it difficult to believe, in spite of reports to the contrary, that the "death camps" actually existed. Mass murders and massacre of social outsiders, political adversaries, and ethnic minorities have been recurrent features throughout human history. But never before had there been a state-initiated and industrially organized mass annihilation of human beings. The setting up of Auschwitz and the other *Vernichtungslagers* or extermination camps, to which an entire people, from infants to the aged, was transported over thousands of miles to be obliterated without a trace and "exploited as raw material" was not only a new mode of murder, but a despotism of darkness.

I found it difficult to talk about Auschwitz. Facts were easy: but the suffering eluded description. *"Those who know do not speak; those who speak do not know."* I could describe what I saw, but nothing could convey the *experience* of so much death. But I was a witness, and if I could not testify, I could be a messenger, and that message (in spite of its shortcomings) had to be delivered. I would not permit myself to forget everything that I had seen. The "unbelievable" had to be documented or those responsible would go free. To overlook men like Phol, Jüttner, Rascher, and Mengele was to turn a blind eye to murder. It was a promise I made to myself, to Marian, and to those I had watched die.

⌘ ⌘ ⌘

After Marian left hospital we had six weeks together before she left to join her uncle in Palestine. The day before she left we climbed the Gurten together. Below us lay Bern, the Nydeggkirche, and Bundeshaus clearly visible. We sat with our arms around each other, gazing into the distance. The peace and tranquillity of those moments was unsurpassed. I turned to Marian and asked her to marry me. She kissed me on the lips and said yes.

Marian and I had not held each other since leaving Auschwitz. Prison camp did little to enhance one's appetite for sex. In many instances desire disappeared altogether, both in feeling and in fantasy, though love, or what passed for it in the camps, was not unknown. Marian showed no inclination to make love, and I did not pursue it. Mengele had told me that due to both the physical and psychological shocks received from entering the camp, most women did not menstruate. He doubted that some would ever regain their periods or become sexually responsive even if they were liberated.

Although we knew nakedness as few others would ever know it, Marian never let me see her undressed. I saw her naked only once. She slept in my bedroom when she came out of hospital. One morning, without thinking, I walked in on her while she was dressing. Although still very thin, she looked beautiful in my eyes. The sight of me looking at her seemed to freeze something inside her. Her eyes held mine, but she seemed not to see me. I left the room, but not before I saw the burn marks on her breasts, and the scar that ran from between her legs to her stomach.

I wanted to get married, but with the war still raging, we agreed it would be better to wait. Religion was another factor. In Judaism luck and contingency are part of the puzzle of divine providence, extending the horizon of expectation and hope beyond the present. Faith and prayer had carried Marian through Ravensbrück and Auschwitz. She felt that she had at last found the right platform, the practice of the mitzvoth, to keep her faith alive and on-going. She had come to think of Palestine, given to Abraham and his descendents by God, as her spiritual home, and wanted to renew her covenant with her forefathers before taking another.

It took many weeks of hard pleading to get Marian a visa. Hitler's rise to power increased the flow of Jews to Palestine to the point that the Arabs rose up, demanding a halt to their immigration. Britain acceded, restricting immigration to 10,000 people a year. This number, totally inadequate, was accompanied by an even more punitive restriction: refugee status was refused to anyone reaching Palestine from enemy territory (Germany, Poland, Czechoslovakia, etc.). Almost all refugees came from enemy territory: they had become refugees to escape being murdered. But this very fact made them unacceptable to the British.

It seemed that Marian and I were always saying good-bye to each other. Parting, so far from thought when we were together, had become a way of life. But it was never any easier. We had heard that the Germans were convinced they had lost the war, and that the army was anti-Nazi because it held Hitler responsible. If this was the case, then the Wehrmacht might possibly force Hitler to sue for peace. But war makes no promises.

Marian left Bern on February 20, 1944. I did not see her again for another 18 months.

27

By 1944 the destruction of Polish Jewry was almost compete. The only light in an otherwise dark tunnel was the decision in October 1943 to set up the United Nations Commission for the Investigation of War Crimes. Even at this late date the stories of German atrocities were not fully believed. Although my report was compromised by having to keep my identity secret, it was one of the first detailed accounts of Auschwitz-Birkenau to reach SOE in London. The weakness of Intelligence is not that it does not collect information but that the information is not used or is skewed to political ends. Although Churchill had said that evidence should be gathered so as to prosecute those responsible for war crimes, no one had lifted a finger to do so. My report was on record, but like so many other firsthand testimonies, was ignored.

Two weeks after Marian left I was in the field again. Although what Father Schefler called my "spiritual equilibrium" had taken a few knocks, I was in good physical health. I had occasional attacks of anxiety, but these soon passed. When Brian asked if I was ready for another assignment I said yes.

British Intelligence had learned that a special SS unit headed by Eichmann was planning to arrest the Hungarian Prime Minister, Miklos Kallay and his cabinet. Anyone who knew that Eichmann was Head of Department 1V B 4 (Jewish Questions and Evacuation) should also have known that his visit to Budapest had more to do with implementing the "final solution" than putting a stop to Kallay's peace overtures. But British Intelligence was not interested in Eichmann's plans for the 825,000 Hungarian Jews. They wanted to know who, after Kallay's arrest, could be trusted to participate in future peace negotiations.

After the German defeat in North Africa, the capitulation of the 6th Army at Stalingrad (with the loss of 150,000 Hungarian troops) and the allied landings in Sicily, Admiral Horthy, the Hungarian Regent, realized that Germany would likely lose the war. With Horthy's tacit approval Kallay sought to negotiate a separate armistice for Hungary. But after Italy's surrender Hitler could not afford the defection of another ally. When he learned of Kallay's peace overtures he ordered *Operation Margarethe,* the occupation of Hungary.

I arrived in Budapest on March 17, two days before the Germans, along with Eichmann and his retinue of SS, entered the capital. There was no fighting. It was, Hitler claimed, another "Battle of the Flowers." The Germans occupied every ministry of importance, every airfield, and every ground base that had strategic value. Kallay was arrested and shipped off to Mauthausen, and Horthy was forced to appoint Dome Sztójay as Prime Minister. Sztójay was Hungarian but pro-Nazi, and with Edmund Vessenmeyer, the Nazi Military Governor, ran the country for the benefit of the Reich. Within 36 hours the public arena was cleared of anyone known to be anti-Nazi or not completely pro-German.

I reported these events, but my main interest was Eichmann. Eichmann had only one task, to clear Hungary of Jews. He moved extraordinarily swiftly. As soon as he established his headquarters in the Majestic Hotel, he told the Jewish leaders to establish a *Judenrat,* or Jewish Council, that ugly institution by which the Nazis had the Jews decide their own fate. "Do you know who I am?" Eichmann asked at the first meeting. "I am a bloodhound." And so he turned out to be.

⌘ ⌘ ⌘

Within days of Eichmann's arrival the round-ups began. The half million Jews living outside Budapest were rounded up with the willing help of the Hungarian Interior ministry and its *gendarmerie* Hungarian police and driven into ghettos before being forced on to deportation trains. The Nazis called the deportation operation *Rehousing and Resettlement.* Although under the umbrella of the Housing Department, it had its own section. The sign on the office door read *International Storage and Shipping Company Inc.* In the six weeks between 15 May and the end of June Eichmann's "shipping" company sent half a million Hungarian Jews to Auschwitz using 145 trains, each hauling between 40 and 50 freight cars.

Knowing the Jews would only trust their own leaders, Eichmann bribed Rudolph Kastner, head of the Jewish Aid and Rescue Committee, with 600 emigration permits in return for his collaboration. Since Kastner and the other Jewish leaders knew that any leak of the pact with Eichmann would have drastic repercussions, they went to great lengths to reassure everyone that they were in no danger. Believing they were going to resettlement camps the Jews boarded the transports without making any effort to hide, escape or resist.

I took a room in a small hotel on the Buda side of the Danube under that huge pile of masonry the Hungarians call Buda Castle. I spoke no Hungarian, but plenty of people understood German. There was even a daily German language paper called *Pester Lloyd.* I had only one contact, a Hungarian Jew called Zoltá, who transmitted my messages, but otherwise remained out of sight. He had seen his cousin, along with dozens of other Jews, taken to Szechenyi Street by the Arrow Cross, where they were lined up facing the Danube and shot. The Arrow Cross murdered 20,000 Jews this way. The bodies of the dead floated downstream as far as Százhalombatta, 30 kilometers south of Budapest.

The Arrow Cross was modeled on Hitler's NSDAP. Founded in 1933 by Szálasi its goal was to realize an order based on the power of the strongest: what Szálasi called a "brutally realistic étatism." Its Arrow Cross emblem (an ancient symbol of the Magyar tribes who settled in Hungary) represented the racial purity of the Hungarians in much the same way as the swastika was supposed to represent the racial purity of the Aryan. The Arrow Cross had their own anti-Semitic paper, equivalent of the Nazi *Der Stürmer,* called *Harc,* meaning "battle." The Arrow Cross became Eichmann's right hand, supporting the 200 *Sonderkommandos* he had brought from Germnay to round up the Jews and execute them if they could not be deported.

The Hungarian holocaust was inaugurated at dawn on May 16, 1944, with the departure of the first train to Auschwitz. The train consisted of 40 sealed wagons packed with men, women and children, a total of 4000 victims. All were gassed. Trains were taken to a specially constructed spur track in Auschwitz, the "Jewish ramp," that provided a direct link to the gas chambers in Crematoria 11 and 111. There was no time for selections, or even for registering the number of victims. Entire trainloads were marched straight into the gas chambers—at the rate of 10,000 a day! When the extermination was at its height, orders were issued that children were to be thrown straight into the crematorium furnaces or fire pits without being gassed first.

To supplement the work of the crematoria, the SS were forced to dig three gigantic trenches, 60 yards long and four yards wide behind Crematorium 2. Here Golgotha dropped its mask. Each of these huge pyres reduced 1,200 corpses to ash in five or six hours. The smoke from the pits could be seen from a distance of 20 miles, its flames illuminating the night sky. *Kommandos* worked day and night, jabbing the smoldering carcasses with long iron pokers, encouraging the flames by dousing them with boiling fat harvested from the burning corpses. The ash was dumped into the Vistula. The bones, after being pounded, were used as fertilizer or gravel for paths between the SS barracks.

The influx from Budapest created a serious shortage of food in the camp. To make up the shortfall the Czech prisoners had their rations cut to almost nothing. Already weak, they succumbed to dysentery and typhus. Mengele's solution was drastic but efficient: gas all 12,000 Czechs. The entry recording the liquidation of the Czechs takes up two lines in the Auschwitz archives:

The Czech section of the Auschwitz concentration camp was liquidated this day due to a prevalence of typhus among the prisoners.
Signed: Dr. Mengele, *Hauptsturmfürher 1 Lagerazt.*

Anyone in Budapest could see what was happening to the Jews. They were taken at all hours of the day and night to Józsefvárosi station opposite Kerepesi cemetery by local *Niles* (Hungarian Nazis) or Arrow Cross men and crammed into freight cars. From time to time Kastner brought fruit and sandwiches for the adults and milk for the children. If they had known that hot ovens were waiting for them and not cold food, they would not have been so trusting. Hungarian guards accompanied the trains until their arrival in Kassa, the railway hub used as a transfer point where the guards were replaced by SS. As soon as they arrived at Birkenau, they were lined up on the ramp and marched to the shower rooms.

When I left Hungary at the end of May Eichmann had succeeded in transporting nearly half a million Jews to their death, more than 50 percent of the entire Hungarian Jewry. Horthy put an end to the deportations early in July, alarmed perhaps by the landing of allied forces in Normandy. Eichmann was furious, but without Hungarian help he was not able to continue shipping "raw material" to the death factory in Auschwitz. But the reprieve was short-lived.

Horthy was forced to resign and sent into "protective custody" in Germany. With Nazi approval the Arrow Cross party seized Budapest and carried on where Eichmann left off. They immediately force-marched 70,000 Jews to camps in Austria, where most of them perished. Those spared the death march were driven into a walled ghetto around the Great Synagogue. Above the main entrance to the Synagogue is an inscription in Hebrew taken from Exodus, *"And let them make me a sanctuary; that I may dwell among them."* For those in the Budapest ghetto, God was anywhere but among them.

Families in the ghetto suffered the same appalling conditions as those in the ghettos of Warsaw and Lodz. Upwards of 10 people shared one room. Starvation was unchecked, typhus rampant. The gutters carried dead rats, garbage, feces and urine. In every corner and doorway people lay prostrate or curled up in fetal position, either dead or too sick to move. Misery, poverty, and suffering was out in the open, without shame or mercy. Nor was this all. Gangs of Arrow Cross men stormed into the ghetto, dragging out 200-300 people at a time. Marched to one of the bridges crossing the Danube, they were shot, their bodies borne away by the waters of the river.

The Arrow Cross government was brutal but short-lived, collapsing when the Russians took Pest in January, 1945. Such was their obsessive preoccupation with "the final solution" that during those last few weeks, with shells from the Red Army's guns already falling on the city, the Arrow Cross used its last resources to shoot 15,000 Jews and set up a human chain of Jewish men, women and children to pass shells from an ammunition depot to the German front line six kilometers away.

Although I was in Hungary for less than three months, I considered my time wasted but for the information about the transports to Auschwitz. British Intelligence should have known that as long as the Germans were in control, any talk of an armistice, with whatever government, was unrealistic. For what it was worth, I reported that Jaross, Minister of the Interior and his Under Secretary of State cooperated with the Germans, that the Economics Minister, Bela Imredy, shipped huge quantities of food and industrial products to Germany, and that Russian collaborators had started a Communist underground movement. With regards to future peace negotiations there was no one in the Sztójay government prepared to carry on where Kallay left off. My reports also included a tally of Eichmann's work: the number of trains dispatched to Auschwitz each week. But this information was considered of little importance. In war humanitarian issues are a distraction.

Budapest is a graceful city. I am glad that I was not there to see it destroyed by the Russians. When the Germans eventually fled the city, only a quarter of the Budapest's buildings were intact, and every bridge over the Danube blown up.

⌘⌘⌘

I had only one tense moment in Budapest. I was standing on the opposite side of the station counting the Jews being pushed on to a waiting transport when an Arrow Cross man strode over, his gun raised. He asked me in Hungarian what I was doing. I showed him my Lloytron ID, and in a voice I hoped conveyed simple curiosity, asked in German, where "all these people were going." He did not reply but returned my ID and waved me on. I knew exactly where they were going and what awaited them: the gas chambers and the final catastrophic panic for air. If ever there was time to recite the 23rd Psalm, it was then.

It was not until after the war that I learned that my time in Hungary was part of an elaborate charade. The British "leaked" the information about Kaly's peace overtures to the Germans in the hope that Hitler would withdraw some of his divisions from the Western Front to protect his Balkan interests. The ruse was successful, thus weakening German costal defenses, facilitating the success of *Operation Overlord* (the invasion of Normandy). Given this sleight of hand, my mission in Hungary had little practical value. Since in war the message is always more important than the messenger, it was quite likely that I was sent to Budapest for other reasons. Such games were played by both British and German intelligence.

28

I called Marian as soon as I returned to Bern. It took all afternoon to get a call through to Haifa. Marian was living in the center of Jewish anti-British guerrilla activity. The hospital in which she worked was a training ground for recruits and a hiding place for smuggled arms. She had left one war zone only to find herself in another. But there was no fear in her voice. She sounded absolutely sure about herself and what she was doing.

I had been recalled because SOE wanted all Anglo-American German speaking agents to join their Resistance network in France in anticipation of the long-awaited invasion to be launched that summer. Our orders were simple: "To conduct espionage in Vichy France and to maintain contacts with underground groups necessary for the planning and execution of the military program." Reading between the lines "the military program" was *Operation Overlord,* code name for the invasion of Normandy.

I traveled to France via Berlin because I wanted to thank Max again for his help and to tell him what I had seen in Budapest. My train pulled into *Friedrichstraße* station just as an air raid started. Everyone dived for cover. The Luftwaffe sent up their fighters and brought down several B-17s. One of these giant bombers must have been hit in the bomb bay. It blew up above our heads. Where a plane had been a moment before there was nothing but a smoke ring. When the all clear sounded, we emerged covered in dust, our ears ringing. Since I was last in Berlin posters had been put up saying, *Our walls are broken but not our hearts.* It was not true. The physical and spiritual destruction caused by the bombing had cut deeply into the Berliner's psyche. In the eyes of many Germans Hitler's promised utopia had started to disintegrate in front of their eyes. There was danger, chaos, misery, and confusion. What lay ahead was anybody's guess.

My meeting with Max the day I left for France was our last. He was arrested and shot after von Stauffenberg planted a bomb in Hitler's bunker, a causality of the purge following the attempt on Hitler's life. Hitler set up special (Gestapo) investigation commissions, 400strong, that rounded up thousands of senior soldiers, ministers, and officials whom the conspirators had planned to place in administrative positions throughout Germany—most of whom had nothing to do with the plot and had not even known of their "selection" for office.

Max's name was found in Stauffenberg's diary. It was enough to condemn him. I am sure Max knew nothing about the assassination plot. He was certainly not one of the conspirators since he had neither the rank nor the position to advance the coup if it had succeeded. It was a tragic irony that he was arrested and hanged, not for spying, but because his name was in a conspirator's diary.

I owed a great deal to Max. He had risked his life on my behalf and Marian's. The evidence I collected against the SS is a modest inscription to a man who never put his own safety before the overall struggle for justice. Max's appearance before the People's Court, after being put through unspeakable tortures by the Gestapo, was, for me, the single most tragic factor of the events of July.

29

France had become a dangerous place for spies. In 1942 the *Abwehr* captured a French radio operator and turned him into a double agent. The subsequent false messages resulted in the capture of 52 agents. The following year the Gestapo arrested nearly all of SOE's agents in and around Paris, and in the first few months of 1944 caught and executed 18 more. The demand for intelligence in the face of the Allied invasion drove the British and Americans to find replacements as quickly as possible.

Brian had prepared the necessary documents and passes for my transition from Albert Oeri to Henri Laval, native of Caen.

⌘⌘⌘

When I arrived in Caenm I checked in at Hotel De La Station. After unpacking, I walked downstairs and talked to a couple of German soldiers standing against the bar. I did not notice immediately that I was being watched by two men seated at a table by the window. Dressed in identical dark gray suits, I should have spotted them straight away as Gestapo. One of the soldiers complained that his buttocks were sore from having to drive an obsolescent French tank. This offhand remark indicated that he was with the 7th SS Division of Prinz Eugen, a second-rate unit employed mostly in anti-partisan duties. Intelligence was sometimes very easy to come by. I might have learned more but for the Gestapo who had come to the bar and were now in earshot. After the soldiers left, they walked up to me, one on each side. I felt a prod in my ribs and found myself staring into the barrel of a Walther pistol.

The bar fell silent. In spite of the gun, which I thought unnecessarily dramatic, I did not feel particularly threatened. One of the men asked for the keys to my room and returned a few minutes later empty handed. Notwithstanding I was marched to the Hotel de Ville ,where the Gestapo had set up their headquarters. I was given a *cahier d'écolier* and told to fill in my name, birth date, school, home address, and religion (never previously questioned in any official state document).

The two men interrogated me for several hours, during which time I was kept standing. They asked the same questions over and over again. "Why did you speak to the soldiers?" "What did you ask them?" "Who are your contacts?" They did not try torture but were very persistent. Finally I was able to convince them that I was Henri Laval, pro-German and a Vichy sympathizer.

After this experience, it was obvious that I could not work openly as I had in the early days of the war. Help came from the proprietor of the hotel who arranged for me to meet Jean-Jacques, a *cheminot* and head of the *Résistance-Fer* in the Caen area.

The *cheminots* (rail workers) knew which trains were carrying troops, weapons, medical supplies, gold, or plundered art—anything the Nazis were sending back to Germany. Their information about the beach defenses and the *Wehrmacht* in the area were invaluable. The *cheminots*, like the *Maquis,* were active saboteurs. I worked with Jean-Jacques over the coming months, and we became close friends.

In the weeks before D-Day we blew up bridges, freight trains, locomotives, electric and telephone lines. The Germans retaliated by hooking up their troop cars to French passenger cars. We countered this by timing a train's movement and calculating the time it took for the French cars to pass a given mark. Instead of unbolting the rails we planted dynamite sticks under the tracks with a carefully timed fuse attached. By the time the Allies landed at Normandy, we had destroyed almost two thirds of the railway system in the area.

But the reprisals were severe. Villagers were shot down in the streets of Brantôme and hanged from lampposts in Nîmes. In Ascq, on the Lille-Tournai railway line, the SS rounded up 60 men and shot them in a pasture facing the station.

Jean-Jacques was a small, wiry man in his forties with a quick wit. A native of Caen, he had sailed the waters of the Norman coast all his life and knew every cove and strip of beach of the coast of Normandy as well as he knew the local railway network. His wife, Yvonne, was a young woman in her twenties. Liaison was central to the Resistance. Yvonne carried messages to and from other Resistance groups in the area at great risk to herself. Since Germans tapped the telephone lines and mail was censored, secret messages and information had to be picked up and delivered by couriers, mostly women. Women often get dropped from memory, then from history. They do not figure prominently in the history of the French Resistance, yet their work was both dangerous and necessary. If caught, they risked deportation. Seven thousand women *résistants* were deported to Ravensbrück, and only half returned.

30

On the Sunday before D-Day I followed the River Orne from Caen to Neumers. The river runs through the city flowing north into the Bay of the Seine. Near the Forét de Grimbosq water and trees come together in dappled light and shadow, making a landscape of natural beauty. It was hard to believe that the fields on either side, dotted with farm houses, would soon be waste ground, a jumble of derelict wire, meaningless ditches, and bomb craters. Death was lying in wait, but for now the flavor of life was doubly strong. The cool air smelt of mown grass and leafy gardens. Away towards Caen there was the sound of a train, and bull frogs croaked continuously in the reeds along the river. How many of us, I wondered, would see this landscape again. If I was lucky, when the war was over, I would meet the survivors—Jean-Jacques and the others, and we would build up our friendships all over again.

In spite of the secrecy surrounding the invasion the Germans had obtained a significant hint of *Operation Overlord* by intercepting conversations between Roosevelt and Churchill. The Security Service of the SS had unscrambled parts of their conversation using the technical resources of the giant Philips works at Eindhoven. Before the British had time to install a new scrambling system the Germans knew that an invasion was imminent and that the main attack would come through France.

Rommel could be seen driving up and down the coast at all hours and in all weathers in his Mercedes supervising the construction of beach defenses. Ordinary soldiers who for the most part had nothing to do were going on maneuvers and putting up signs: *ACHTUNG MINEN.* No mines, in fact, were laid. But German officers had developed a taste for Camembert and Pont-l'Evêque. They put up the warnings, because they did not want the cattle disturbed.

On the surface the French and the Germans got on well enough. But behind the soldier's backs the French sent little signals to each other: they raised their eyebrows, shook their heads, smiled, made faint gestures of scorn and defiance—as if to say these Germans are not really very clever, since they believe that favors are being done for them willingly, whereas we know we are obliged to. The Germans called for French champagne, "please Mam"zelle!" played billiards in the cafés, and complimented the serving girls, but they were still the enemy—in spite of the posters on the walls depicting a smiling German soldier giving out chocolate to school children under the caption, *Abandoned citizens, trust in the soldiers of the Third Reich.* Other posters were not so benign. Most of them began with the word *Verboten* (forbidden). It was forbidden to walk outside after dark; forbidden to keep any firearms; forbidden to help escaped prisoners, the Resistance or English soldiers; forbidden to listen to foreign radio stations; forbidden to refuse German currency. Beneath each poster was the same warning in black lettering: *ON PAIN OF DEATH.*

⌘ ⌘ ⌘

On the night of June 4 the French Service of the BBC broadcast the second of two lines from Paul Verlaine's poem, *Chanson d;Automne:* "Wounding my heart with a monotonous languor." The first line—"The longs sobs of autumn's violins"—broadcast on June 1 warned us that that the landings were imminent; the second line, that the invasion would begin within 48 hours. It was the eve of the liberation of Europe. The largest fleet the world had ever seen was preparing to cross the Channel. Jacques and I could not sleep. One of the great moments of history was about to break.

The next morning Jacques and I cycled to Caen in our *cheminot* caps and overalls. While *résistants* laid explosives along the track from Caen to Bayeux we planted dynamite in the signal boxes. The fuse on one stick was old and blew almost immediately. Germans rushed from their huts, shouting and running in all directions. I thought our war was over before it had begun. Jacques and I picked ourselves up and pretended to repair an earlier act of sabotage. The Germans questioned us, but nothing more, convinced that we would have run if culpable.

A few minutes after midnight we heard the throb of aircraft and saw hundreds of green and red navigation lights twinkling between breaks in the cloud. Moments later the sky was filled with thousands of paratroopers in combat gear falling slowly downward all along the Orne from Franceville Plage to Touffreville. The great moment had arrived. But the Germans had also heard the aircraft overhead. Before the first paratroops landed the air crackled with the sound of machine gun and small-arms fire.

Suddenly there was a big explosion near the Varaville Bridge about a mile east of us. We guessed that paratroopers had blown up the bridge before attacking the command post. Jacques raced off to tell the paratroopers that the post was defended by mines and a 75-mm gun. I grabbed some sticks of dynamite and made for the marshalling yards but was stopped by some soldiers from the 5th Parachute Brigade. Their faces and equipment were smeared with black and brown paint, and they carried so many weapons that they looked like walking arsenals. Grenades hung from their belts; they had fighting knives in their gaiters and clips of cartridges in the lining of their steel helmets. They had become separated from their main force and asked me to take them to the battery south of the Merville-Franceville Plage. The battery carried four guns in a steel-doored concrete emplacement six feet thick and was protected by an anti-tank ditch and a belt of barb wire.

Flak guns fired sporadically as we neared the beach but otherwise there was nothing to suggest that the invasion had begun. I wondered if all battles began so innocuously. At every step I expected to hear a shot or a challenge ring out from the darkness. But the only challenge was from other paratroopers moving out from their landing-zones. To their call of "V for...," an officer in our group quickly added the other half of the password—"Victory."

When we reached the battery, we found that an advance party had cut the outer wire, marked the paths through the minefield to the inner fence, and neutralized a number of trip-wire booby traps. We moved only when the moon was hidden by cloud, crouching low to avoid being seen. As the paratroopers prepared to make a frontal assault two towing gliders landed between the battery and the perimeter wire. The gliders made a loud *whoosh,* which immediately awakened the Germans. They started firing, and so did we. Bullets screamed into the bushes or struck rocks and screeched piercingly away. Too late to do anything: just lie with heart beating: then instant darkness, followed by another volley of rifle fire.

Then one of the paratroopers threw a flare. We all froze as the sky lit up. Suddenly there was a maelstrom of fire from both sides. Shrapnel burst above us in an instantaneous black-grey cloud of smoke. Caught up in the heat of battle, I threw a stick of dynamite at the battery and dropped to the ground. A moment later there was a tearing, earthshaking explosion. Moments later the gun crew, soot stained and blinded, staggered out from behind the steel doors of the emplacement.

After the Germans surrendered, I waited to be told what to do like a boy on his first morning at school, while others, ignoring me, went about their own mysterious and definite tasks. My hands were shaking. I was completely unprepared for the mayhem, chaos, and noise. Just for a short time I had lived in a meaningless and heroic limbo on the edge of panic. I had not stopped to think that I might be killed. When we stormed the emplacement I felt an adrenalin rush that swept all else aside in a sort of reckless fatalism. A wild reality intervenes in the heat of battle. The situation makes its own rules. In the end all commands are reduced to just one or two very simple propositions: either to attack or hold on, to kill or be killed.

No one who looked out to sea on the morning of June 6 will ever forget the spectacle of that vast invasion fleet crowding the Channel. The sea itself was scarcely visible between the swarm of landing ships bearing tanks and men and guns. As the leading assault craft reached the shallow water, the Germans opened fire. While the troops were in their landing craft they were safe enough with the bullets hammering the amor-plated sides, but directly they showed themselves they were exposed to enemy fire. Everywhere the calm surface of the sea was whipped up into ghastly discolored foam by thousands of falling bullets.

As soon as the landing craft reached the shore and the ramps came down, men ran across the obstacle strewn sand to take cover in the doubtful shelter of a seawall. Weighed down by their equipment, unable to run in the deep water and without cover of any kind, they were at the mercy of German fire. Dead and wounded by the hundreds washed back and forth in the blood-red swell. Ammunition boxes, weapons of all kinds, jeeps, and tanks littered the sand. Small islands of wounded dotted the beach, others lay shoulder to shoulder, crouching behind obstacles, sheltering among the bodies of the dead—and in front of them the barb wire hung with the corpses of the men who had tried to cut a way through the German defenses. Many of these men, wrenched from the peace of an English summer, would not have had time to get used to the noise of warfare or to master their fear.

By June 11 thousands of men, vehicles, and supplies had been landed across the beaches. The capture of Bayeux, the first city of France to be liberated, permitted the British and Americans to link up and create a front nearly 30 miles wide and six miles deep. In spite of this formidable force Caen remained in German hands. Nothing could have prepared Caen's inhabitants for the air raid that followed. The air was full of the tumult of high explosives. The whole of the German lines seemed one mass of fire and flame. When it was over, a great silence fell over the city, broken only by the cries of the wounded and the noise of falling masonry from burning buildings. Among the causalities were Jacques' sister and her cousin. They died in the cellar of their house that had collapsed on top of them.

After the battle of Caen, Rommel sent Hitler an urgent memorandum in which he forecast an early Allied breakthrough:

> The consequences will be immeasurable. The troops are fighting heroically everywhere, but the unequal struggle is nearing its end. I must beg you to draw the conclusions without delay. I feel it is my duty as Commander-in-Chief of the Army Group to state this clearly.

Hitler did not draw the conclusions. He told Speer that Rommel had lost his nerve.

The next day two generals from the German High Command arrived at his home. After they left Rommel told his son Manfred, "I have just had to tell your mother that I shall be dead in a quarter of an hour...the house is surrounded and Hitler is charging me with high treason. In view of my services in Africa I am to have the chance of dying by poison. If I accept none of the usual steps will be taken against my family." He then turned to his aide-de-camp and said: "In a quarter of an hour, you, Aldinger, will receive a telephone call from the Wagnerschuke reserve hospital in Ulm to say that I have had a brain seizure on the way to a conference."

Rommel got into the generals' car. Twenty minutes later the telephone rang. Rommel was dead.

The next day Frau Rommel received a telegram from Hitler.

Accept my sincerest sympathies for the heavy loss you have suffered with the death of your husband. The name of Field Marshal Rommel will be forever linked with the heroic battles in North Africa. Adolph Hitler.

31

Yvonne said a prayer every time Jacques and I left the house. It was a kind of propitiation. We took comfort from her words, although we could never quite believe in them. It was against logic to think that we would all survive, particularly during those early days when causalities were so heavy. There was hardly a moment when one didn't hear the distinctive sound of a Schmeisser submachine-gun. British Bren-guns and Brownings made a *tat-tat-tat* sound, but the Schmeisser was more like a piece of calico being torn, and the noise hung in the air after the gun had been fired.

Although it was a time of great camaraderie, danger, and excitement, there were also, as frequently happens in times of uncertainty, instances of cowardice and treachery. Jean-Jacques was denounced by a collaborator and arrested after the liberation of Toulon. Yvonne asked for permission to visit him, taking with her some pills that would induce a high fever. She hoped the Germans would think his illness was contagious and transfer Jean-Jacques to a hospital, where it would be easier to organize his escape. But the Germans refused her permission to see him.

When the *cheminots* recovered Jean-Jacques' body, they saw that he had been tortured half to death. The Gestapo had burned the soles of his feet and pushed the fingers of his right hand into the space between the hinges and door and slammed the door shut. From the appearance of his clothes, the blood must have gushed from his hand like a fountain. Knowing they would return and crush the fingers of his left hand, he hung himself on his leather belt.

⌘⌘⌘

After the capture of Caen I moved into German-held territory, first to Lisieux, then to Evreux and then Paris. Keeping ahead of the Allied advance was difficult because of the damage done to railways, bridges, and roads. Sometimes I hitched a ride with the Germans, passing myself off as a collaborationist, and picked up useful information. I was never sure which intelligence would be most valuable because we were not privy to what high command had planned. Although there was a reason for this (we might have been captured and forced into talking), it meant passing on information that might only be of limited value.

On my way into Paris I spotted a train held up in a damaged marshalling yard carrying V-1 flying bombs and V-2 rockets in converted dining cars and passenger coaches. It was an easy target. When I reached Paris, I got in touch with a radio operator, whose address had been given to me by the *cheminots*. I had made it a rule always to check a wireless post, no matter how secure it was believed to be, because it could be in German hands. Both sides sent agents to posts they knew were compromised for the purpose of maintaining a channel of communication down which, at some time, it might be possible to pass deceptive information.

Because I was in a hurry to let London know about the V-weapons before the yard was repaired, I did not check out the building as thoroughly as I should have.

Réne lived on the third floor of an apartment block in the 12th Arrondisssement behind the Gare aux Marchandises. On the ground floor was a shop that sold religious books and articles. I walked up and down the street a few times but saw no one watching the building. I rang the bell on the side door. It was opened by a thickset man whom I recognized as Réne from his description. He led me into his apartment, pried open a floorboard, and removed a shortwave radio and cipher book. Moments later the door burst open, and three Gestapo, two of them carrying machine pistols, charged into the room. Réne dived for the cipher book and was shot dead immediately.

As soon as Réne's body hit the floor, I turned on the Gestapo and shouted, "You fools!" Looking directly at the German whom I took to be in charge, I demanded, "Who ordered this arrest?"

The man was taken aback, confused by my German and self-assurance. He said they had been watching the house for several weeks and that the raid had been cleared with his boss in Gestapo Headquarters. I told him I was passing false information to the British—that he had not only blown a channel that SOE trusted as a reliable source of intelligence, but also my cover. Without waiting for an answer I ordered the man who shot Réne to pick up the transmitter. I said the situation might still be saved if we left the building so that it appeared I had been arrested and then made my escape.

But this was asking too much. No, I would have to return with them to headquarters and make my explanation there.

"Very well then," I said.

I had no intention of going to Avenue Foch (a bizarre choice for Gestapo headquarters, given the fashionable address). I picked up the cipher book and walked to the door. I was first down the stairs, followed by the man carrying the transmitter. The staircase was narrow and poorly lit.

Just before we reached the final landing I turned and pushed the transmitter hard against the German's chest. As he fell back into the arms of the man behind him I bounded down the stairs and out of the building. By the time the Gestapo reached the road, I was lost in the traffic. I had been lucky. The Gestapo man was young and, typically, had responded to authority.

I never learned whether Réne had been betrayed or the Gestapo had picked up the presence of a receiver. Either way it was a victory for the Gestapo and a blow for us. Réne's death abetted my escape, but it was a heavy price to pay. I had been on the move since leaving Caen, sleeping little and always looking over my shoulder. In this cat-and-mouse game staying alert was critical. If you let your guard down, as I had, the consequences were nearly always fatal.

⌘⌘⌘

I stayed in a safehouse near the Gare St. Lazare belonging to the *Résistance-Fer*. Food was hard to come by. Only one out of four people received their ration of potatoes. The staple was a variety of turnip normally given to cattle. But for the Germans and those who curried favor with them, life went on as before. Nightclubs like the Lido, Shéhérazade, and Don Juan had everything in the way of food and drink one could wish for, as well as star cabaret shows. For most people the best they could hope for was a seat in the Gaumont Palace, where the projectors were kept running by a brace of bicycles generating pedal-power.

As far as the Allies were concerned, Paris was simply "an ink spot on the map," to be bypassed as its armies headed towards the Rhine. Eisenhower wanted to avoid a head-on attack, knowing that to dislodge the Germans might mean house-to-house fighting similar to that in Stalingrad. Paris was under the command of General von Choltitz, who had commanded the German forces in Holland and ordered the bombing of Rotterdam, one of the more vengeful acts of the war. Hitler had instructed Choltitz that at the first sign of unrest he was to introduce the severest measures: "…public executions for example. The Seine bridges will be prepared for demolition. Paris must not fall into the hands of the enemy except as a field of ruins."

Choltitz, with the sound of rifle fire crackling in the street below, ignored Hitler's orders and told the Americans to march on Paris while he was still in command (and by implication, arrested, before he could carry out Hitler's orders). When Bradley told Leclerc, "On to Paris," the French general moved swiftly, entering Paris with three tanks just before midnight (the others were still fighting their way through the outskirts of Paris). The Germans, believing that a full armored division was on its way, laid down their arms.

By dawn the fighting was over.

As the sun set on August 15, the feast day of St. Louis, the patron saint of Paris, we were all on the streets celebrating the liberation of the capital. As the brilliant day faded into darkness the streetlights in Paris came to life for the first time in five years. The blackout was over. It was a time of terrific exhilaration but also of hurt and retribution. Women who had had German lovers had their hair shaved and swastikas painted on their foreheads with iodine. Men who had collaborated with the Germans were dragged into alleyways and beaten up or shot.

But these reprisals did nothing to overshadow the spontaneous outbursts of cheering when Leclerc and DeGaulle marched down the Champs d'Elysées.

That night there was dancing in the street.

But to the astonishment of everyone the Luftwaffe bombed Paris. The city might be liberated, yet the war was far from over.

32

After the liberation of Paris, de Gaulle gave orders to incorporate all Resistance factions into the regular army. There was a good deal of opposition to these orders. Many of the *résistants* who had lived for years with their guns on or near them would not give them up but wrapped them in oilcloth and returned to their village.

I contacted MI-6 headquarters in Paris in the hope I would be recalled to Berne but was told nearly all our agents had been "removed from the field" (a euphemism for liquidated) and to return to Berlin. The front was, in any case, moving too quickly for effective scouting on the ground.

⌘⌘⌘

By mid-September the Americans had crossed the Moselle River between Metz and Nancy, had fanned through the Ardennes, liberated Luxembourg, and pierced the Siegfried Line, threatening several German cities. In little more than three months from D-Day the Allies had advanced to a continuous front from Ostend to the Swiss border.

MI-6 arranged for me to be taken from Paris to Hodge's First Army Headquarters at Spa, 15 miles from the German border. I was given papers identifying me as an officer in the *Grenzpolizei*. Since their duties included "observation and control of suspicious travellers," it gave me freedom to travel without raising suspicion. I could count on local support to make my way east to Bonn and from there to Berlin.

The road to Spa was choked with wreckage and the swollen bodies of German soldiers and horses. Bits of uniform were plastered against burnt-out tanks and trucks, and the dead lay in piles in sodden ditches. The Americans fired bursts of rounds from their automatic rifles into the bloated bodies to empty them of gas before they were burnt. Somewhere the families of these men dreamt of seeing them again. But they had fallen among the dead, to be counted among the nameless and missing.

I was advised to wait until dark before making my way to the border because German mortar fire on the road between Spa and Aachen was heavy. Company headquarters had plotted where the Germans were from information passed over the radio from a scout plane. I reached Malmedy without incident and had the cover of heavy forest to within 20 miles of Bonn. German patrols were not silent and were easy to avoid.

When I reached Reinbach I caught a bus to Bonn.

⌘ ⌘ ⌘

The following day I was in Berlin.

In spite of the bombing, mobile repair teams were able to maintain the operation of the major railroads. On the way to Berlin I had shared a carriage with some wounded soldiers from the 11 SS Panzer Corps who had fought at Arnhem. It was the only real victory inflicted on the Allies after D-Day (the Germans had found the battle plan on the pilot of an American glider that had been shot down). Both sides suffered heavy casualties. When I asked about the front they repeated Göebbels' stock phrases about "secret weapons" that would turn the war in their favor. Germans soldiers killed and missing by that time (November 1944) amounted to just over four million. Yet these men still believed they were fighting a just war and that they would win it.

Air raids on Berlin had reduced much of the city to rubble. I looked for a landmark, but none was visible. Whole streets had disappeared. Squares and gardens were covered in piles of bricks, stone and mortar. It took most of the morning to find my apartment building, or what was left of it. It had taken a direct hit and was completely destroyed. I understood why so many people walked around with wooden expressions. But I saw few tears. Tears, in any case, were a useless protest in the face of such devastation.

The area around the *Leipzigerstrasse* and the *Friedrichstrasse* looked more like a wound in the earth than the center of a city. The three big railways stations, *Potsdamerbahnhof, Anhalterbahnhof,* and *Lehrterbahnhof,* had their roofs blown off. The *Tiergarten* was pocked marked with shell holes. When I was last in Berlin. this deer park was reduced by the urgency of the need for firewood to a desert of tree stumps. Now even these were gone.

Nothing remained of the ministerial buildings on either side of the *Wilhelmstrasse.* Hindenburg's old palace, which Ribbentrop had taken over, was gutted. Through the open windows and gaping holes nothing was visible but debris. The Foreign Office was destroyed, blackened with fire and in ruins. Göebbels' Propaganda Ministry had received a direct hit. Hitler's Chancellery, as luck would have it, was still more or less intact. So too was the *Kaiserhof,* the hotel just round the corner that had been his headquarters before he came chancellor. Allied bombing had inexorably changed the face of the city.

My only contact in Berlin was a radio operator called Walter Reinecke, a German-Jew with the code name *Owl.* His case officer told me that he was nervous about any contact so I should not rely on his help. The Gestapo employed Jewish "fingermen" to roam about the city in search of remaining Jews, and Reinecke had been nearly caught several times. In France no one paid much attention to the rule that an agent should keep clear and independent of other agents. But France was not Germany, and few British or French agents were Jewish.

I met the Owl only once, if hearing his voice can be said to have met him. While sitting in the little church in *Elizabetstrasse* a voice whispered in my ear that I was to drop my messages in a bin outside the church after Sunday evensong. I never saw him face to face, even after the war. The radio operators were the unsung heroes of the Resistance. Every radio set had a local oscillator to "change" the incoming signal into a fixed frequency. An oscillator radiates sound waves as it operates. It is these emissions that reveal the presence of a receiver. The Germans were able to track down these signals in less than 15 minutes.

There were many bombed houses, most of them broken up and broken open, but some were still habitable. I moved into one that had suffered little damage near the Rudolph Virchow Hospital. I was not the only squatter. There were three others, two of whom were boys, members of the *Edelweisspiraten* (the Edelweiss Pirates). The Pirates were a street gang that rejected the Hitler Youth and dodged conscription. They seemed to spend all their time dodging the Gestapo and covering the walls of pedestrian subways with anti-Nazi slogans. It was a dangerous game. If they were caught, they would be sent to a concentration camp. In Cologne the ring leaders of the Edelweiss Pirates were publicly hanged as an example to others.

The third occupant was Walter Tesmer. Walter worked in Himmler's SS *Führungshauptamt*, the Operations Headquarters of the SS. He knew about the boys but ignored their presence. Walter's department was responsible for the organization, supply, training, deployment and mobilization of the *Waffen*-SS and the *Allgemeine*-SS. Because he had access to information about German forces through occupied Europe he was an invaluable contact.

Walter was a tall spare man who had risen quickly up the ranks of the SS till someone learned that his first wife was Jewish. Although Göebbels' first wife was also Jewish, it made no difference. Walter had his promotion blocked at the rank of Major. Officers in the SS were promoted to the next higher rank after three years. Walter had missed out on two promotions, and his loyalty to the SS was severely dented. After his wife and daughter were killed in a daylight-bombing raid, he lost confidence in Hitler's "new order" and believed that the war was a disaster.

When I returned to Berlin I reverted to being Albert Oeri. Since German factories needed raw materials more than ever, my Lloytron credentials gave me access to almost any industrial unit. Hits on factories had the effect of dispersing production into smaller component producing works on the outskirts of the city. Nearly all these light industries, especially those making munitions and accessories for tanks and aircraft, needed materials that Lloytron could supply, but because of the disruption to roads and railways could never deliver.

I spent most nights with Walter. We both enjoyed listening to music, and he had a very good radio. Music, most often Wagner and Beethoven, was continually broadcast to keep the population cheerful.

Listening to the radio was one of the few pleasures left, particularly the evening concerts.

The night the Gestapo broke into the house Walter was still in his uniform. When the Gestapo threw open the doors and stormed into the room, the last thing they expected to see was an SS officer. One of the Gestapo said that they had been told the house was a hideout for the *Edelweisspiraten* and begged the major's apology. They did not glance in my direction. A salient feature of the SS was its military ordering of rank and status. It was not the first time I had benefited from this regard for rank.

Although Berlin was being bombed night and day, and people looked dazed and shell-shocked, the slogan *Victory or Death* appeared on posters all over Berlin. There were some, like Walter, for whom such propaganda only confirmed that Hitler was mad. Far fewer people seemed to worry about being denounced to the Gestapo for defeatism: there was a pervasive atmosphere of impending downfall in personal lives as much as in Germany's existence. The ubiquitous initials *LSR* for *Luftschutzraum*, or air raid shelter, was now said to stand for *Lernt schnell Russich*: "Learn Russian Quickly." And most Berliners had entirely dropped the *"Heil Hitler"* greeting for *"Bleib* übrig!"— "Survive!"

But most ordinary Germans still put their trust in Hitler. Even when the collapse of the Reich was inevitable, many drifted with the tide because they knew that any internal resistance would engulf Germany in chaos. There were seven million foreign workers in Germany working as slaves. Most of them had been forcibly deported from the conquered territories and maltreated. If the civil government broke down, there was nothing to stop them going on the rampage. Moreover Allied air raids had created havoc with essential services. People were more dependent than ever on the State for food, clothing, fue,l and other necessities. Instead of rising in revolt against Hitler, as the Allies hoped, Germans were forced to defend the very person leading them to ruin.

33

News that the Russians had liberated Auschwitz in January 1945 did not reach Berlin until many weeks later. Walter had not even heard of the camp. But as information about the brutal conditions and gas chambers filtered down, he realized, as did many others, that there would be no retreat into a negotiated peace. For the Allies, the only possible response to war of annihilation was an equally intractable policy of unconditional surrender.

Several months before the Soviets liberated Auschwitz, the underground learned that Himmler had given orders for the destruction of the camp and that no one was to remain alive. Because of the sheer size of the camp, a mass breakout was almost impossible. Forceful escapes could only be launched by the Jewish *Sonderkommandos,* since they were the only ones who had time to get weapons and form fighting groups.

The *Sonderkommandos* were the brainchild of Reinhardt Heydrich, chief of the Reich Security Main Office and second in importance only to Himmler. Jews working in these units were temporarily kept alive to clear the gas chambers, service the ovens, and perform other various gruesome duties. Because the *Sonder* men were privy to information about Nazi methods that the Nazis did not wish to reach the outside world, the groups were murdered at regular intervals; new *Sonderkommandos* were selected from the subsequent transports.

The first task of the new *Sonder* men was to dispose of their predecessors' corpses. *Sonderkommandos* had a life expectancy of three months at most. Heydrich boasted that he got this idea from Egyptian history, where a similar necessity to preserve the secrets of the tombs of the Pharaohs found the same solution: the death of all those who had built them. In a manuscript found among the ruins of the crematoria a Polish *Sonder* man had scrawled:

The dark night is my friend,
tears and screams are my songs,
the fire of sacrifice is my light,
the atmosphere of death is my perfume.
Hell is my home.

When a rash of selections led the *Sonderkommandos* to believe the SS had begun their purge of the camp, they decided to fight their way out. Armed only with stones, three hand grenades, a couple of flat-nosed pliers to cut through the barb wire, and a small amount of explosives, they mounted a credible rebellion.

When the SS entered *Krema* 4 on October 7, they were met by a sudden hail of stones. Shooting broke out, and the crematorium went up in flames. Seeing the blaze, the prisoners in *Krema* 2 thought the uprising had begun. They overpowered the German *Kapo* and threw him, along with an SS officer, into the burning oven, tore down the fences, and fled. The prisoners in *Krema* 3 and 5 could not join in, because the camp siren had sounded the alarm by this time, and they were surrounded by mobile SS units.

Hell-bent on escaping, the fleeing prisoners from *Krema* 2 ran in the wrong direction: not northeast towards the Vistula but southwest, within the confines of the camp's outer fences. Trapped, they barricaded themselves in a barn.

The SS set fire to the barn, killing all those inside. The remaining insurgents were taken into the woods and killed by flame-throwers.

It was a day of reckoning. None of the *Sonder* men escaped, and 450 had been killed trying. But three SS officers were dead, and *Krema* 4 blown up. Although the revolt was a failure, it became a symbol of resistance. At the site where millions of innocent victims had been murdered, the first SS met their fate, felled by the hands of prisoners.

The destruction of truckloads of files: hospital records, dossiers on thousands of interrogations, and carefully falsified death certificates were burnt in accordance with secret orders issued by the Commissioner for Reich Defense:

All files, particularly the secret ones, are to be destroyed completely. The secret files about the installations and their purpose must be destroyed at all costs. Under no circumstances can they fall into the hands of the enemy, since after all they were secret orders of the Führer.

Only one file escaped destruction, the *Verbrennungsbuch* (The Book of the Burned), a register of victims cremated in Crematorium 1, along with some *Auschwitz Death Books* listing the death certificates of 68,864 registered prisoners.

While evidence documenting the crimes of the SS was going up in smoke, 2,000 prisoners were put to work in the storerooms of Canada packing everything of value to be shipped to Berlin. Everything else was burned or, as in the case 20,000 pairs of children's shoes and 293 bales of human hair (weighing 7000 kgs), simply abandoned.

The last spasms of killing occurred on January 6, 1945, to the sound of Russian guns booming in the distance. After months of interrogations, the SS finally identified the four young Jewish girls from Warsaw who had smuggled explosives out of the munitions factory for the insurgents. Twice that day inmates in the women's camp were marched out into the snow to watch a hanging. Two women were executed at noon and left on the gallows till the second pair, their hands tied behind their backs, were brought out and hanged after dark in the glare of the camp's lights. It was the last official execution at Auschwitz.

On January 8 the SS dynamited the already largely dismantled *Krema* 2 and *Krema* 3 and the resistant structures of the remaining crematoria. At the same time orders were given for a general evacuation. Women too sick to march were disposed of. Those still on their feet were ordered to dig out and burn the corpses tossed into mass graves behind the crematoria. Left behind was 112 tons of human bone meal ready to be shipped for the manufacture of phosphate.

When the Russian reconnaissance scouts emerged from the snow-laden forest, there was nothing to see of the crematoria but the snow-covered rubble of the four structures.

On January 20 the SS command sent orders to murder all the

prisoners remaining in the camp, but with Soviet troops in the neighborhood, the SS calculated that if they liquidated the remaining survivors there would not be enough time to dispose of the bodies before evacuating the camp. 58,000 thousand prisoners were marched off into the Polish winter, most of them dressed in rags. For those unable to keep up with the furious pace of the march, the evacuation amounted to a last ruthless selection. The evacuation journey was a *Todesmärsche* (death march). Astride the columns the guards hovered like angels of death. Prisoners who staggered, lagged behind, or fell were beaten without hesitation with rifle butts or shot. It did not matter that they died along the way; what really mattered was that they should not tell their story. Upon reaching Gliwice, the women were loaded onto open freight cars and deported to Bergen-Belsen and Ravensbrück. Male prisoners were dispatched in open cattle-cars to Gross-Rosen, Mauthausen, and Buchenwald.

The chaotic evacuations, forced marches, and executions during the last months of the Nazi regime showed just how deep-seated German anti-Semitism was. When no one could believe any longer that the war could still be won, 6,000 prisoners were taken from Dachau on a *Todesmärsche* to the mountains of Tyrol and machine-gunned.

When the camp was liberated by American troops, they found 9,000 bodies strewn round the camp, and a further 4,000 in the boxcars of an abandoned transport. The victims were Hungarian and Polish Jews who had been shuttled round from camp to camp for more than a month. A third of the 700,000 prisoners driven out of the camps lost their lives while marching or in the transport trains that shunted backwards and forwards in search of somewhere to dump their human freight. The camps to which they were shipped had no food and were hopelessly overcrowded.

In Bergen-Belsen the prisoners were simply left to starve, although two miles away there was a *Wehrmacht* training school that had 800 tons of food and a bakery capable of producing 60,000 loaves of bread a day. At the Lüneburg trial the Commandant, Joseph Kramer, confessed that he had not asked for help, because it would have required "special papers." When Bergen-Belsen was liberated, the British found 13,000 unburied bodies, some partly eaten.

Yet typically people refused to believe that Hitler knew about these marches or condoned them. Although residents were close enough to see the victims as individuals, not as "subhuman" or criminals, it was rare for anyone to offer help. After the war, people cited danger to themselves as the reason they were unable to pass the inmates food or water. But at the same time no one could remember any instance in which the SS actually arrested anyone who dared to assist a prisoner in any way.

The last SS man to leave Auschwitz closed the iron gates and cut off the lights from the main switchboard. Birkenau sank into darkness. When the Ukrainian reconnaissance scouts emerged from the woods, all they saw were rows of barracks, miles of barb wire, and empty guard posts. But as the scouts approached the camp, they were suddenly besieged by the sick and half-dead abandoned by the SS.

Since three out of four prisoners lost their entire family, awakening from the nightmare was no less painful than captivity. Sentenced to carry their pain and sadness to the grave, there was nowhere for them to pay their last respects. The enormous cemetery of European Judaism, Auschwitz, was a cemetery without a grave.

34

The house in which Walter and I were living had escaped one near miss, but neither of us thought to leave. Then in early February the Americans staged one of their biggest air raids over Berlin. When we heard the sirens, Walter and I made for the cellar. The bomb blasts followed one another in a succession of thunderclaps.

Just as we reached the cellar, the house was ripped apart by a violent explosion. Walter was lifted off his feet and flung down the stairs. The next minute the house came crashing down.

I found myself on the cellar floor, a whirlwind of bells ringing in my head. The first recognizable feeling was numbness, then trying to find out which parts of my body were broken and which parts were still there. Either way the situation felt hopeless.

But as the minutes ticked by and I found myself still breathing I thought perhaps that I should not give up, and that I should do something about it.

I looked at Walter. His clothes and face were covered with plaster and dust. He was holding his left arm, wincing with pain. His skin had only a burn-like mark but below the surface the bones were broken.

Suddenly there was another explosion. The floor heaved and rolled under us, choking the air with more dust. When the dust settled, I saw light coming from a hole in the cellar roof that had not been there before.

At that moment I heard Walter cry out. I turned round and saw the fin of a 400-lb bomb sticking out of the rubble. It was either a dud, or the debris had broken its fall; either way we did not wait to find out. I struggled to my feet, grabbed Walter by his one good arm, and together we scrambled out of the hole into what was left of Berlin.

The city lay dying in blood and flames. The streets were a succession of craters, choked with smoke and dust and heaps of masonry. Buildings that had not received a direct hit but were caught in the firestorm were still burning with scorched holes in place of windows. Bodies were everywhere; many had been burnt to a cinder; swept up in the firestorm, they had become living torches. Most were foreign workers (identifiable by a letter painted on their clothes to denote their country of origin), who were forbidden entry to underground bunkers and cellars. The few souls who dragged themselves out from their cellars were black with soot. Some wore nothing but the wet blankets they had thrown over themselves to ward off the flames.

For four days we could not see the sky. We saw only a blood-red ball behind the dust and smoke that covered the city. It looked as if the earth was in mourning.

Walter led me to a *Gasthöfe* for SS officers near the Tetlow canal in Mariendorf. It was only three miles away, but it took two hours to get there. The roof was damaged, but the house was otherwise habitable. An SS orderly put a splint on Walter's arm and a couple of stitches in my forehead. The other SS were from many different sections: the Security Services, the *Waffen-SS, Kripo,* and the *Gestapo.* They were Hitler's executioners, complicit in the extermination of millions and the murder of untold numbers of civilians. But for the moment, the war made us more or less equal. Bombs do not distinguish the guilty from the innocent.

⌘⌘⌘

During my four months in the Gasthöfe I met several senior SS who made for Alt-Aussee, a crescent of mountains that separate German Bavaria from Salzburg. This was the starting point of the escape routes that took them to South America, Canada, and the Middle East. Among the Nazis who wrote themselves false discharge papers while I was at the *Gasthöfe* were two Brigadier Generals: Ernst Grawtiz, the chief medical officer of the SS, who directed the experimentation program carried out on the women in Ravensbrück, and Wilhelm Albert, chief of the Security Police at Lodz, who was responsible for the liquidation of the Lodz ghetto. I took note of who came and went, lest any of them be indicted for war crimes.

The Germans were exceptionally good at restarting factories and rescuing undamaged plants. All over the 20 *Verwaltungsbezirken* or districts of Berlin, industry, both heavy and light, though badly hit, had not closed down. In fact, by the end of the war an astonishing 80 percent of German industry was still intact.

I spent the last months of the war tracking down these factories in the outer suburbs. I passed on my findings to Reinecke but thought it unlikely that Intelligence would make much use of it. By this time industrial centers were not the primary target for Allied air raids.

35

With the Americans across the Rhine, Montgomery about to attack the Ruhr and the Russians on the Oder, Hitler must have realized the war was lost. He returned to Berlin in the middle of January, making his home in the massive concrete shelter built in the Chancellery gardens.

Twelve weeks later Zhukov broke through the German lines on the Oder and the Neisse and reached the outskirts of Berlin. German radio first pictured the Russian offensive as a steamroller, then as a landslide, then as an avalanche, and by April, as an Apocalyptic "Bolshevist flood." On April 22, two days after Hitler's fifty-sixth birthday, the first Russian shells began falling in the Chancellery garden.

Göebbels pleaded with all Germans to take up arms and "work a miracle." The "miracle" was to be realized through faith in Hitler. "Where in these bitter days does the homeland's almost god-like strength come from? From the Führer. We shall never succumb, we can never be altogether broken, because the Führer dwells within us." Hitler, for his part, had nothing to say that could bring comfort to his hearers in the presence of visible doom. Even the most credulous Nazi must have found despair implicit in the words with which he declared that not even the Russians could conquer a triumvirate composed of himself, God, and the German people.

When I returned to the Gasthöfe on the evening of April 23, the day Berlin radio announced Hitler's vain glorious gesture that he would sacrifice himself to save European civilization from Bolshevism, I found it empty. Walter had left a prophetic note saying that he would not be coming back. As with every German male, regardless of injury or sickness, he had been pressed into service, given command of a *Panzerjagd* Division, consisting of boys from the Hitler *Jugend*. Each boy was given a bicycle with two panzerfaust anti-tank launches clamped on either side of the front wheel with which to ram a T-34 or Stalin tank. Göebbels said that the boys in Hitler *Jugend* had "volunteered" for the "honor" to be accepted into the SS and to die for their Führer in the defense of Berlin.

But they had little choice. If they were found hiding or carrying a white flag, they were hanged as traitors by the SS as a warning that "he who was not brave enough to fight had to die." When trees were not available, they were hung up on lamp posts, executed by a small group of SS fanatics. I was sorry that I was not able to say good-bye to Walter. We had become friends. He must have suspected my cover but never tried to catch me out or caution others when I was present.

From the time the Russians entered Berlin on April 20 until General Weidling surrendered the city 12 days later, I rarely left the Gasthöfe. Stalin concentrated a far more powerful force to take Berlin than Hitler had deployed to invade the whole of the Soviet Union: 2.5 million men, 41,600 guns, 6,500 tanks, and 7,500 aircraft. These are the facts: the reality was ruin, shattered bodies, suffering, and death.

The air echoed with the thunder of heavy artillery and rocket-firing katyushas. Clouds of smoke and dust from falling masonry reduced visibility to almost zero: only the fire-streaks of katyusha rockets were visible. No bombardment in the war had been so intense. The earth shook, and I felt my eardrums were about to burst.

The bombing and shelling created cracks in the walls, and dust from plaster and pulverised masonry seeped into the air. But unlike so many others trapped in bomb shelters and cellars, I had an adequate stockpile of food and water. I did not have to risk being caught in cross-fire to snatch food from an abandoned shop or siphon water from the nearest street pump. Nor did I have to fear that my wife or daughter would be snatched from my arms and raped.

My only fear was that the Gasthöfe might be blasted by an antiaircraft gun or howitzer, or stormed by one of Russian assault groups that made their way from house to house, along the rooftops, and from cellar to cellar. Armed with grenades, submachine-guns and flame-throwers, they rarely had time to distinguish who was who. A civilian was lucky if he or she was forced out of their cellar at gunpoint and into the street, whatever the crossfire or shelling.

During a lull in the fighting I risked going out to get a copy of *Der Panzerbär*, the last newspaper to be printed in Berlin. Scraps of bodies poked from the earth. The streets were laid waste. Houses were reduced to a shattered chimney or a broken wall. But Göebbels' headline affirmed victory: "A Mass-Grave for Soviet Tanks! Berlin fights for the Reich and for Europe." Incredible as it may seem, there were some in the *Volkssturm* who believed this cant. I saw a unit of these boys, aged 14 and 15, dressed in old black SS uniforms and French steel helmets waiting to run at Russian tanks without even knowing how to fire their rifles. Captivated by the idea of fighting for "the final victory," they died believing they were fighting for Germany.

Hitler had always said that if Germany lost the war, he would leave no one to triumph over its defeat. "If the war is lost," he told Speer, "the people will be lost too; it is not necessary to worry about what they will need for survival. We might sink, but we'll take the world with us."

Everything, simply everything essential to the maintenance of life, was to be destroyed. He supplemented his earlier "scorched earth" order with one of "total annihilation by explosives, fire or dismantlement." It was a death sentence for the German people. Speer countermanded the order but was too late to save the thousands of civilians sheltering in the underground when a tide of water released by the destruction of the locks of the river Spree swept through the subway.

The last days of savage house-to-house fighting and street battles had been a human slaughter, with no prisoners being taken on either side. No one was prepared, however much horror propaganda, they had heard from Göebbels, for the shock of Russian revenge. The Russians gave no mercy. Every opportunity was taken to drum into them the scale of German atrocities. To reinforce the message, the Red Army exhumed the bodies of 65,000 Jews massacred near Odessa, and ordered them to be placed alongside the road most used by troops. Every 200 meters a sign declared, *Look how Germans treat Soviet citizens.*

Rape and looting took place in front of one's eyes. Women quickly learned to disappear during the "hunting hours" of the evening.

Daughters were hidden in storage lofts for days on end. Mothers emerged into the street to fetch water only in the early morning when Soviet soldiers were sleeping off the alcohol from the night before. Sometimes the greatest danger came from one mother giving away the hiding place of other girls in a desperate bid to save her own daughter. Estimates of rape victims from Berlin's two main hospitals ranged from 95,000 to 130,000. One doctor deduced that out of approximately 100,000 women raped in the city, some 10,000 died as a result, mostly from suicide.

General Wilding, the commander of the German troops in Berlin, surrendered the city on 3 May, just 13 days after Marshal Zhukov ordered his long-range artillery to open fire on Berlin. There was no radio or newspaper, so vans with loudspeakers drove through the streets, ordering the Germans to cease all resistance. Suddenly, the shooting and bombing stopped. The unreal silence meant that the ordeal was over.

Hitler's all-absorbing narcissism and destructiveness had turned Berlin into a lunar landscape. Gone were the public monuments, the elaborate façades, the library, and the university. That wide and lovely boulevard, the *Unter den Linden,* had disappeared, buried under rubble. Even the supposedly impregnable *Tiergarten* flak-tower was in ruins, its heavy concrete slabs crushing Rembrandts, Titians, and Rubens along with the best of Schliemann's Trojan excavations, among them the golden mask of Priam. Ten square miles of central Berlin was reduced to rubble, a million people killed, and twice that number left homeless. Stalin saw Berlin as Russia's rightful reward, but Zhukov gave him a city of gutted buildings and traumatized people. There was little to claim, and the waste was terrible.

36

On April 30, just eight days after celebrating his 56th birthday, Hitler shot himself in the mouth. We heard the news of his death the following day. Hamburg radio, one of the few German radio stations still able to function, interrupted its program to tell listeners to stand by for "a grave and important announcement." This was immediately followed by excerpts from a number of Wagner's operas and the slow movement of Bruckner's *Seventh Symphony*.

Then, at 10:20 p.m., after a muted silence, an announcer said:

> Our Führer, Adolph Hitler, has fallen this afternoon at his command post in the Reich Chancellery, fighting to the last breath against Bolshevism and for Germany. On April 30 the Führer appointed Grand-Admiral Dönitz as his successor. Our new Führer will now speak to the German people.

Dönitz, who did not suspect suicide, told the nation that Hitler had died a hero's death while defending the Fatherland and that the oath of allegiance sworn to the Führer now applied to himself.

Hitler's death should have brought his life to an end, but Stalin, who ordered Hitler's remains to be taken to Moscow, told Truman, for reasons best known to himself, that he thought Hitler was still alive. This prompted the Americans to conduct an 11-year investigation into the possibility that Hitler was hiding out in the foothills in the Andes or in a remote part of Argentina. The charred corpse taken to Moscow was identified as Hitler's remains by forensic specialists overseen by SMERSH (Soviet Counterintelligence). Further proof was given by two former dental assistants to Hitler's dentist ,who identified Hitler's teeth and bridgework. These findings were kept secret, either because Stalin did not trust them, or because he wanted to keep the evidence up his sleeve in case someone showed up claiming to be Hitler.

In April 2000 a fragment of Hitler's skull went on display in the National Archives of Moscow as part of an exhibit called "The Agony of the Third Reich: Retribution." Although Hitler's body was destroyed in 1970 on orders from Leonid Brezhnev, the skull and jaw fragments were saved, along with remnants of Hitler's uniform and a bloo-d stained mattress said to have been part of the sofa that Hitler was sitting on when he committed suicide.

WH Auden's poem "Epitaph on a Tyrant," written in September 1939, the day Germany invaded Poland, depicts Hitler as a man driven by the fanaticism of his sentiments:

> Perfection, of a kind, was what he was after
> And the poetry he invented was easy to understand;
> He knew human folly like the back of his hand,
> And was greatly interested in armies and fleets;
> When he laughed, respectable senators burst with laughter,
> And when he cried the little children died in the streets.

37

I had no reason to remain in Germany after the fall of Berlin. I hitched a ride to Freiburg in an American Army truck and crossed the border into Switzerland. A week later we heard that Jodl had signed an unconditional surrender. The war in Europe was over. This then, was the end, after those long years of war. Hitler's thousand-year Reich had lasted just 12 years. Germany was in ruins, and 50 million people had died. What good had it all been? For what purpose had so many people given their lives?

There were no victory parades or dances in Switzerland, no one shouted or sang, or ran shouting and singing into the streets. There was a small party at the legation, but few handshakes and no cheers. Most staff had not been touched by the war. Its end meant little change in their lives, as it did for the Swiss generally. The country had had much to answer for. Given Switzerland's neutrality and geographic position, it could have offered protection to those persecuted by the Nazis, or introduced a policy of aid and rescue on an international scale. By asking Nazi Germany to mark the passports of Jewish citizens with a "J" (it chose not to recognize anyone persecuted for racial reasons as worthy of asylum), and delivering captured refugees over to their persecutors, many people were driven to certain death.

I was glad the war was over. Well, not quite over; the Japanese would not surrender for another six months. Perhaps my brain was too full of memories to be really excited by the thought of peace. All I wanted was to find Marian and be with her. I called her as soon as I learned the arrangements that had been made for my demobilization. The broken connection and interruptions reminded me how little time we had spent together, and even these fleeting and threatened with uncertainty. Sometimes it is the hidden aspects of war that are the most difficult to bear.

My only remaining commitment was to give my files on the SS to the Jewish Congress in Geneva. When I called Geneva, I was told to pass them to UNWCC (United Nations Commission for the Investigation of War Crimes) or one of the American war crimes investigation groups in Germany.

No one had much faith in UNWCC after Belsen. When the camp was liberated, Guy Lambert (deputy under-secretary in the War Office) denied that any crimes had been committed and ordered British troops not to collect evidence that might be used against the Nazis because the victims "were not British nationals." UNWCC would deal only with cruelties and massacres against "nationals" of countries recognized by the United Nations. Because Nazi legislation deprived Jews of their nationality, people who were formally German, Austrian, Polish, etc., were regarded as stateless and could not be represented on the Commission. Since this ruling completely undercut the effectiveness of UNWCC as an instrument for investigating war crimes, I turned to the Americans.

The American war crimes teams reported to Brigadier Hugh Scott-Barrett, head of the Judge Advocate General's office JAG) in Berlin. I had had enough of the war, of cities transformed into moonscapes, and ghostlike people living in damp cellars. But under the circumstances I had no choice but to return to Germany.

Brian arranged for me to stay at Von Seeckt's army barracks in *Wilhelmstadt* in the southern part of Spandau, seven miles from the center of Berlin. Although the suburb was important industrially and as an armaments center, it was surprisingly unscathed. The army barracks consisted of a series of large pink rectangular blocks with pink roofs, its walls decorated with frescos of Pan-Germanic supermen and robot-like infantrymen.

The barracks were occupied by soldiers from the 21st Army Group. They had cleaned up the mess left by the Russians who had removed all the furniture, including door handles, power points, taps, and light bulbs. To make the place habitable the British press-ganged 300 German women from a nearby tenement to clear up the rubbish. I was given a sparsely furnished room that overlooked the stables. It was a pleasure each morning to watch the horses being taken out for exercise, clattering over the cobbled streets on their way to the woods towards Gatow.

Spandau was the first part of Berlin to be captured by the Red Army and was close to the Russian sector. Since one could move freely between the sectors, there were always Russians (though seldom vice versa) in "British" bars and cafes. The barrack cells always carried a hard-mouthed crowd of Russian deserters and drunks arrested by the Military Police. There were hundreds, perhaps thousands, of Russian deserters, mainly from the Ukraine, drawn from second-grade troops. Their officers took it for granted that these men would indulge in looting, rape, and profiteering, and did little to stop them.

Almost every morning I walked to the American sector over the Havel or the Spree, filled with all kinds of rubbish from old cars to dead trees, past twisted girders and pitted blocks of flats. *Trümmerfrauen* (rubble women) were on almost every street, forming human chains with buckets to clear the rubble and salvage bricks.

But for all the destruction, the real evil of war was the consequent human damage. Thousands of returning troops and released POWs shambled about, their feet bare, swollen, blood-covered, crumbling within their tattered and filthy uniforms. A surprising number were amputees, without feet, released by the Russians without crutches. Sometimes all that was left was the trunk. Amputated up to their hips, they sat in old wooden boxes supported by wheels, pushing themselves forward like raftsmen. Where they were going, or how, they did not know, nor, apparently did anyone else. Their eyes, often sunk in hollow sockets, searched for some recognizable landmark. Some were mere boys, conscripted out of school to be sent to the eastern front. At first I felt little sympathy for these men, particularly the SS among them. But then I realized that they too had lived through events that would mark them for life.

Starvation was visible in the faces of children and adults alike. More than 70 percent of the population was without bread. Montgomery had cut the monthly rations in the British Zone to 1,000 calories. When pointed out that Belsen rations were 800 calories, he answered "...the big overgrown Germans have got to tighten their belts... I believe that 75 percent of the population remain out-and-out

184

Nazis." I saw no "big overgrown Germans" and whether they were Nazis or not was beside the point. To make matters worse, Montgomery had forbidden food parcels into Germany. For ordinary Germans in the British Zone the actual calorific ration was equal to two or three slices of bread a day and a cup of bean soup.

Scott-Barrett was not in Berlin as I was told, but "traveling," and no one could tell me when he would return. Nor was I able to reach any of the 17 American JAG investigation groups who were combing the internment camps for SS. I was given an introduction to Clio Straight, who ran the prosecutions for JAG, but he was always "unavailable."

Straight was a lawyer from Waterloo, a small town in Iowa, where he arranged loans for local farmers. He had requisitioned an office in the Deutsche Bank in Wiesbaden but spent most of his time chasing the investigation teams and Intelligence Corps for information. JAG was so badly resourced that by August not a single German had been put on trial in the US Zone. All attempts to create an Anglo-American records center failed through lack of staff. Believing that there was no point in pestering the Americans further, I pinned my hopes on CROWCASS (Central Registry of War Criminals and Security Suspects) being set up in Paris.

Meanwhile the Gestapo and SS were fleeing Germany in droves. There were reports from Stockholm of Nazis parachuting to asylum and confirmed sightings from Spain of German submarines taking people to South America. Gustav Wagner, the "Angel of Death" in Sobibor, was in an internment camp in Bavaria. No one questioned him, and he was released at the end of May. Ernst Heinrichsohn, who supervised the trains leaving Paris for Auschwitz, was under arrest in Bavaria but was freed a year later because no one thought to question him. Adolph Eichmann stayed unrecognized in an American POW camp until he saw his picture in an Allied newspaper and then escaped without much trouble. Himmler's Adjutant SS General Karl Wolff had papers to prove he was a nonentity and was let go. Richard Baer, the last commandant of Auschwitz, and SS General Oskar Dirlewanger (who massacred the Polish partisans) also had false papers and were released. There were hundreds of thousands of former camp inmates in DP (displaced persons) camps who could have identified SS personnel and former tormenters if the investigators had been more resourceful.

In fairness to the investigation teams they were asked to do a difficult task amidst conflicting and confusing orders, without any training or preparation and with no help or facilities. They thought they had time on their side: no one had told them about the network of agents smuggling out Nazis.

Among the best organized of these "ratlines" was the Intermarium (between the seas) run by the Catholic Church. Its relief agencies in Rome smuggled out 30,000 Nazis and neo-Nazis. It even organized the escape of an entire *Waffen-SS* division—some of whom had served at Treblinka, Belsen, and Sobibor.

Archbishop Ivan Buchko (the senior *Intermarium* representative in the Ukraine) successfully intervened with Pope Pius X11 to win freedom for the 11,000 men interned at the Rimini POW camp north of Rome. Since the 14th *Waffen-SS* division had collaborated with *Einsatzgruppen* units in the Ukraine, they were facing repatriation to Russia. Pope Pius used his office to have the troops reclassified as "confines" rather than prisoners of war. As a result Buchko was able to get the British Government to extend "free settler" status to the Rimini internees and to assist them in resettling in Canada, Australia, and other Commonwealth countries.

The SS and the Gestapo did not rely entirely on the Vatican. They had their own pipelines out of Europe. The best known was ODDESA (Organization of Former SS Members). It was run by Hitler's favorite commando, Otto Skorzeny, who went on to advise Juan Perón about setting up a Fourth Reich in Argentina. Another "successful ratline" led through Rome, where the Austrian Bishop Dr. Alois Hudal had made a secret pact with the Italian police to take wanted Nazis (Eichmann among them) to selected churches and monasteries until they could be smuggled out of the country to Latin America.

Meanwhile, the Swiss government, for the sum of 200,000 Swiss francs per Nazi, helped others to fly out on regular scheduled airlines to Brazil, no questions asked. Britain was little better. Its immigration policy after the war favored members of the SS over non-whites and Jewish Holocaust survivors. Among the immigrants were more than 70

Auschwitz guards and 120 SS and Gestapo suspected war criminals.

Although photographs were beginning to appear of exhumed bodies of slave workers and prisoners murdered by the SS, tracking down the perpetrators was not a priority. The Allies were more eager to track down the Nazi's top scientists. The Russians forcibly transported a trainload of German technicians to Moscow under *Operation Osavakim.* The British shipped whole laboratories, including the Göring Aeronautical Research Institute and its revolutionary wind tunnels, back to England, along with 200 tons of documents.

But these operations were dwarfed by *Operation Paperclip.* The Americans sent over 3,000 specialists to seek out and arrest the best scientists working in the camps and other institutions. Their biggest coup was the "capture" of 400 scientists working on the V2 rocket program at Nordhausen. When the Americans entered Nordhausen they found 3,000 bodies, rotting and unburied, stacked inside the building. Thirty thousand others had already been cremated, having died of exhaustion, starvation, and disease. Among the scientists offered lucrative contracts were Von Braun, who had personally picked labor slaves from the Buchenwald concentration camp, and SS Major General Walter Dornberger, who was interrogatied by the British War Crimes Investigation Unit in connection with the use of slave labor. Like other Nazis admitted under *Paperclip*, the military sanitized Dornberger's past and maintained the public pretense that no incriminated Nazis had entered the United States. Dornberger later rose to become vice president of Bell Helicopters. In recognition of his time with Hitler's V-2 program he called a range of Bell Helicopters the "V22."

Not all Nazis were so lucky. Himmler was arrested at Lueneburg; Dönitz, Jodl, and Admiral von Frideburg were taken into custody after returning from their headquarters in Muerwik; Speer was arrested while shaving at Glücksburg; Göring surrendered to an American colonel; von Ribbentrop was arrested while living openly in his Hamburg apartment; and Julius Streicher was found painting on his veranda. These Nazi leaders had stayed in Germany in the erroneous belief that they would be needed by the Allies to help rebuild Germany. It was a measure of their collective fantasy that the world would accept any form of succession within the Third Reich, assuming that it had any territory left.

After nearly a month of fruitless effort, I considered leaving my files with one of the Military Governors and quitting. But then I heard that they were employing SS as political advisors. One of the advisors in the American sector was a protégé of Hjalmar Schacht, who was in custody in Nuremberg. Given this scenario and the incriminating nature of my files, I thought better of it.

Unlike the British and Americans, the Russians had begun trying and executing German war criminals in 1943. The news of these hangings came as a great shock to Hitler, who considered the SS to be above the law. As his anxiety grew, he tried to infect the whole of Germany with his own fear of Allied retribution. "If we lose the war, gentlemen," he told a conference of armaments-industry executives in July 1944, "then your only choice will be whether you help yourself make the transition from this world to the next, or whether you let yourself be hanged, or let them give you a shot in the neck, or starve to death, or work in Siberia—these will be the only possibilities open to an individual."

38

While waiting to hear from CROWSCASS I worked part-time for the Royal Army Service Corps. This involved driving round Berlin interpreting for troops having problems guarding coal trains, food, and petrol depots. Anything of value that was not watched disappeared. There was a general feeling at the time that people had become nastier rather than kinder after the war. But since the average German spent most of his time waiting in line for food or a stamp on a form and was afraid of facing another winter, altruism was a luxury few could afford. Food was scarce and the water, foul (in most places there was none), and there was no gas or electricity. The Russians had taken the electric motors from the S-Bahn trains, which added to the problems faced by those trying to repair the city. Despite the wreckage of human life and property, civilian morale never really cracked, which says much for the resilience of human nature. On the whole I found the German people longsuffering, and grateful for simply being alive.

Food rationing and price controls led to a flourishing black market, most of which took place in nightclubs and black market restaurants. Although these markets moved in and out of the Russian, British, and American sectors depending on expediency, their center of gravity was almost always the *Kurfürstendamm*. Among the many clubs in the *Kurfürstendamm* was "The Royal."

"The Royal" was the most up market of the *Kabaratten*. It was a brilliantly illuminated and lavishly furnished set of rooms lined with red and gold velvet wall coverings with padded leather chairs and sofas. It was always crowded with British and American officers, foreign correspondents, and "big shots' in the black market. Although fraternization between Allied troops and Germans had been forbidden by Roosevelt ("There must be no fraternization! This is absolute!"), no one took any notice of the order.

The girls employed by the club were lovely and beautifully dressed. Among them was Sylvia Hasse. Silvia was very pretty, with a smile that lingered in one's memory long after she had turned her head. The girls in the Royal were not prostitutes, but few principles could hold out against the sway of the black market. The acute shortage of food and other essentials led girls from the best families to prefer promiscuity to rubble clearing and starvation. Very few women could not be bought at a price nor would refuse at all cost to surrender their bodies. As Brecht said in his *Threepenny Opera*, "First comes food, then comes morals."

Sylvia and I became close friends, but not lovers. She undid the separateness and aloneness I had felt since the beginning of the war. We were a little in love with each other but never spoke the words that would make our feelings known.

Sylvia's parents were among the 250,000 killed in Berlin during the two weeks of the Russian siege. Her mother had refused to leave her husband when the order came through for all women and children to leave Berlin and all men to stay and fight the Soviets. She had insisted, however, that Sylvia join the stream of evacuees heading towards Magdeburg, begging and scavenging to stay alive. When Sylvie returned home, she found her mother dead and their house all but destroyed. To protect herself from Zhukov's Russians who prowled the streets looting and raping, she locked herself in the cellar until the first Allied troops arrived. Even then, for the benefit of any Russian who was hanging round, she wore a red kerchief fashioned out of a Nazi flag when she stepped into the street.

Like other girls Sylvia added to her earnings by selling eggs and vegetables brought from outlying villages to those who could afford them. Although much of the illegal trafficking was conducted in private houses it was still dangerous. Racketeers did not confine themselves to buying and selling. Until the German police force was armed in 1946, there were between 40 and 50 murders a month. The motive was nearly always robbery. The black market gangs were made up of ex-SS men, Poles, Russian deserters and German gangsters and their profitable dealings did not stop them from robbing anyone whom they thought had money. Whenever possible I left my jeep with its army markings conspicuously in front of Sylvia's house.

During my last six weeks in Berlin I saw Sylvia almost every day. At the weekends we went to Grunewald, an expanse of woodland and lakes a few miles west of the city. That summer, as if to make up for all the gray years of the Reich, was gifted with a charmed light that made everyone hold their breath. Grunewald had miraculously escaped the bombing. It was a carpet of many colored flowers: a breath of beauty in this unquiet grave of a city. We laughed a lot and talked endlessly. It was my first real taste of normal existence for a long time.

The Americans, especially, felt that the Germans had not "fully" acknowledged their responsibility or accepted their guilt. To be accepted as "not a Nazi" one had to be perceived as distinctly anti-Nazi. It was felt that the Germans should be grieving for the victims of Nazi death camps rather than be preoccupied with their own losses. But anyone who had been in and out of Germany during the war knew that the lives of millions of Germans had ended prematurely or had been painfully interrupted by a war they neither wanted nor supported.

But the idea persisted that any "good German" would have left Hitler's Germany, or at least performed some small-scale daily sabotage against the Nazis. But what might appear as an unnecessary compromise was a dangerous option for the vast majority of people. It was all the "average" man could do to get himself and his family through the war one day at a time. Hitler's policies were not foreseen, and when the worst occurred most people could not believe it. Sylvia noticed the isolation and disappearance of Jews during the war. But to jump from expulsion to Auschwitz was beyond her and most people's imagination. *The population hardly realized what was happening,* Eichmann stated with barely concealed satisfaction in a note about the deportation of German Jews, and it was true.

The fear that allegations of atrocities would be dismissed as propaganda persuaded the Americans to set up screenings of films taken of Belsen and Buchenwald after their liberation. I did not want to see these films, or be reminded of those potentially disabling memories that I tried to forget. But when Sylvia was asked to attend a screening (required of any German applying for a job with the Control

Commission) she asked me to go with her.

The film was shown in an army cinema and called *Atrocities—The Evidence.* The cameraman had an eye for the shocking and for what would disturb his viewers the most. One sequence showed the main camp in Buchenwald strewn with corpses, in many cases piled five or six feet high. Seated among them were women peeling potatoes and cooking scraps of food, smiling at the camera. One had to have lived with the dead to understand their indifference.

Another scene showed dozens of naked bodies being pushed into a pile by a bulldozer. A British soldier drove the bulldozer, beret pushed back, a cigarette dangling from the corner of his mouth. Sitting calmly above the corpses about to be picked up by the bulldozer's shovel, the young soldier might be reclining in a deckchair; for him, the distended corpses might have been large rotting vegetables. How had he become inured so quickly? Yet another scene showed a small boy walking calmly towards the cameraman along a road. Bodies were laid out neatly on either side, some of them covered, some not, their long thin legs pointing toward the child. The caption read: "A small boy strolls down a road lined with dead bodies near camp at BELSEN." What was he doing there? How had he got there? What would he say to his mother (if alive), and what would she say to him?

The film represented a brief but unforgettable picture of Belsen before its liberation and, in the eyes of the Commission, evidence of German collective guilt. But these dreadful pictures, which by no means told all, issued from a world beyond civilized imagination. How could anyone "really" be made to feel that they had contributed to the rise of a regime whose atrocities, committed in their name, they were now held responsible?

Sylvia sat through the film in silence. When we turned to leave, there were tears in her eyes. There was no point in telling Sylvia that she had not seen the worst—that the worst was beyond description. I did not mind talking about Auschwitz but found it impossible to say what it meant to be there. The factual elements only made up part of the experience of camp life: the other part, the unspeakable part, is what happens to you inside.

Sylvia did not know about the gassings—hardly anyone did outside

192

the inner circle of SS. But she said she knew something was happening. She used that untranslatable word *ahnem* (a kind of "sixth sense") to describe knowing that something dreadful was happening to the Jews. But to find out, to look for an explanation, would have been very dangerous. I said there was nothing she could have done about it— whatever "it" was, but she was not convinced.

A more critical issue than individual guilt were the factors that allowed a destructive character like Hitler to take power. The German people gave Hitler the mandate for licensed gangsterdom on a heroic scale and paid the price. In the end he joined forces with his enemies in order to complete the destruction of his own people by destroying the last remaining life-support systems. In the last months of the war Hitler's war machine no longer had war as its object, but the annihilation of its own servants.

39

After six years of war some 50 million Europeans had been uprooted from their homes and left wandering across the ravaged countryside. The wandering masses poured into Berlin ignoring the signs posted on all the main roads: *Attention refugees! Newcomers banned from settling in Berlin. Use detours. Avoid entering city limits. Continue westward.*

Half a million Germans passed through Berlin in August alone. Having reached their goal, they were immediately directed to leave again, since there was no food for them and nowhere for them to stay. Carrying their bundles of what earthly goods they had managed to save, holding their underfed sickly fretful children, they tried to board one of the few erratically scheduled trains that would take them out of Berlin. The chaos at the stations was a microcosm of the chaos in Germany. People stood in dense rows on precariously narrow platforms, ready to jump up onto the running board the moment a train arrived, desperate to get somewhere where they could find food and shelter.

Sylvia gave a room to a family who had trudged half a dozen times between Magdeburg and Berlin, a round trip of more than 70 miles. They had been rejected from 51 towns in-between. When she saw them, footsore from walking in worn-out shoes stuffed with newspapers, they had been trekking back and forth so often that they had lost all sense of time. The sum of their belongings was stuffed into a small cart, including a small supply of potatoes replenished by farmers along the road. These carts became a symbol of the collapse of Germany and the resilience of the people, especially the women, trying to hold their families together.

I kept waiting for someone from CROWCASS to contact me. When I did hear from them, it was to be told that they were currently sorting through 80,000 names on a "black list" sent to them by the headquarters of the Commander, Allied forces. There was nothing I could do but wait while the politicians argued by what means and by which laws and in which courts the murderers of 10 million innocents should be apprehended and tried.

The Nuremberg Trial was the only demonstrable evidence that the Allies were serious about trying Nazi war criminals. The only questionable judgment concerned Albert Speer. The atrocities committed during Hitler's dictatorship had not swayed his loyalty to Hitler or his Nazi beliefs. In a letter written after his release he said:

> I still consider it essential today to take upon myself the responsibility, and thus the blame, for all crimes which were committed after I became a member of Hitler's government. It is not individual acts or omissions, however grave, which weigh upon me, but my conduct as part of the leadership... However, to this day I still consider my main guilt to be my tacit acceptance of the persecution and the murder of millions of Jews.

If Speer had said this at Nuremberg, he would have been hanged. At the trial he denied knowing about the fate of the Jews. It was a lie. His signature was in the guest book at Mauthausen. Mauthausen was the most lethal death camp in Austria. No one visiting the camp could have avoided seeing the cruelty practiced there on a daily basis. The American, French, and Russian judges all agreed that Speer should be executed. It was the English judge, Sir Geoffrey Lawrence, who wanted to spare his life—not for the reason given in the judgment ("...in the closing stages of the war he was one of the few men who had the courage to tell Hitler that the war was lost and to take steps to prevent the senseless destruction of production facilities") but because he had been impressed with Speer's "honesty" and "intellect" and by the fact the he was not a "ruffian." As a compromise and after a long argument, Speer was given 20 years.

40

I had hoped to pass on my files within a matter of days. Days had stretched into weeks, and weeks into months. Nobody, it seemed, was interested in the information I had collected, or if they were, were in no hurry to receive it. Meeting Sylvia had given meaning to the weeks of fruitless waiting, but when my stay slipped into the second month I decided to leave my files with the BDC (Berlin Document Center) and hope for the best. Since their offices were swollen with 10.7 million record cards and around 600,000 personal files of the SS (found by the US Seventh Army, who had stumbled on them in a paper mill near München, where they were about to be pulped), it was unlikely that my files would see the light of day.

Just before leaving Berlin, I was approached by a man who introduced himself as Isik. Isik was short, dark-eyed, with uneven broad shoulders. We were about the same age, in the mid-twenties, but he looked much older, perhaps because he had lost whatever boyhood a man carries with him. Isik had little time for small talk or trivia. He told me that he was with DIN (the Hebrew acronym for *Dam Yehudi Nakam* : Avenge Jewish Blood), and said that he had heard I had a list of SS and that if the War Crimes Group was not interested in it, he was.

All the men who joined DIN had lost somebody in a death camp and had pledged to hunt down those responsible. Because every man they sought had committed murder many times over they did not limit their vengeance to those who had done them personal harm. There were more of these men, *Ziele* (targets) than would ever be brought to trial: the thousands of SS who staffed the concentration camps, the *Einsatzgruppen* who had filled the mass graves from the Baltic to the Ukraine, men of the Security Police and the *Gestapo*.

DIN's active members were divided into four units, one for each of the four military occupation zones. When a suspect had been identified, he was dragged into a waiting car and driven to a deserted area. There, for the first time he was called by his name, told who his captors were, what he was dying for, and shot. Among DIN's victims were some very high-ranking SS officers, including Brigadier General Dr. Wilhelm Albert, SD Chief in Lódz, and General Odilo Globocnik, the SS head of *Operation Reinhard.*

I agreed to meet Isik the next day and give him a photocopy of my files. I knew that by giving him my files the men on my list would not be tried, judged, or sentenced, but executed. It is part of everyone's experience that there are times when good must stand aside. The SS on my list were among the most fanatical Nazis who routinely killed without reason or motive. The problem of nonretaliation was not restraint, but justice.

I met Isik as arranged. He spoke German with a Baltic accent. "Are you from Latvia?" I asked.

Isik shook his head, "Lithuania."

I asked him how he found his way into DIN. I had seen hundreds of Isiks in Auschwitz: Latvian and Lithuanian Jews transported in cattle cars from the ghettos of Eastern Europe. But they were not individuals whose stories you knew, and very few dedicated their lives to avenging the past.

He told me his story....

⌘⌘⌘

I was born in Cheznick. It is a small town on the edge of Rudnicki forest, a few miles south of Vilnius. Jews have lived there for more than 800 years. Cheznick, like the rest of Lithuania, changed hands many times. Life was always hard. But even after Vilnius was annexed by the Russians we did not imagine that the clouds rolling over Europe were going to rain blood. We went on picnics to local lakes and rivers, we played soccer, and if we had a good month at the sawmill, where I worked with my father, we went to the Yiddish theater in Vilnius or the hot springs at Drozgenik.

We listened to Hitler's speeches on the radio. We did not know what to make of him, or how seriously to take him. Even after *Kristal Nacht*, which had its equal in Poland, we did not expect an upsurge of anti-Semitism.

But that changed after the fall of Warsaw. Vilnius became the center for every Jew in Poland seeking asylum. The refugees hoped to get papers for America, Shanghai, Palestine, anywhere that would put them beyond the reach of the Germans. Many of them took shelter in the mill. We fed them and gave them clothes and blankets. My father set up a refugee committee. We raised money to ransom the refugees caught by Lithuanian border guards and buried those who were shot.

My family had lived in Cheznick for hundreds of years. Many of those years were a journey through hell, but they had never thought of leaving. My sister got married about this time; another reason for staying. Her husband was a Talmud scholar who taught at the yeshiva in Vilnius. We were a close community, accustomed to living together, working together, sharing everything; it was easy for us to extend the practice of sharing to the sharing of danger. When I was not helping my father at the mill I was smuggling refugees over the border into Byelorussia. I was old enough to know the risks; but I never thought to kill Germans, only save Jewish lives."

In the summer of 1940 Russia "incorporated" Lithuania, Estonia, and Latvia into the Soviet Union. We were back under communist rule. Farms and houses were confiscated. Anyone thought to "pose a danger to communism" was bundled off to Siberia. Eight thousand people were deported from around Vilnius. It didn't matter whether you were communist or not. Jewish Communists had no rights.

When a year later German tanks crossed the border, the Russians were just as surprised as we were. They couldn't believe that Hitler had stabbed them in the back. Focke Wulfs and Bf-109s flew so low over Cheznick that they almost clipped the trees. The first German soldiers entered the *shtetl* on bucket-seat motorcycles. Then came tanks, armored cars, and artillery. We watched them from behind closed windows. Endless columns of troops marched through the village, some throwing notices into our doorways. "We have come to liberate you from the Jews and their leaders, Roosevelt, Churchill, and Stalin who brought Bolshevism, abuse, and exploitation to the world."

Our Polish neighbors, the Kofnas, were on the street waving to the Germans. Gita Kofna spent more time in our house than her own. When her husband lost his job, my father lent him a horse to cart wood to Salcinikai and Chizhevsk. As more and more Germans marched through the *shtetl*, Polish cheers got louder and louder.

The Germans did not march through Cheznick and away as we hoped. They took the best houses as command posts and barracks. The occupants were kicked out onto the street or made to cook and clean for them. Reb Eretz and his family, who owned the inn on the high ground near the synagogue, were bundled into a truck and taken away. Later we learned that they had been taken to Treblinka and gone up in smoke. Even then my father did not think we should leave. A German had told him it would be a short war, "Here today, Moscow tomorrow."

But others were not so encouraging. "Too bad that you are Jews. Bad times are in store for Jews."

As the front line moved eastwards, the German soldiers in Cheznick were replaced by Gestapo. Our new overlords were Himmler's *Reichkommissars*, sent to oversee the extermination of the Jews and the commissars. They ordered Rabbi Ezrahi to set up a *Judenrat*, or council of elders, and when no one volunteered, they threatened to kill him. Eventually 12 men were selected by lottery, including my father. They had to help the Germans with supplies and carry out their orders but also carried the blame for anything that went wrong."

Soon after the councilor's names had been given to the *Reichkommissar,* the police chief told Rabbi Ezrahi that a Jew had tried to kill a German soldier. A Polish policeman had heard a shot and thought a villager had attacked a German. The shot had been fired by a soldier testing the sights on his rifle, but the Germans weren't questioned. The *Judenrat* was ordered on pain of death to find the culprit within the hour. My father and the others rushed round the *shtetl* trying to find the person responsible.

After an hour, when nobody had been found, the Germans grabbed hold of Amshel Nehemia, a 67-year-old scholar, marched him into the *shulhoyf* (the synagogue courtyard), and shot him. Everyone, even the children, was forced to watch the execution. It didn't end there. The *Reichkommissar* told us that the *Judenrat* had tried to bribe him with eggs and chickens to pardon Amshel. There was no truth to this, but my father and the others were punished by being made to crawl round the square on hands and knees shouting, *"Geborene Welt- und Reichsfeinde"* (born enemies of the world and Germany).

In the weeks that followed we were subjected to daily abuse. The German commander insisted on being carried round the square like a king. He picked on four men to carry him while he dropped burning paper on their heads. Another time he rounded up a group of children for some misdemeanour and sentenced them to execution. His idea of clemency was to accept the offer of some 70-year-olds to be hanged in their place."

Our women were not spared either. The Germans were drunk most nights. They staggered out into the marketplace and made my mother and other women dance for them, much to the amusement of the Poles. They looked on, making lewd gestures, shouting in Yiddish, *"Yidden, in shul arain!"* (Jews, go to hell!). The Jews and the Poles had always been good neighbors. Now they were laughing at us. It was difficult to understand, especially as the Poles themselves were victimized. We thought it was because they were Catholics and believed that we had crucified Jesus. We had all heard stories of Jews who had stones flung at them or worse at Easter.

Everyone in the village was put to work: repairing roads or enlarging the German barracks at Titiance. The women cleaned house for the Germans, did their cooking and laundry, and were made to pick out the weeds and moss from between the cobblestones. The Gestapo issued one demand after another. First it was for food, then clothing, then carpets and furniture, then the few valuables we had— candlesticks, jewelry, and our winter coats. From all corners of the village people carried their possessions to the Beth Midrash, which the Germans turned into a warehouse. Before long we were sleeping on boards, our only covering a horse blanket."

I knew exactly who I wanted to kill if I got the chance. First was Hans Hingst, the *Gebietskommisar* for Cheznick, and his aide, Franz Murer. Then the *Gebietskommisar* for Vilnius, Dr. Wulf, who went everywhere with a pack of *Hundestaffel* (killer dogs) that terrified everyone. Then Piaski, the police chief, who only opened his mouth to curse and scream at you. Later there were the men in the Police Battalions and the *Einsatzgruppen*. They were all murderers.

We did not think things could get worse, even though we heard rumors that Jews were being murdered, and not just by Germans. When the Gestapo arrived in Jedwabne, not far from Vilnius, they asked the Poles if they had plans for the town's Jews. They said that all the Jews should be got rid of. Encouraged by the Germans, the Poles armed themselves with axes, clubs, pitchforks, and iron bars, and chased the Jews into the town square.

Knowing what was in store for them, some women drowned their babies in the village pond before drowning themselves. The youngest daughter of a teacher in the Tarbut School was decapitated, and her head used as a football. Because there were too many Jews to be murdered by clubs and axes, mayor Karolak had the survivors driven into a barn belonging to Bronislaw Szeleszynski, a local carpenter. The building was doused with kerosene and set alight. Small children were tossed by pitchfork on to the flames.

As soon as the fire died down, the Poles began hacking at the smoldering corpses to remove their gold teeth. Of Jedwabne's 562 Jews only seven escaped the killing. After the massacre the Poles destroyed all records of the Jews' existence: birth certificates, marriage certificates, death certificates, business records, everything. If you went to Jedwabne today and asked the townspeople about the Jews, they'd say, "What Jews?"

It was only after Pessa Kofna told us that German killing squads had murdered Jews in the next village that my father told me to take my mother and brother into Byelorussia. But she would not leave him. She did not believe that anyone would kill women and children, and if she was to die, she wanted to be buried in the cemetery along with her ancestors.

A few weeks later a supply driver for the German command in Vilnius confirmed what Kofna had told us. The Germans had rounded up the population on the pretext of checking papers, then led the men off to be shot. My father immediately called a meeting of the *Judenrat*. Rabbi Ezrahi said that we should buy guns and die with honor. Others said that the Germans were only after Jewish property and money and not Jewish lives. They were still arguing when Chelm Piaski, the police chief, walked in and told them that he would save Cheznick if he was given 1000 rubles in gold. Somehow the money was raised. We thought we were safe.

On the eve of Rosh Hashanah, the Jewish New Year, Dr.Wulf and some officers of Strike Commando 3 entered Cheznick. The men in Strike Commando 3 reported to Walter Stahlecker, head of *Einsatzgruppen* A. Each member of the *Einsatzgruppen*, even if he worked at a desk, was required to kill at least one Jew. In this way no soldier could stand above the others; if the war was lost, everyone would share the guilt.

Wulf told Piaski to assemble everyone in the square. This was always a sign of trouble. The presence of the *Einsatzgruppen* confirmed it. Piaski read out a decree signed by the *Gebietskommisar* telling us that we had two hours to hand over our remaining valuables and line up on the main road. No one mentioned the gold given to Piaski or his promise to protect us. He would have denied it anyway, and the accuser would be shot.

It was too late to hide or run. Lithuanian *shaulisti* (shooters) appeared out of nowhere. They took up positions throughout the village, on the corner of every street and alley as well as in the market square. Piaski ordered the *shaulisti* to go from house to house and take what they could find. The Lithuanians went mad, smashing down walls, even stripping people of their clothing. Everyone fled from their homes. The Germans were waiting outside with baskets, telling us to throw in anything we had hidden on ourselves. My father tried to bargain with the Germans to spare his wedding ring, but to no avail. We lost everything.

We lined up, the entire Jewish population of Cheznick: men, women and children, aging parents, the sick and babies in arms. But the Germans had not done with us yet. A *shaulisti* read out names from a list he had been given by a local Pole. It was a list of the prettiest girls in Cheznick. Esther Hendl, the girl I was in love with, was among them. The girls were marched off to the schoolhouse. They came back with their clothes ripped, their faces scratched. Some cried nonstop;

others stared blankly into space. Esther wouldn't look at me. Blood was streaming down her legs into her shoes. After the Germans had done with them, they were passed to the *shaulisti*.

The *shaulisti* took up positions alongside us, and a German gave orders to march. We set off, thinking we were going to the Jewish ghetto in Vilnius. The last thing we saw as we left the village was our Polish neighbors plundering what was left in our homes.

We reached Beizevsk on the outskirts of Vilnius at sunset and were driven into the Horse Market. Exhausted, many people fell asleep. Others recited Palms. I found Esther, sat down beside her, and put my arms round her. After dark a dozen SS men from Strike Commando 3 roared into the village on motorcycles. Their caps carried the death's head insignia and they aimed their huge flashlights on us. When they saw someone with a beard, they dragged him to his feet shouting, "Death to the Jews!" and beat him senseless.

As they kicked their way among us, their flashlights fell on Rebecca, one of the girls abused by the *shaulisti*. They dragged her to her feet and told her to undress. When she did not move, they told her to obey or they would shoot her. They started to tear off her clothes. She fell to the ground and huddled up into a ball. They stepped back, laughing, drew their guns, and shot her. Having had their fun, they climbed back onto their motorcycles and drove off.

Early the next morning the Germans started shouting and pushing everyone back onto the road. I was sure there would be more killing before we reached Vilnius. I told my parents I was going to run for it when we reached Bieniasonie, where the road passed through the forest. When we got to the village, I broke from the column and ran into the forest. As I dived between the trees, I heard bullets whistling all around me.

A couple of *shaulisti* came running after me, but the undergrowth was too thick for them to see anything. They fired ahead of them hitting only the trees. After a few minutes they gave up and retraced their steps to the road. Just as the *shaulisti* emerged from the forest, my brother decided to run after me. He had no chance. The Lithuanians shot him down before he had taken a dozen steps. I heard my mother cry out, then silence.

When the column passed on I carried my brother's body into the forest. I spoke his name and thought I saw a glimmer in his eyes. Even though he was dying, I felt he knew I was there. By the time I laid him on the ground his eyes had a different look. Life had gone out of him, and I knew he was dead.

The Germans took the villagers to Panerai, a site on the edge of the forest 10 km southwest of Vilnius. Four huge pits had been dug in the forest. Standing beside the pits, holding machine guns, were men from Strike Commando 3. With them were some local auxiliary police and a few Lithuanian and Latvian collaborators. On the other side of the pits stood a field kitchen, with food and vodka.

The first group of 40 or 50 people were brought forward. They were told to undress and sort out their clothing into piles—one for shoes, one for underwear, and one for shirts and so on, and then jump into the pit. Those who hesitated were beaten and pushed in. Some mothers jumped in, holding their children; others threw their children in first and then jumped in after them. The sight of so many naked bodies excited the Germans. If a girl was pretty, she was dragged into the bushes and raped. Then the shooting started. Even in the midst of the gunfire I could hear wailing and crying. The bodies were covered with lime and sand; then the next batch of people was brought forward."

I knew that sooner or later it would be my parent's turn. When I saw them, they were holding each other's hands, their lips moving in prayer. *Shaulisti* pushed them to the edge of the pit. It was the last I saw of them. Shots rang out and they fell, murdered and buried in a mass grave with Esther and the rest of our neighbors. You don't choose your memories: they choose you. I cannot forget what happened at Panerai. I never will.

When the shooting stopped, the 2,300 Jews of Cheznick were no more. In just one day the Germans had obliterated 800 years of history. While the freshly covered graves were still moving and spouting blood the Catholic priest in Cheznick was telling his Polish parishioners that the Jews had at last been called to account for the killing of Christ.

The Germans returned to Vilnius at sunset, congratulating themselves on a good day's work. When it grew dark. I followed them, going to Niemiecka Street. where my sister lived. I had not seen Hannah or her husband for six months when we came together in the synagogue for the naming ceremony of their baby girl. In the meantime the Germans had turned the Jewish quarter of Vilnius into a ghetto, crowding 76,000 Jews into a small area between the synagogue and the bus station.

I told my sister and Elchik about the killing. I pleaded with them to escape with me into the forest. Living in a ghetto did not guarantee their survival. The Germans had already begun taking Jews from the ghetto, spreading the rumor that they had been taken to a labor camp in Ponar. Their actual destination was Panerai, where my parents had been shot.

Sara Menkes, a 19-year-old girl who had been among the victims, had miraculously survived the shooting. She pushed away the dead bodies that lay on top of her, crawled out of the pit, and walked back to Vilnius. She told her story to the Hashomer Hatzair, a Zionist youth group, and they printed a leaflet urging all those able to fight to do so:

Jewish youth do not believe those who are trying to deceive you. All the Gestapo's roads lead to Panerai and Panerai means death. Those who are taken out through the gates of the ghetto will never return. Ponar is not a labor camp; all of them are shot. Brethren it is better to die fighting like free men than live at the mercy of the murderers.

Elchik said he couldn't leave, notwithstanding Menkes' story. The Nazis had closed down his school, and he would not abandon his students. He told Hannah that she and the baby should go with me. But Hannah refused, insisting that her place was beside Elchik. But it was too late anyway.

The next morning the Germans surrounded the ghetto. Everyone in my sister's district was told to leave their homes and line up. We knew what this meant. There had been round-ups before.

The Germans started going through the houses. Anyone caught hiding was shot. The street was packed with people. Then Hannah, in fear for the baby, ran back into the house, the baby in her arms. Elchik and I ran after her. She wanted to hide the baby in the hope that someone would smuggle the child out of the ghetto to the Sisters at the Covent of St. Catherine in the Aryan quarter. There was very little time. We could hear the Germans kicking down the doors of the house next door. Hannah wrapped the baby up tightly and put her behind the curtain next to the wash basin. Then Elchik and I grabbed Hannah and pulled her outside. A moment later the Germans entered the house.

The next few minutes I will never forget. We heard a shot from inside the house, and Hannah ran back. Elchik and I ran after her, calling her back. The Germans had found the baby and shot her. One of them was holding the dead child by the legs, swinging her like a rabbit. My sister went crazy. She threw herself at the man but was shot before she could reach him. Elchik turned on the man who killed Hannah and was shot too. I backed out of the door, my hands in the air.

We were marched to a field beside the station. People were praying and crying and calling for their children. Every now and then the Germans broke into the crowd, hitting people with their rifle butts in order to keep everyone quiet. Some of the *Einsatzgruppen* had knotted whips, similar to horse whips, with which they lashed out, hitting young and old alike. After a couple of hours the guards became bored and started throwing their empty beer bottles at us. Anyone hit by a bottle was dragged out, beaten, and shot, in front of smiling Polish onlookers.

Later, much later, an empty train pulled into the station, and we were pushed into boxcars. Everything I had seen during the last few days convinced me that this was a one-way trip with only one end. It was dark, and the ramp was a melée of bodies. The guards were behind us, pushing and shouting, driving us like cattle. I jumped on the track, slipped under the car, scrambled over the rails, and ran out of the yard. An hour or so later the train left for Treblinka, taking with it 2,000 Jews. They were not seen or heard of again."

Although there was nothing left for me at Cheznick, it was the only home I knew. I made my way back to the village through the forest. When I got back, I saw that most of the houses, including our own, were occupied by Germans or Poles. At night I crept into the village and stole food and drink. During the day I hid in the forest, sleeping in an abandoned woodsman's hut. The Germans I could avoid. The real enemy, when it came, was winter. You can't hide your tracks in the snow.

There were several partisan groups in the forest. I had to join up with one of them before the weather changed. I had my chance a few weeks later. I heard gunfire and when the shooting stopped, I went to see if there was anything I could retrieve. In a clearing I found a badly wounded German soldier. He held up his hands and begged me not to kill him, even though I was unarmed.

Then I heard voices and the snapping of branches. Coming towards me were a dozen or more men with drawn guns. I could tell from their clothes they were Russian. If they had been Polish AK, they would have shot me. The major target of the AK around Cheznick was not Germans but Jews. They even joined the *Einsatzgruppen* on search-and-destroy missions. Their slogan was *Polska bez Zydow* (Poland without Jews). Not one AK unit helped the Jews during the Warsaw ghetto uprising, whereas a thousand or more Jews converged on Warsaw to help the Poles fight the Germans.

The Russians saw me standing over the German. Seeing that I was unarmed, one of them thrust his rifle into my hands and said, "Shoot."

I had never killed anyone. I took the gun. The man was wounded, obviously dying.

"Shoot," the Russian said again.

This time I pulled the trigger. The Russian said there was nothing partisans could do with a wounded German. Moreover he still had his rifle. He could have killed me. I was naïve and inexperienced, but I soon learned.

The leader of the partisans was a tough-looking man with a high forehead and arched nose called Vyacheslav. Vyacheslav and the other partisans had been released from jail to do heavy labor for the Russian army but chose not to return when the army withdrew. I told Vyacheslav that I wanted to join him. Most Jewish partisans had a dual agenda, fighting Germans, but also saving Jewish lives, which was of no interest to the Russians.

My hesitation in front of the wounded German did not convince Vyacheslav that I was ready to kill. But when I told him that I knew the forest and where they could hide in safety, he nodded and said "Okay."

I killed my second German a few days later. An *Einsatzgruppen* patrol had strayed into the forest looking for Jews. We came across the patrol near Olkenik. Olkenik had been cleared of Jews but Polish informers told the Germans that some Jews had escaped and were living or hiding nearby. Since we outnumbered the Germans two to one, we could have ambushed them easily. But Vyacheslav said he wanted to give them a taste of their own medicine. After taking their rifles we marched them to the edge of the forest and made them take off their clothes.

Their command center was 200 yards away across an open field. I can tell you they did not look so brave and arrogant at that moment, and not one of them was singing. As soon as we pushed them into the open they started shouting and yelling and waving their arms. They had not run more than 50 yards when Germans began pouring out of the command post, amazed to see their messmates running naked towards them. Vyacheslav took the first German. I shot the second. The rest fell in a hail of gunfire. An eye for an eye, as they say. But I had a lot more than one death to avenge.

We set up camp in a swampy area in the center of a marsh which very few people knew about. Floating marsh grass and algae covered black ponds twenty feet deep. If was very dangerous if you didn't know where you were going. Mists rising from the swamp helped to hide the fires we built for cooking and warmth. I got food by posing as a Polish partisan and making contact with farmers and villagers who lived in the timbered villages on the edge of the forest. Life was not easy. The farmers and villagers organized defense teams and rang church bells to alert the Germans whenever they saw anything suspicious. There were betrayals and ambushes and narrow escapes. We regularly lost people.

During the next three years we fought many actions, derailed trains going to the eastern front, and blew up locomotives with explosives that had been parachuted by the Polish army in exile. Combat was unpredictable and murderous. The Russians were brave fighters; nothing unnerved them. But their drinking was a problem. It caused military misjudgements, brawls among themselves, and sexual attacks on women.

By May 1944 the battlefront was nearing Vilnius. The ground began to shake with the sound of heavy shells. At night the sky was criss-crossed with huge red arcs of Russian rockets. Most Jewish partisans joined the advancing Red Army, eager to fight the Germans openly. They felt they had nothing to lose. If they stayed where they were they would either be murdered by the AK or blown up by shellfire.

By June the Russians reached the outskirts of Vilnius. Heavy fighting broke out in a wide circle that threatened to encompass us. It was time to leave. Vyacheslav and the others hoped to be absorbed into the 8th Army and return home after Poland was liberated. It was not an option for me. I had lived under the Russians before. Stalin had no time for Jews. Jews returning to their homes would find them occupied or in ruins and hear their Polish neighbors tell them that Hitler had not done a good enough job.

I caught a train to Warsaw carrying hundreds of *Volksdeutschen* fleeing the area before the Russians arrived. I took another train to Vienna and contacted Berihah, the underground organization set up by Jewish members of the Polish resistance to smuggle Jews out of Europe. While waiting for my papers, I met a partisan who had fought the Germans in Parczew near Lublin. He asked me if I was still interested in killing Germans. He didn't have to ask twice. I joined DIN. That was six months ago....

⌘⌘⌘

I gave my files to Isik and did not see him again. Some weeks later I heard that several senior SS on my list had committed suicide.

41

I left Germany for the last time on December 10, 1945.

Saying good-bye to Sylvia was difficult, although our parting was there from the beginning. Since the outbreak of the war I had not had a personal life. If I went out with a girl, it was because it was necessary to be seen with a girl. Fear of surveillance and arrest meant that I was always on the move. Friendships had, with rare exception, been purely symbolic relations that enabled me to remain within myself. Sylvia allowed me to be myself again, to *feel* again. And for this I will always be grateful to her.

Brian arranged a flight for me to Cairo from where I took a bus to Port Said, where Marian was waiting for me aboard the *SS Portland*. I was 27 years old. If someone had asked me what I had done during the last five years and nine months I had no ready answer. War, for all its activity, is peculiarly bankrupt of meaning.

I saw Marian before she saw me. She was looking over the ship's rails at the Sudanese dockworkers loading cargo. I was halfway up the gangplank when she turned and saw me. We waved to one another, and she ran to meet me. When I took her in my arms, the emotion left me breathless. Our lost years were finally behind us. There had been so many false starts and separations that at times I wondered if we would ever be together again.

Our cabin had two small bunks, one on top of the other, and while sex was possible, she said we should wait until we were married. I knew from her letters that she had become increasingly devout, agreeing with the Torah that sex was an adjunct of marriage. Although I wanted to take her into my arms and make love to her, I was so happy to be with her, that to wait another few months before we were married was not an issue.

The passengers on the Portland were mostly Australians who had been seconded to SOE Cairo, where they had provided intelligence for Allied missions in Yugoslavia. Because Marian was afraid of being drawn into talking about the war, we kept to ourselves.

Later, much later, when she admitted spending time behind barb wire, and the truth about Auschwitz was more widely known, people said to her, "Why didn't you run?" "Why didn't you fight back?" "Why didn't you do something?" Some people even asked her if she had been able to survive because, perhaps, she had slept with an SS man...? People wanted stories of heroes. Those who spent time in the camps could only offer stories of survival. The only response was silence. How could they know that in camps like Auschwitz survival was not in one's hands?

Although there was little deck space on the Portland, most of it being taken up with cargo hatches, we could always find a place to sit by ourselves. The American marines were friendly and keen to tell us about their near misses from German torpedoes. Survival depended on luck (how often had I heard that!), since the Liberty ships had a top speed of only 10 knots, half that of submarines. When they raised their eyes to the sea it was to watch for telltale silver streaks on top of the water, not to appraise the setting sun.

It took five weeks to reach Melbourne. Although the Japanese had surrendered three months earlier we made a wide detour because of the fear that not all enemy submarines had returned to base. Each evening we watched the sunset, the horizon filled with rising tides of gold and violet, red and yellow. Sea and sky were caught in a dream of light that carried everything before it.

⌘ ⌘ ⌘

We docked at Port Melbourne without the usual fanfare given to returning troop ships. During the war I had experienced real feelings of pleasure when a fragment of my childhood stirred into life again. But one could not let them take hold.

It was not the same for my parents. Years of silence, unbroken by any official news of my whereabouts, had made every day a question mark. It had taken its toll. They had aged. I felt desperately sorry that the nature of my work had restricted communication to an absolute minimum. Even so, it was a wonderful homecoming: the renewal of ties and memories broken by war for nearly eight years.

To the world at large we were just another couple returning back after the war. No one knew about our time in the camps. Marian, certainly, did not want to talk about the past. To live daily in the shadow of death is not something that is easily communicable. Few victims believed that anyone could understand the horrors they had been through or what it did to a person. Marian closed off the past as a means of denying what she had experienced. I had my nightmares, images that struggled to create substance from ruin, but had little difficulty rebuilding my trust in the world.

My father's health had deteriorated. He had been marking time with his machinery business and passed it to me to look after. The period immediately following the war was a time of unprecedented growth due to the stability of the economies of the world and the increased level of investment. During the boom, which lasted well into 1970s, there was a steady increase in the price of wool that meant money was available for agricultural implements and machinery.

But my first thought upon returning was our marriage. Marian wanted a Jewish wedding, but I could not find a rabbi who would marry us until I converted. Instruction took at least a year because the convert is expected to experience each of the Jewish holidays. Nor was this all. After instruction I had to appear before a *Beit Din* (rabbinical court) who would examine me and decide whether I was ready to become a Jew. Only when I passed the oral examination are the rituals of conversion performed. I would be circumcised (or, in my case, a pinprick of blood would be drawn for a symbolic circumcision), immersed in the *mikvah* (a ritual bath used for spiritual purification), given a Jewish name, and introduced into the Jewish community.

I had no religious objection to becoming Jewish, although I did not accept the Jewish pretension (shared with the Nazis) that they were a "Chosen People." I was prepared to do what I had to, but only if Marian and I could live together in the meantime. The ordinary Jewish term for marriage is *Kiddushin* ("sanctification") and implies a strict morality for both parties. The Rabbis we spoke to reminded us of the prohibition against unmarried couples living together and would not waive the lessons or the learning of the 613 *mitzvoth* of the Torah.

Just when it seemed that we had reached a stalemate, I found a rabbi who had given up on the commandants and would marry us without preconditions.

Rabbi Levi had a rich, ringing voice and wore a loose black overcoat that he never removed. Because his relaxed version of the *mitzvot* was not acceptable to Orthodox Jews, he was refused permission to read publicly in the synagogue. But since Marian did not insist on being married in a synagogue, he could ignore the restrictions imposed upon him.

Physically Marian had changed very little. She was still very slender, lovely to look at, and when she talked, her hands and eyes entered the conversation as they always had. But emotionally there was much that still troubled her. She could not avoid the many links to her own personal Holocaust. The associations were idiosyncratic (men in uniform, exhaust gas from a car, a line of people queuing up at a bus stop, barking dogs). When we finished a meal, she sometimes asked me if I wanted some *nachschlag* (the supplemental food given when an inmate performed extra work). Brutality leaves a permanent feeling of vulnerability.

Marian and I were married in March 1946 in my parent's garden. My mother and father escorted us down the aisle, as is the custom in Jewish ceremonies, to the *chuppah* (a silk canopy), where Rabbi Levi waited for us. After the traditional blessings were recited and rings exchanged we were declared man and wife: *"Harei at mekudeshet li betaba"at zo kedat Mosheh veyisrael"* (Behold you are consecrated unto me, with this ring, according to the Law of Moses and Israel).

Immediately after the marriage in Jewish weddings it is customary for the bride and bridegroom to spend a little time alone together. Circumstances prevented this, but it would not have changed anything.

42

Marian and I had lived through the worst that the world had to offer, and had rarely experienced shared moments of tenderness. After our wedding, I wanted to hold her in my arms and bring all our lost moments together.

But it was not to be. When I touched her, she began to shiver uncontrollably. She said the touch of my hands reminded her of the *Frauenblock*. Tears ran down her face. There was nothing I could do or say that would have made any difference. We lay together for a while, not speaking, then I returned to my room.

In the days and weeks that followed it became clear that sympathy and understanding alone would not silence her memories. Deeply upset, feeling both guilt and blame, Marian agreed to see Dr. Levin, a Jewish psychotherapist.

Dr. Dorothea Levin was born in Berlin. She had lived under the Nazis until 1939, immigrating to Australia when her family home was expropriated. Although she had no personal experience of life in the camps, the fact that she was Jewish and from Berlin created a tie that helped Marian take her into her confidence. After their first session, Levin told me what I already suspected: that no words could articulate the full measure of Marian's ordeal and that she (Marian) felt that those who had not undergone the same experience could never imagine or understand what it was like. While therapy consisted in unblocking the past, healing relied almost exclusively on the curative powers inherent in her own nature. As a first step, Dr. Levine suggested that we join a survivor group. "When you try to forget the past, it doesn't go away. It comes back in states of anxiety. Listening to other people's experience may help her bring her own into focus."

At about this time my father's secretary retired. Among the people I interviewed to take her place was a young woman, Lynn Taylor. Lynn came from a long-established farming family. She had four brothers. The resemblance between the siblings was striking. All had the same aquiline nose, wide-set eyes, full mouth, and when they got together, one heard nothing but laughter. In many ways Lynn was the opposite of Marian. Marian's nature was essentially inward and shy. Lynn was high-spirited, optimistic, and impulsively hospitable. People naturally found Lynn easy to talk to. After Auschwitz, there was little give and take with Marian in the ordinary commerce of life. There was much with Lynn.

Marian's and my first session with a "survivor group" was not a success. Our hostess, Dora Koch, was a small frail woman with a wan smile. There were five or six couples in the room sitting in a circle facing one another. There was a set pattern to these evenings. The host or hostess began by talking about his or her experiences, after which each new member was expected to tell their story. If there were no new members, the group would discuss anything anyone cared to bring up.

Dora told us that she was married in Vienna to an Austrian Jew. When the Nazis stormed into Austria, her husband was arrested and she did not see him again. Because she was Aryan, she did not have to wear the yellow star but had to move house with her daughter every few months because her neighbors were suspicious of her background. One night the Gestapo smashed in her front door and arrested her for carrying forged papers for the Jewish Underground.

Dora spoke quite normally to begin with, but when her memory returned to the past, her voice broke and her eyes filled with tears. Dora and her daughter were herded into a boxcar filled with women fighting their way to the single window to say good-bye to their husbands and children. After days without food and water, they arrived at Auschwitz.

Dora held her daughter's hand, saying all the while, "Don't worry, we'll be all right. Don't worry, we'll be all right." It only took a few moments and the girl was gone, pulled away by the SS. She ran after her, screaming, but was caught by a *Kapo*, knocked down, and beaten. When she got to her feet, her daughter, along with scores of other children, was being marched to the gas chamber. "I feel now some-times, did I do my best or didn't I? I should have said, 'Run!' But I didn't

...I let her be taken away, and I survived. If I forget anything, this I will never forget."

It was fearful to have to outlive the death, or rather the murder, of those you love, but it is equally agonizing to have to outlive one's own death, as Dora insists she did, embracing an agony beyond suffering that turned the remainder of her life into a vacuous "no" life. This was a unique psychological wound that only graduates of Auschwitz could comprehend.

There was nothing Dora could have done. By the time they reached Auschwitz, it was already too late: one could either hasten death or momentarily postpone it; there was no other alternative. Everything happened so quickly that you didn't even have time to see your mother or sister vanish.

The rest of her story was familiar: selections, the ruinous regimen of physical labor, the fight for a scrap of floor space, for something to eat. She escaped the gas chamber because she was transferred to Dachau in 1944, just months before the camp was liberated.

Dora and I were the only non-Jewish members of the group. She could not forgive herself for jeopardizing her daughter's life by taking the risks she did. She could have avoided being picked up. She wasn't identified as a Jew. She didn't have to carry papers for the Resistance. Although closely involved with the Jewish community, she blamed the Jews, albeit unconsciously, for what happened. But how was she to know? How was anybody to know?

It is not uncommon for survivors to feel guilty for having survived while others, perhaps more deserving than themselves, had been swept away. "Why me? Why did I survive and not my daughter? Why not the children?" The camp was a fertile soil for survivor guilt, for at its most fundamental, it was a competitive world. The overwhelming relief of not being chosen for extinction was coupled with the knowledge that one survived because someone else died in one's place.

Mourning provides relief. But the dead did not die in Auschwitz; they just disappeared. There was no focus for Dora's tears. The dead that went up the crematoria chimneys were left floating in the air. There was no grave, no ashes, no tomb, and no burial place. There was nowhere to direct one's pain, one's sadness, one's anger, or one's guilt.

That life goes on after death is a platitude; that death may also go on after death was part of a post-Auschwitz experience for many.

Although the terror came to an end more than 50 years ago, Dora was one of those who still could not forget, and for whom the question, "Why?" remained unanswered. What she called her absent past is permanently present inside her. She inhabited two worlds—the world of then, when her daughter was wrested from her, and the world of now, which always fell under the shadow of the past. It was not a matter of forgetting. She didn't choose her memories. Always before her eye, images from the past blocked her entrance into the sunlight—"living without being alive," as she put it. Her time in Auschwitz collapsed conventional distinctions between living and dying as separate and antithetical states of being. The *Shoa* is a narrative without closure, and there are few happy endings.

Dora's story could have been told by almost everyone present. There was no ready-made right thing one could say, that one could hand over like a bunch of flowers as a sign of sympathy. One could only express, with the gestures usual on such occasions, that one is faced with something incomprehensible. To speak about the past would only have rubbed salt in her wounds. To look forward was equally inappropriate. For the future to have meaning, it must have some purpose. But its significance is lost without children or family. Even the recollection of the days when her life had been good could not prevail against her loss.

We sat there, in silence, like the friends who came to see Job, knowing that nothing we could say would touch the heart of what she felt or experienced. The language problem for a survivor is compounded by the existential incomprehensibility of what was endured. There was no reason for the Nazi's criminality. It was totally irrational. When all that the mind can grasp is that there is no meaning to be grasped, there is no possibility of bridging the gap through language.

It is said that suffering ceases to be suffering the moment it finds a meaning. But where was the meaning in Auschwitz? The missing victims, the missing meaning of their disappearance, the missing God—the paradox of presence known only through absence—is part of every survivor's experience.

After Dora stopped speaking, a couple of people looked at Marian. Because she kept her head down, they looked at me. It was our turn to speak. I hesitated to say anything. Compared to other survivors' experiences, my time in Auschwitz had been bearable. In that atmosphere of mutual self-sorrow I could not bring myself to tell them that I was a *Prominenten* and had the *protekcja* of an SS officer who arranged my escape. I had been beaten. I had been hungry, and there were times when I thought it was all over.

But I never saw anyone I loved being pushed into the ovens. Like others, I had to create an invisible wall, shutting myself off from anything that threatened my survival; like others I organized illegal food, found influential friends, protected my status. But I was not paralyzed by unanswerable questions. Although I saw more death than most I did not let the improbability of survival chasten my confidence in life. I had been rewarded by an intense memory of several people whose courage had shown me the power of the human spirit—that spirit that could withstand the utmost assault. Against the background of the camp and its brutal stupidities, they were victorious against the things that sought to destroy them. They gave me the courage to hope when things were very bad.

I looked at Marian. I knew what she was thinking. *How could I say what I went through, when it is still incomprehensible to me?* One of us had to say something. I knew enough about the last days of Auschwitz to tell a credible story....

⌘⌘⌘

We were arrested while trying to leave Germany in June 1944 and were deported to Auschwitz. I was assigned to an artisan labor squad, which gave me access to the women's camp. I was able to keep in touch with Marian and smuggle letters in and out.

A year later, on January 17, all work came to a halt. Word spread that the SS had orders to kill everybody. No one was to be left alive to be freed by the Russians. Even so, everyone in the men's camp started shouting out addresses to the women on the other side of the wire where they would meet after the war in case they got separated. Although I could not believe that the Germans would simply let us walk out, I followed the others and ran to the wire. When I saw Marian, I shouted her mother's name, making a B with my fingers for Berlin.

The next day Soviet artillery started pounding the outskirts of the camp. We prayed that we would be liberated before the Germans got around to shooting us. Then, shortly after midnight, the SS ordered a general evacuation. They dynamited Crematorium V, the last one still standing, and set fire to the large warehouses. The women were lined up in single file and marched from the camp.

Marian, as we had arranged, walked at the tail end of the column with prisoners from the infirmary. Those able to stand wrapped themselves in whatever they could find and ran out, desperate not to be left behind. But only a handful of the hundreds of sick prisoners saved their lives in this way. Guards stood at the gate, examining everyone by torchlight. It was another selection. Anyone who looked too weak to walk or was judged to be too old or feeble was sent back to the infirmary. Those who tried to slip past the guards were pursued with sticks and revolver shots. When the last woman marched out of the camp it was the men's turn.

Once outside the camp the SS ordered us into ranks of five. The cold was intense. We shivered in our clothes, tucked our hands under our arms, and stamped our feet. The sky was thick with stars, giving just enough light to see the man in front. We huddled together, but there was so little warmth in our bodies. I thought, *If the SS doesn't kill us, the cold will.* Finally the order to march was given, and we started forward, toward Wodzisław Śląski, 35 miles away, on the German border. It was an impossible distance, in midwinter, for many of us.

I looked back at the camp. It was in darkness. The only light was from a bonfire near the administrative block where the crematory records were being burnt. The guards were nervous, hurrying us along with rifle butts and shouts. We could hear shellfire. The shots seemed to be getting closer. Some of the SS became alarmed and took off. It must have entered their heads that the war was lost and that they would be held accountable. Our death was their survival. Every few yards we passed a corpse: someone shot for not keeping up, or fallen from exhaustion. I worked my way forward till I caught up with Marian. I took her arm, and we fell back to the rear of the column, where the line had broken down and was partly abandoned by the SS. We passed several Polish villages, houses with curtains and lights behind them. I could not believe we shared the same world.

Hearing gunfire and shouting in front of us, the guards ran ahead. I took Marian's hand, and we bolted into the darkness. We stumbled through the snow, not knowing where we were going. We came to a fence, which we crossed, saw some lights, and entered a barn. It was pitch dark, but we found some straw and spread it over ourselves.

Next morning we were found by some villagers, who mistook us for English and looked after us until the Germans evacuated the village.

The roads were full of vehicles—Red Cross trucks carrying German wounded, artillery pieces, and retreating soldiers. It really did look as if the last bugle had sounded for the Germans.

After three days the Russians arrived. Suddenly we heard a new language and saw people we had not seen before—from the Ukraine, the Urals, from Siberia and Mongolia, and they brought with them something we never thought we would see: Freedom!...

⌘ ⌘ ⌘

My concocted story had a plausible ending that satisfied everyone. Marian looked grateful. A man opposite me said that, had the Polish villagers suspected we were Jewish, they would have betrayed us. Another said the Russians were no better than the Germans and that if we had not spoken English, they would have shot us.

My story brought the session to a close. As far as Marian was concerned, nothing had changed. For my part, I could not see how these Holocaust revelations could bring her to herself or lead either of us to a happy ending.

43

A few weeks after the meeting at Dora's house I took my first business trip with Lynn. I did not call Marian while I was away. When I returned, there was nothing in Marian's voice to suggest that I should have. We had begun to live separate lives.

Our second "survivor's meeting" was no more successful than the first. Neither of us wanted to go, but Dr. Levine was convinced that Marian would benefit from prophylactic group therapy. But on this occasion, we were spared more harrowing recollections of life under the Nazis. The talk was all about God.

Because Jews had entered into a covenant with God, they believe they had His divine protection. *"Ye are the children of the Lord your God"* (Deuteronomy 14:1). Hitler turned the notion of the Jews being a *"chosen people"* upside down. As someone said, "To confront God, how dare I? But I must say it… Where was He? When we were on the ramp at Auschwitz and an SS man grabbed a baby from her mother's arms and threw the baby against the wall and the baby's head smashed open in front of its mother's eyes…. Was God watching this?"

But for two Orthodox Jews, who neither asked questions nor sought answers, the group was almost equally divided between those who clung to their faith and those who had lost it. Marian belonged to the former. Her faith was not compacted into a moment as with a blinded Paul on the road to Damascus but arose out of her experience in the camps. "During the worst times, the times when there was nothing else, I had only my faith, and without it, I could not have survived."

For my part, there were times when I thought the world too evil for a good God to exist. The squat brick chimneys belching out human ash confirmed our corporality, but I never doubted our spiritual nature. Our "safe arrival," as Father Schefler put it, did not apply to our bodies, but to the "I" we know ourselves to be. I acknowledged the existence of that mysterious reality we call God, and our place in his life. But it fell short of that religious experience by which, according to St. Paul, we know what God is.

The question faced by those who survived Auschwitz and did not lose faith in God and the Covenant was, "How to vindicate divine justice by allowing evil to exist?" If God is the cause of everything in the universe, he must also be the author of all its evils and responsible for all its sins. "How could God let them take my children and your children and kill them?"—a question which is answered the moment it is asked. If God had eliminated sin, the script of creation would have denied free will. Clearly it is better to leave human freedom intact, in spite of the wickedness that sometimes ensues. While God shows forbearance to the sinner, he must abandon the victim. This is the inescapable paradox of divine providence.

Those who had lost faith in God thought of Him as the parent who abandoned them. *"I am the God of your father Abraham. Do not be afraid, for I am with you; I will bless you and will increase the number of your descendants"* (Genesis 26:24). He brought them out of Egypt, he parted the Red Sea, he gave them manna to eat in the desert, and then he turned them over to Hitler. It looked as if Hitler was God's instrument and they were being punished for their foreswearing of the Torah. *"The Holy One, blessed be He, said to Israel, My children, I have created the evil impulse, and I have created the Torah as an antidote to it; if you occupy yourself with the Torah you will not be delivered into its power."* The preservation or loss of life is decided by one's attitude to his Word. The obedient man chooses for himself life; the disobedient man, death. But if you take this prophetic idea of life's dependence on God to its remorseless conclusion, one is faced with the absurd contention that six million people deserved their fate.

Equally silly, I thought, was the idea that God had allowed them to suffer so they could claim the rewards of adversity. *"Behold, happy is the man whom God reproves; therefore despise not the chastening of the Almighty.... He delivers the afflicted by their affliction, and opens their ears by adversity"* (Psalm 90:15; Job 5:17). This may be true, but only partially so. Drowning in daily episodes of atrocity, it was absurd to talk about the ennoblement of one's character. There were very few souls who did not put survival before morality.

Behind the questioning was a scarcely concealed censure of God: Where was he?

But the real question was, "Where was man?" What happened to the millions who died did not happen because God wanted it to happen. It happened because man turned his back on reason and yielded to prejudice and hate. As the testimonies at Nuremberg made abundantly clear, sin resides in the minds and wills of men. It is only if we turn the Holocaust over to God that it becomes an incomprehensible event. The *Shoa* is neither incomprehensive nor inexplicable, but an eminently human event that points to the frailty of man's will to do what is morally right.

Although Marian continued to see Dr. Levin, we did not attend any more group discussions. I found myself spending more and more time at work, which is to say with Lynn, since we worked very closely together. Time had not changed Marian's attitude towards sex. We lived together, not unhappily, but it was not the union we had both hoped for.

But by now I had to admit, that in spite of my deep fondness for Marian, I was in love with Lynn. When I told Marian about Lynn, it was less of a surprise to her than her admission to me. She had been waiting for just such an opportunity to tell me that she wanted to return to Israel. We parted as the closest of friends, whose love for one another had, at times, been the deciding factor between life and death. Although the war had interrupted our relationship, and was the start of our troubles, it was by no means a posthumous victory for Hitler. Despite everything, both of us found happiness in a world he wanted to destroy.

Marian returned to Israel just before the 1948 war and worked for the *Magen David Adom* (the Jewish Red Cross) in Tel Aviv. After the war she joined a kibbutz near the Sea of Galilee and opened a school for immigrant children. Her identification with the struggle to create a Jewish homeland restored much of her sense of well-being.

In one of her letters to me—for we have kept up over the years—she wrote:

... and even if you have to face the terrors of the past, there is still that area of human faith, that certainty of understanding and of being understood, no matter how dark the night.

This is almost like what is expressed by Christ's saying, *"Peace I leave with you; my peace I give you. Do not let your hearts be troubled and do not be afraid"* (John 14:27).

Lynn and I were married soon after Marian returned to Israel. Although we have visited Europe several times, Hitler's death camps were not among our list of things we wanted to see. I have no wreaths to lay and no ghosts to bury. What happened in Auschwitz can never suffer from too much memory; but for those who lived though the experience, the difficulty is not one of remembering, but forgetting.

Afterword

Thucydides said that the massacre of the civilian population of Melos, which exposed the ruthlessness of Athenian imperialism, was not a one-time-only event outside the course of history but indicative of patterns that would repeat themselves as long as human behavior remains the same. This tendency to commit wicked actions and make ruthless political judgments can be reduced, if we are to believe Bertrand Russell, to a conjunction of the clever but wicked:

> We can make lots of wonderful gadgets, including an atom bomb.... But we have not been able to achieve that moral and political growth and maturity which alone could safely direct and control the uses to which we put our tremendous intellectual powers.

Popper, on the other hand, believes that we are good, perhaps a little too good, but we are also a little stupid:

> The main troubles of our times...are not due to our moral wickedness, but, on the contrary, to our often misguided moral enthusiasm.... Our moral enthusiasm is often misguided because we fail to realize that our moral principles, which are sure to be over simple, are often difficult to apply to the complex human and political situations to which we feel bound to apply them.

One may agree with Bertrand Russell; one may agree with Popper; one may agree with them both, for the Bible lists among the effects of sin both a darkening of the mind and a weakening of will.

Since goodness is the sustaining principle against evil, the solution to the problem of evil is self-evident. But, as Russell and Popper point out, for the solution to be universally accessible and permanent, it

225

would involve some transcendence of human ways. The dark forces of passion and violence rest on man's proud contention to be just a man, and its tragedy is that, if evil is not to repeatedly assert itself, to be just a man is what man cannot be.

The "final solution" legitimized the horrendous destructive and nihilistic passions that reached their climax in Auschwitz. Hitler's world was to be *Judenrein* (Jew free), a word that has no counterpart in any other language. Auschwitz was to be a museum for an "extinct race." It can still evoke a sense of horror with its gallery of pitiful relics behind glass walls: the meticulously salvaged heaps of dentures and artificial limbs, rooms full of shoes, dolls, and human hair, and photographs of open-mouthed corpses and numbers tattooed on the arms of living corpses. But the many thousands of tourists who visit Auschwitz each year see only the superficiality of terror. Even those who lived through the experience cannot tell the whole story. The past belongs to the dead.

Dachau has become a place of remembrance. Little of the original camp remains. The walls of the administration offices are hung with photographs of the industrial relics of mass murder: blood-stained uniforms, torture chambers, firing-squad walls, mass hangings, and emaciated and sprawling bodies. At the end of the *Lagerstrasse* is a monument of atonement to the legions of unjustly slaughtered, a round chapel shaped like a huge winepress built of unhewn rocks, along with a Jewish memorial where Jewish visitors, wrapped in the white-and-blue flag of Israel, come to chant the Kaddish. At the extreme north end of the camp there is a Carmelite Convent founded by Maria Theresa, where the Carmelites stand before God in intercessory prayer. "There is nothing love cannot face; there is no limit to its faith, its hope, and its endurance."

The only admissible comment on these words involves a transition from the written word to the memory of deeds. I am thinking of Father Schefler, who not merely surrendered to death, but gave himself away, body, mind and heart, in the service of others. He convinced me that we can hold on to our humanity in the very worst of times, and that, with God's help, evil would be undone and that goodness and mercy will have its day.

ALSO BY VERNON L. ANLEY

An Unholy Love

What happens at death?
And what does life—and love—
mean in the light of it?

This remarkable journal, written by a dying man in the last months of his life, is the record of a crisis of faith that forces him to reevaluate aspects of Christian dogma and doctrine. **Beautifully written, and deeply moving**, it goes beyond conventional boundaries in its attempt to understand man in his wholeness.

    O.M. KORTLANG

This beautifully written book **takes the reader on a spiritual odyssey** that transcends religious speculation in its apprehension of the imperishable power of love. It is for anyone who fears the unknown, or is in doubt about their own salvation.

    S. L. MCCALLUM, *La Source*

An intimate story that does not shirk to question many of religion's truths, without losing sight of man's ultimate destiny. It **leads us to discover something about ourselves** which might have lain undeveloped and unknown. *An Unholy Love* can be read many times over. **I could not put it down.**

    J.L MOORE

About the Author

DR. VERNON L. ANLEY was educated in Australia and in England. After leaving university he worked for the Ministry of Overseas Development in the West Indies before resuming an academic career in Europe and the Far East.

He has coauthored a number of academic books, written travel guides on the Hejaz and Yemen, radio scripts, and articles on linguistics and education.

A Carnival of Lies, a novel about the complex developments in Germany between 1939 and 1945, is an outstanding work from which no one interested in the subject can fail to profit. His visits to Hitler's death camps in Germany, Poland, and Austria raised question about human nature and death which he attempts to answer in An *Unholy Love*.